Passion Misplaced

"My lord," she exclaimed, lifting out the diamond bracelet and trying it on her slender wrist, "it is exquisite. You are so generous. But"—she wrapped her arms around his neck and pulled his head down to look up at him under seductively lowered lids as her tongue flicked over her full red lower lip—"I can be generous too." Her mouth clung to his as she pressed herself into to his arms.

Why, Gareth asked himself as his hands traced the ripe curves of Maria's truly voluptuous figure, should he be thinking of a pair of startling blue eyes set under delicately arched brows when deep rich brown ones, warm with passionate invitation, were promising him a world of physical delights? He could not imagine why the image of another woman's delicate eyebrows—or her beautifully sculpted lips—should intrude into his consciousness at this particular and very inopportune moment. Or why, he wondered as his lips explored Maria's, should he be speculating on whether or not such passion could be aroused in an Ice Princess?

Fortune's Lady

Evelyn Richardson

A SIGNET BOOK

SIGNET
Published by New American Library, a division of
Penguin Putnam Inc., 375 Hudson Street,
New York, New York 10014, U.S.A.
Penguin Books Ltd, 80 Strand,
London WC2R 0RL, England
Penguin Books Australia Ltd, Ringwood,
Victoria, Australia
Penguin Books Canada Ltd, 10 Alcorn Avenue,
Toronto, Ontario, Canada M4V 3B2
Penguin Books (N.Z.) Ltd, 182–190 Wairau Road,
Auckland 10, New Zealand

Penguin Books Ltd, Registered Offices:
Harmondsworth, Middlesex, England

First published by Signet, an imprint of New American Library,
a division of Penguin Putnam Inc.

First Printing, March 2002
10 9 8 7 6 5 4 3 2 1

 REGISTERED TRADEMARK—MARCA REGISTRADA

Printed in the United States of America

PUBLISHER'S NOTE
This is a work of fiction. Names, characters, places, and incidents either are
the product of the author's imagination or are used fictitiously, and any
resemblance to actual persons, living or dead, business establishments, events,
or locales is entirely coincidental.

In memory of Melinda Helfer

Friend,
Mentor,
and
A Champion
For so many of us

Chapter 1

"Gareth, my dear, do try for a little more enthusiasm. This is a rout after all, not a funeral, and it is Lady St. John's rout at that. There is not the least reason to be so Friday faced. Do look as though you are enjoying yourself. You promised you would." The Marchioness of Harwood tightened her grip on her son's arm as they mounted the magnificent marble staircase in the countess's splendid mansion in Grosvenor Square.

"Yes, Mama, I shall—" Angrily he bit off the meek reply. For years he had responded unquestioningly to her every whim with "Yes, Mama. Of course, Mama," too well trained to do anything but her bidding, catering to her every desire just as his father had done, but no longer. He was finished with all that. Now he was head of the family, Gareth de Vere, sixth Marquess of Harwood. And he did *not* want to be here. "No, Mama. I promised you I would escort you, but I would never have been so rash as to promise to enjoy myself."

He loathed *ton* functions such as this, the crush of people elegantly attired, expressions of polite boredom carefully pasted on their faces while their eyes restlessly scanned the fashionable throng as his were doing now, seeking something, anything, to make this night different from countless other nights at one select gathering or another during the height of the Season.

As they crossed the threshold Gareth's gaze swept the brilliantly lit ballroom. His breath caught in his throat at the sight of her, slightly off to one side, standing next to a marble pillar. She was exquisite in a way that made every other woman there seem overdressed and tawdry. Dark hair threaded with a rope of pearls and arranged in a simple knot, a gown of white net over a white satin slip, devoid of fussy ornamentation but designed to show off the tall elegant figure to perfection—she was as pure and as perfect as a snowflake. Surrounded by a crowd of admirers, she still somehow appeared to be alone, aloof from idle conversations and petty intrigues, the gossip and the *on dits* being exchanged all around her, whispers that could make or break a reputation.

Tall and stately, she observed the scene with the disdainful serenity of one who knew herself to be above it all, sure of herself, fully conscious of her worth on the marriage mart, utterly confident of her power to attract the eager young bucks who flocked to her side. And he hated her for it, for this air of calm self-assurance. He knew what it meant for the dozens of men doing their utmost to win her attention. It meant they would be her willing slaves, falling all over themselves to earn just the tiniest smile from those beautifully sculpted lips, a look of approval from the sparkling eyes set under delicately arched dark brows, slaves just as his father had been.

"Lady Althea Beauchamp," his mother remarked, following her son's gaze. "The Duke of Clarendon's only child. She is an incomparable among incomparables, with a fortune besides. You would do well to marry someone like that, Gareth."

"I have no need to marry a fortune, Mama. I have one of my own."

"Faugh. A fortune won at the gaming tables. Too utterly vulgar." The Marchioness of Harwood sniffed disdainfully.

"No more vulgar than losing a fortune at the gaming tables as my father did."

"Your father was always a gentleman. No one could ever accuse *him* of doing anything that was bad *ton*."

"Except losing a fortune."

"Concerning oneself with money is bad *ton*. Your father never paid attention to money."

"Too true, especially when he owed it to every member of his club, every friend he could find, and every tradesman with whom he had even a passing acquaintance."

It was an unanswerable statement and all too unpleasantly true. The marchioness treated it as she treated all unpleasant things in her life; she ignored it. "Dear Lady Granville." She turned to smile at the woman next to her, whose long ostrich plume wafted dangerously close to the elaborate diamond aigrette adorning the marchioness's toque. "A sad crush, is it not? But we could not miss Lady St. John's rout for the world. And this must be your daughter, Amelia. Charming. Utterly charming. Do you not think so, my dear?" Lady Harwood turned to her son.

"If you say so, Mama." Gareth remained unmoved by the hurt expression in the shy brown eyes smiling so hopefully up at him. Undoubtedly the lovely Amelia would soon be making sheep's eyes at other, more susceptible young men who would quickly make her forget all about the callous behavior of the Bachelor Marquess. If Gareth had thought for one moment that the girl was truly upset by his cold response, he might have softened it with a rueful smile or some sort of acknowledgment, but he had met too many eager young women to be flattered into thinking they were interested in anything but his title and his fortune. Why, therefore, should he pretend to have any interest in them?

His glance strayed back to the young woman his mother had identified as Lady Althea Beauchamp. At least it could be said of her that she did not appear to be exerting the least bit of effort to enthrall the willing victims clustering around her. Her air of distant abstraction implied that she was thinking of something quite above and beyond the crowded ballroom, only becoming aware of her surroundings when a remark was addressed so obviously to her that a reply was unavoidable. Even then she acknowledged it with a barely discernible nod in the direction of the speaker.

As a tactic it worked to perfection; the less interested

the lady appeared to be, the more the men crowded around her. Gareth could not help chuckling sardonically. Much as he disliked the implications of her colossal arrogance—that it sprang from being followed by a constant coterie of worshipful admirers who hung on every word and were ready to sell their souls for a smile from their goddess—he had to admire her independence, her refusal to laugh and flirt, to adopt the coy manners that all her peers seemed to think were guaranteed to drive a man to distraction, or at least most men, Gareth amended silently.

She had no need for such manners. Her stunning beauty was enough to draw every eye in the room, yet she appeared totally unconscious of it all, as unaware as a marble statue surrounded by connoisseurs exclaiming over its flawless lines and exquisite craftsmanship. Gareth swallowed hard, refusing to acknowledge the quickening of his own pulses as he watched her. After having so many women—Portuguese *condesas* and Spanish *marquesas* during his service in the Peninsula, opera dancers and expensive Cyprians at home—there was no reason he should be so affected by this particular young woman, no reason at all. But he was drawn to her in spite of himself.

"Come, Mama. I see the Countess of Rothsay and Lady Edgcumbe over there across the room." He guided his mother through the press of people as best he could, toward a group of dowagers arranged like generals along one wall and surveying the scene with critical eyes, deploring the coming manners of the jumped-up Miss Thorp or the daring décolletage of Lord Hilverton's dashing young wife.

Procuring his mother, Lady de Vere, a chair next to the countess, Gareth escaped before she could protest. While the marchioness enjoyed a good gossip as well as the next person, she infinitely preferred being seen on the arm of a handsome imposing gentleman, even if it was only her son. "Dear Gareth, so attentive. He absolutely insisted on escorting me to the St. Johns' rout, and now he will positively wear himself out keeping me supplied with refreshments and doing everything in his power to assure himself of my comfort." The marchioness smiled triumphantly at the countess, whose resolutely dull brood of children remained immured in their respective country estates. Furthermore, her husband was never seen anywhere but traveling between their residence in Berkeley Square and the card room at White's, leaving the countess utterly dependent on Lady Edgcumbe for amusement and companionship.

"Then we should have warned your son that the refreshments are at quite the opposite end of the room." The countess, gleefully noting Gareth's hurried departure, was perfectly capable of giving as good as she got.

"Ah, no, you are wrong, my dear. I am sure he has gone to speak with Lady Althea—such a delightful young woman with the exquisite breeding and manners that are so rare among young people these days. Gareth, as you know, is so sought after himself that he has become very particular and only an incomparable of incomparables can arouse his interest."

"And of course the young lady stands to inherit such a large fortune." The countess was not about to allow her old friend to have the last word. She had been at school with little Sally Farnborough, and not a day had gone by without that pert young lady hatching yet another scheme to catch herself a wealthy husband.

"I had not realized that your son was in the market for a wife. One hears that he is so unusually particular that he only seeks out the company of, er, *professional* women." Not to be outdone by her companion, Lady Edgcumbe smirked maliciously.

"Oh, my dears, have you ever seen such absurd headgear as Lady Marston is wearing? She looks a positive dowdy in that quiz of a turban, but then she never did have the least modicum of taste." Once again the marchioness resolutely ignored the unpleasant implications swirling around her.

"Do you not know that she is greatly *epris* with Lord Wilverdale? And it is said that Marston positively welcomes the distraction, which frees him at last."

Both ladies turned to look at Lady Edgcumbe in some

surprise, but the countess was the first to speak. "I had no idea that Marston had an eye for the fair sex."

"He does not. He merely wants to be left in peace to hunt and gamble with his cronies, and his wife's constant demands for attention were making it impossible."

"A situation with which our dear countess is intimately acquainted," the marchioness could not refrain from adding.

Meanwhile, less conscious of the direction in which he was moving than the ladies who were observing his progress, Gareth made his way slowly toward the corner of the room where Lady Althea was holding court.

"Gareth . . . Gareth . . . I say old fellow . . ."

Drawn inexorably and inexplicably toward the young woman at the other side of the room, his eyes fixed on the lovely face, Gareth did not even hear his own name spoken until he nearly collided with a pleasant-faced young man sporting a cravat expertly knotted in an oriental.

"Been out in the sun too long, old man, or has rustication caused you to forget the existence of your old friends?"

"Ceddie! I beg your pardon. I did not see you in this crush of people."

"No need to point that out. I have been positively shouting for your attention this age." Turning his head as far as the stiff points of his collar would allow him, the honorable Cedric Fontescue regarded his friend curiously. It was not like Gareth to be woolgathering. Ceddie had known him since their schooldays together at Eton and if anything could be said of Gareth de Vere, it was that he was awake on every suit, even to the point of being uncomfortably acute. Under the gauge of those penetrating gray eyes, one felt one's very soul revealed.

Those eyes were not focused on Cedric now, however. Instead, they kept flicking off to one particular corner of the room. Ceddie turned to followed their gaze. It must be something highly unusual to distract a man who was ordinarily so bored by gatherings like this that he almost never attended them. Or, on the rare occasions he did, it was to head straight to the card room to fleece some unfortunate who had the temerity to boast that he could beat the Marquess of Harwood at his own game.

"I should not have thought you would waste a glance on Lady Althea, even if she is the catch of the Season. It is not like you, Gareth." Ceddie too could be remarkably acute when he chose to be.

The slight tinge of color that crept over the marquess's high cheekbones was so faint that it almost seemed to be a trick of light from the massive crystal chandelier above them. Ceddie's eyes narrowed as he observed his friend more closely. This was a change indeed. "Even you, Gareth, devastating as you are to the fair sex, would lose there. They say she has not looked twice at anyone, even Wolverton. In fact, she is so unimpressionable that they are calling her the Ice Princess. But she is quite lovely, is she not?"

"Lovely? My dear Ceddie, where are your eyes? She is exquisite," Gareth drawled as his gaze swept the young woman in question with the coolly detached air of a connoisseur. "And furthermore, she is thoroughly aware of it. No, Ceddie, highly cultivated works of art do not appeal to me. They are far too expensive and exhausting to maintain. Give me a true woman, a passionate creature of flesh and blood who demands a fair price for her favors, not a man's soul."

"Like the divine Maria?" Ceddie grinned. "Surely she costs you a pretty penny. I saw her new barouche and its handsome pair in the park the other day."

"Like the divine Maria. She is expensive, but she named her price at the outset and has never wavered from it. And she is worth every penny. Not only is she, ah, extremely skilled, she is content to accept my, ah, protection without demanding eternal devotion, constant companionship, or even my occasional escort. She is a delightfully practical creature who does not bore one with tears, tantrums, or jealous fits, all of which I am certain our celebrated beauty over there has on a regular basis."

"But surely with that face, that fortune, that lineage, she is entitled to a little show of temperament."

Gareth snorted. "Perhaps those poor deluded fools hanging on her every word are prepared to suffer, but I, Ceddie, am no fool. I suffer no illusions about beautiful incomparables."

"No, that you do not." Ceddie regarded his friend thoughtfully. "But I am not so sure that your cynicism makes you any happier than their delusions make them."

"Ceddie, your skill at the card table is infinitely superior to your talent for philosophy. I suggest you abandon your attempts to analyze my state of mind and stick to piquet—so much less complicated, is it not?" Gareth took his friend's arm and, without a backward glance at the offending Ice Princess, steered his friend toward the refreshment room.

Chapter 2

Dismissed so contemptuously by the Marquess of Harwood, the object of his disgust had just become unpleasantly aware of his scrutiny. Oblivious to the crowd of young men around her and wishing that she were anywhere but where she was, Lady Althea gazed desperately across the crowded ballroom seeking she knew not what, a friendly face perhaps, or the knowledge that there was at least one person in that glittering crush of people who thought there was something more to life than spending one's days with dressmakers in order to appear more noticeably fashionable than the rest of the world.

As her glance swept over richly turbaned heads clustered together in gossiping groups, their feathers and jeweled aigrettes waving as they exchanged the latest *on dits*, it encountered, for the briefest of moments, the scornful stare of a haughty dark-haired man on the other side of the room, who appeared to tower over the rest of the throng. He seemed to be less a participant than an observer of the fashionable crowd before him. His gaze passed from her to the rest of Lady St. John's guests and Althea realized, with a shock, that to him, she too was part of this indistinguishable crush of social aspirants hoping to win distinction in the rarified atmosphere of the haut monde. In fact, if she had been asked, she would have had to admit that the cynical stranger's sardonic expression had grown even more derisive in the few seconds that his glance had met hers.

Althea drew an angry breath. The insolence of the man was infuriating in the extreme. How dare he pass judgment on her? How dare he condemn someone he did not even know, someone he had never encountered before in his life?

"My dear, I *do* wish you would not scowl so. It makes you look positively hatchet-faced, and if you do not have care, you will get wrinkles." The Duchess of Clarendon, about to lead her daughter toward more promising company than the group of young bucks surrounding her—men of greater fashion than eligibility—allowed herself the faintest of reproving sighs. An air of aloof superiority was one thing; after all, a certain amount of pride was expected in someone of Althea's distinction, but the ferocious frown wrinkling her brow was quite another. Her daughter's undeniable beauty quite naturally attracted universal admiration, but sooner or later her obvious disgust with the Season and its time-honored rituals was bound to put off even the hardiest of suitors.

But at the moment Althea's expression was more than one of vague distaste, it was almost angry. In an attempt to determine the source of her daughter's annoyance the duchess surveyed the room. It seemed that Althea's eyes had strayed to and then been hastily averted from one particular area of the room dominated by a tall dark-haired gentleman. "Harwood." The duchess snorted. "Do not bother to dignify him with the slightest glance, my love. No well-brought-up young woman would have anything to do with a man who spends his time in gaming rooms among such company as should not even be mentioned. Fortunately for all of us, it is a well-known fact that he is a confirmed bachelor who has never acknowledged any woman with anything more than the briefest of nods. One wonders that he is here at all. But look, there is the Duchess of Wroxleigh with her son Rupert. The Fortheringay family isn't so distinguished as the Beauchamps, but they do have extensive holdings in Hampshire and Wiltshire as well as several plantations in the West Indies. You could do worse than becoming the next Duchess of Wroxleigh."

Althea eyed the chinless, sandy-haired young man with some misgiving. Perhaps it was only shyness that gave his face the vacant expression of a flounder, but it did not look promising for any sort of conversation, intelligent or otherwise.

"My dear Duchess, it has been an age since I last saw you. And this must be your charming son." Althea's mother propelled her daughter forward with a firm but imperceptible thrust of the elbow. "How delightful that he and Althea are at last able to meet. This is her first Season and she quite longs to see a friendly face."

"Rupert!"

Prompted so peremptorily, the unhappy Rupert shuffled forward, his pale, freckled skin turning even paler. "Ah, er, yes, delighted."

Feeling sorry for someone who was obviously more miserable at finding himself in the countess's magnificent ballroom than she, Althea could not help warming to the unfortunate Rupert at least a little. "And how are you enjoying your stay in London, my lord?"

"Not at all."

Even Althea, firm believer in plain speaking that she was, found this to be a little blunt for her tastes. "Ah, then you must be missing the peace and quiet of the country, or perhaps you are an avid horseman who finds the metropolis far too confining?"

"Umm."

"Dear Rupert is a quiet lad. He minces few words, so very much like his father and not at all like these gentlemen of today, who are all flattery and no character, all talk and no action." Rupert's mother fixed a wasp-waisted young buck sporting a quizzing glass and elaborate cravat with a basilisk stare and sniffed disapprovingly. "I am sure he is longing to have you join him in the quadrille, Lady Althea." Striving to prove her son the man of action she claimed him to be, the Duchess of Wroxleigh gave him a none-too-gentle push in Althea's direction, and they were off to the dance floor where couples were just beginning to take their paces.

Watching her partner stomp through the figures of the

dance, Althea kept telling herself that he must shine in the saddle or in something that would account for his singular lack of conversation, not to mention grace. Victim of an overbearing mother herself, she knew what it was to be told constantly how to behave, to have the words taken out of her mouth before she could even frame a reply. *But at least I have the appearance of looking awake on all suits,* she told herself as she tried to smile encouragingly at her glassy-eyed partner whose expression had not registered the slightest change since the very beginning of their encounter. *And if someone were to take even the smallest interest in me I should at least have the civility to respond.*

She was thankful to her partner, however, for freeing her from her mother's watchful eye. With her daughter safely on the dance floor, partnered to a peer of unimpeachable credentials, the Duchess of Clarendon was free to search the ballroom for other eligible prospects, though there were few who could match her daughter in family and fortune.

The duchess allowed herself a tiny smile of triumph as her glance fell on Lady Belinda Carstairs. The chit was well enough dressed, for her mother frequented only the most select of the fashionable establishments in Bond Street, and she carried herself gracefully enough, but she could not hold a candle to Althea. Her color was unbecomingly high and her nose was a vulgar snub. The duchess was forced to admit to herself rather begrudgingly, however, that Lady Belinda seemed to be enjoying herself. Still, she lacked the distinction that Althea's air of cool detachment gave her.

Her Grace's smile disappeared quickly enough as she caught sight of her daughter and Rupert going through the figures of the dance. Puppets would have been more animated and certainly more self-possessed than the heir to one of the kingdom's most important families. No matter, the duchess consoled herself. Though Rupert's mama had done nothing to ensure that her son had any style or address, a strong-willed mama-in-law with a distinct air of fashion and boundless determination would be able to work wonders with the lad in spite of his unprepossessing countenance.

At last the dance ended. Lady Althea was restored to her mother and Rupert bolted like a frightened rabbit toward the refreshment room and several glasses of fortifying punch. The duchess nodded condescendingly at Rupert's mother. At least her daughter, though less animated than a mother might wish, was not an arrant coward. "So charming to have encountered you and your son. I look forward to further acquaintance, but now I see Lord Foxworthy nodding in our direction. Such a distinguished gentleman and quite taken with Althea, if you will forgive a mother's natural partiality."

Reestablishing her grip on Althea's elbow, the duchess propelled her toward a portly self-satisfied–looking gentleman whose thinning locks betrayed the number of years he had spent waiting until a partner worthy of his name could be found among the crop of hopeful young misses who frequented the most select gatherings each Season.

But before the duchess was within speaking distance of this eligible prospect, her daughter broke from her grasp. "There is Grandmama. She looks quite worn out with the closeness and the heat. I shall take her to the card room and send someone to procure refreshments."

"Really, Althea, there is no need to concern yourself. You can see that she is quite enjoying her conversation with Lady Alderly."

But her daughter had already escaped and was eagerly accosting her grandmother. "Grandmama, here you are at last. I have come to take you with me to the card room."

The Dowager Duchess of Clarendon looked up and smiled. "How very kind of you, my dear." She turned to her companion. "If you will excuse me, the heat and the crowd are quite overwhelming."

"I agree it is rather close in here and naturally you wish to join your charming granddaughter."

"Thank you, my dear." The dowager patted Althea's hand as they made their way to the card room. "Though

I suspect you are rescuing yourself quite as much as you are rescuing me."

"You know how I detest these affairs, Grandmama. I feel like a prize thoroughbred at Tattersall's being scrutinized and rated on all my finer points by people I have never met and care even less about. Mama is thoroughly put out because I do not revel in it the way she does."

"Well, she was a great beauty in her day, and to her, such attention and admiration are the very stuff of life."

"But not to me. I loathe being stared at, and I am bored to distraction by the conversation, if I am fortunate enough to be conversed with at all. I would much rather play whist. At least in the card room I can put my mind to good use."

And so can I." Althea's grandmother grinned conspiratorially. "You are not the only one forced to endure dull conversations, if what you rescued me from can even be called conversation. I have known Lydia since she was a schoolgirl, years before she met Alderly, but despite her years and experience, she is as empty-headed now as she was when I first met her."

At last they reached the card room and the dowager paused in the doorway surveying the dozen or so baize-covered tables in search of worthy opponents. Close behind her, Althea tried to peer over her shoulder without appearing to do so. One of the few benefits of her enforced visit to the metropolis was the opportunity to match her wits and card-playing skills against truly challenging opponents. While her grandmother was a formidable adversary and her parents competent enough in their own right, Althea had grown accustomed to their styles of play. The card rooms of the *ton* offered a wide array of experienced players and, if it could be said that she looked forward to anything at all in the mansions of London's most renowned hostesses, it was the chance to pit herself against those who had spent the better part of their adult lives haunting gaming tables where the stakes were higher than most average men could even comprehend.

A burst of raucous laugher to one side of her made

Althea long to push through the doorway quickly and escape into the peace and quiet of the card room. "You ain't the Duke of Wroxleigh yet, Fotheringay, but I see your expectations alone were enough to get you a dance with the Ice Princess, you lucky dog. The rest of us are never even allowed to get close enough to the Ice Princess to feast our eyes on . . ." The laugher drowned out the young buck's words, but the meaning was clear enough to send the hot blood rushing to Althea's cheeks.

"Aye, she wanted me well enough, but she is not my type." Rupert, a little worse for the glasses of punch he had gulped down after their dance, laughed uproariously.

"Not your type? What is wrong with you, man? The woman is a goddess."

"Nose ish too long." Rupert hiccoughed. "Lipsh are too thin, and the neck ish too scrawny. A man wants a real woman to love."

Glancing out of the corner of her eye at Rupert's narrow shoulders, sickly complexion, and protruding middle, Althea ground her teeth. *Scrawny neck!* At the moment she could think of nothing more satisfying than wrapping her hands around his skinny neck until the pale protuberant eyes bulged out even more, miserable worm! Althea had not deigned to exchange glances with him, had only given him the very tips of her fingers to clasp during the dance, and yet he now had the unmitigated effrontery to pass judgment on her. Oh, it was beyond all bearing.

"Ha, ha." A pimply young man even less prepossessing than Rupert giggled. "You devil you, Fotheringay, but the fortune is nothing to sneeze at."

"Perhapsh, but if I were married to the wench, I would be forced to spend so much on a cozy armful in order to keep me happy that I would need a second fortune."

Althea's clenched fingers dug into her palms until they tingled. For once in her life she agreed with her father—she wished desperately she were a man. Then she could demand satisfaction from the insolent puppy. As it was, she was simply forced to ignore it, to put it from her mind and try not to imagine how many other similar conversations were going on about the ballroom.

Chapter 3

Catching the encouraging glances of Lady Denbigh and the Countess of Northcote who were taking their places at one of the baize-covered tables, the Dowager Duchess of Clarendon turned to take her granddaughter's arm and lead her over to join them. After exchanging the briefest of pleasantries, the group fell into profound silence as they drew cards to determine their partners and the dealer. Quiet reigned as they examined their hands. Looking across the table at the calm reassuring face of her grandmother, whom she had been lucky enough to get as a partner, Althea felt the tension that had been gripping her neck and her shoulders from the moment she had entered the ballroom slip away. Here she was on familiar ground. Here no one was looking at her, judging her, calculating how much she was worth or whether she would bear healthy heirs. Here, if anyone thought about her at all, it was to wonder what cards she held in her hand.

But Althea was not entirely correct in thinking herself unobserved. All during her conversation with the Countess of Rothsay and Lady Edgcumbe, the Marchioness of Harwood had kept a sharp eye on Lady Althea Beauchamp, and the more she considered it, the more convinced she became that a young lady of such excellent background and expectations would not only be the perfect wife for her son, but an appreciative and generous daughter-in-law, one who was bound to sympathize with the trials and tribulations of a poor widow whose husband had left her less comfortable than she ought to be, and whose son had not the least notion of the necessary expenses of a lady of fashion. She had observed with some satisfaction the rigid expression on Althea's face as she performed the quadrille with the unimpressive-looking young Fotheringay and had noted the exact moment that Althea and her grandmother headed toward the card room. Excusing herself to the countess and Lady Edgcumbe, the marchioness had made her own way to the card room, nodding to acquaintances while keeping a sharp eye on the Dowager Duchess of Clarendon and her granddaughter.

It took no great powers of observation to establish that the two of them were very serious card players indeed. In fact, not one of the four ladies seated at their table was looking at any of the others, but concentrated instead on the cards in their hands with the intensity of true devotees.

A sly smile of satisfaction crept across the marchioness's face. It was perfect. Her misogynist son might resist dancing with the highly eligible Lady Althea Beauchamp, but he would not be as likely to resist a game of cards with her, particularly if he were engineered into it by the one woman he could not ignore—his mother. Nodding in a self-congratulatory manner, the marchioness slipped back out of the card room and returned to her place among the sharp-eyed dowagers clustered along the perimeter of the ballroom to learn more, if she could, about Lady Althea Beauchamp's prospects. If Gareth would not make a push to reinstate the Marchioness of Harwood to her former position of preeminence in fashionable society, then his mother was going to have to take matters into her own hands.

Meanwhile, left to her own devices, the Duchess of Clarendon, without appearing to do so, also reconnoitered the card room and, assuring herself that her daughter was quite beyond her reach, went in search of her husband.

She found him at last, deep in discussion of poor

laws and taxation with Castlereagh and Lord Eldon. Favoring her husband's companions with a brilliant smile, she apologized for interrupting them. "Forgive me. I apologize for breaking into such an enlightening discussion, my lords, but I do feel that all of you need some relief from this high seriousness. We are, after all, at a ball."

"Of course, my dear. Would you care to honor me with the next dance?" Her husband responded gallantly enough, but it was clear, as he led her reluctantly away from his cronies, that he infinitely preferred politics to dancing.

"It is not that I wish so much to dance, my lord, as to remind you that we do have a daughter making her come-out. Politics come and go from year to year, but Althea has her first Season only once. I cannot manage anything so critical as finding a suitable husband for her on my own, you know."

"But my dear, I was working on that very thing."

The duchess's finely arched brows rose in disbelief.

Even now, after twenty-five years of marriage, her expression of patent incredulity caused a flush to rise to her husband's bony cheeks. He knew, and he had always known, that it was only his fortune, his family, and his title that had won the beautiful Miss Dorothea Williston, toast of a long-ago Season, as his wife.

The Willistons were a respectable family, though not wealthy or illustrious enough to command the attention of the *ton* until the second daughter, Dorothea, made her appearance. Exquisitely beautiful and possessed of a captivating manner, she had taken the *ton*, including the Duke of Clarendon, by storm. Even now, the duke could not believe that it had been he, among all her suitors, who had had the good fortune to win her hand.

Though he was well enough convinced of his own importance as one of the last of the illustrious Beauchamp line, and fully cognizant of the respect he commanded as the Duke of Clarendon, he still carried within him the knowledge that Henry Beauchamp, scorned by his schoolmates at Eton as a prosy old bore, offered no competition to the dashing fellows who made up the lovely Dorothea's circle of admirers. And despite a quarter of a century as the acknowledged victor in the competition for her hand, he could still never quite believe he had won it.

"And how, pray tell, does a discussion of taxation with Castlereagh and Eldon have anything to do with finding a husband for our daughter?"

"Eldon has a son and Castlereagh has a brother."

The duchess was nonplussed. "William Henry Scott? Charles Stewart? My lord, Althea can command a duke at the very least, and a wealthy one at that."

"Perhaps, but who is to say that the right political connection is not more powerful than money or a title? The Beauchamps have been helping to govern this land since the Conqueror. I will not let that glorious tradition die out simply because I have been blessed with a daughter instead of a son."

"But Stewart? He is a second son, and a rather harum-scarum one at that, while Scott simply has no cachet at all."

"Well, Castlereagh's wife is not likely to give birth to an heir now. And both men move in the highest circles."

"*Political* circles." His wife snorted in disgust. "I can see that it is all up to me to make Althea a match worthy of her since neither my husband nor my daughter will make the least push to do so."

"No, no, my dear. I promise you, I shall speak to St. John and Montague at White's tomorrow. They both have sons of a marriageable age. You may count on me, I assure you." The duke, appalled by the thought of having to spend a second Season assiduously attending all the *ton* functions, hastened to reassure his wife of his total support.

Somewhat mollified, she allowed him to lead her onto the dance floor. Her husband was not a graceful dancer, but he did creditably enough and at least he did not disgrace himself like Lord Kiloran who insisted on capering around the floor as though he were half of his advanced age. And there was no denying that with his silver hair, angular features, and long patrician nose her husband looked every inch the duke he was.

The slight frown that had begun to wrinkle the duchess's brow disappeared. She was suffering a temporary setback; that was all. A recalcitrant daughter and a husband oblivious to the finer points of matchmaking in the *ton* were daunting to be sure, but her daughter was an incomparable of incomparables and her husband was a man of rank, wealth, and power, even if it was only political power. She was just going to have to be more forceful in her representations to both of them of the necessity of their joining with her in her efforts to find Althea a husband worthy of them all.

The duchess began her campaign to enlist their compliance immediately after the ball as they drove back to Clarendon House. Chatting brightly, she ignored their silence as they gazed out the carriage windows at the elegant facades of the houses they passed with their well-scrubbed steps, brilliantly polished brass, and exquisite fanlights over imposing doorways. "My dear"—she turned to her daughter—"you were quite the toast of the evening. Even in such a sad crush it was abundantly clear that you were the object of all eyes, and certainly the center of the largest crowd of admirers. Why the group around Lady Mary Sotherton was nothing to the one around you."

Althea sat mute, having learned from years of experience that it was useless to point out that her popularity was largely the consequence of her being one of three unmarried daughters of dukes present that evening. And since one of them had a dreadful squint and a laugh like a donkey and the other was the only daughter of a man whose heavily mortgaged estates were in dire need of an infusion of money from a wealthy son-in-law, it was not entirely surprising that she attracted attention. The duchess would simply ignore such a rational response or would label it unattractively pert.

"If I were such a fortunate person, I would feel exceedingly gratified. Were you not? Come now, Althea, do not be sullen. It is not in the least becoming. Were you not gratified at the very particular attention you were shown by such eligible young men as Fotheringay?"

Althea gritted her teeth as the image of the bragging, tipsy young lord and his friends rose before her eyes. "Yes, Mama," she responded dully.

"Really, Althea. You could show a little enthusiasm for all that I am doing to ensure that you are suitably launched. Even dukes' daughters with expectations can end up on the shelf if they do not exhibit a little animation."

"Yes, Mama." It was also useless to express the heretical notion that being "on the shelf" appeared, to Althea at least, to be a delightfully comfortable place to end up. Untroubled by interfering husbands or parents, free to pursue one's own interests, and not obliged to spend hours with dressmakers in order to appear to advantage at yet another stultifying function, being "on the shelf," seemed like a paradise compared to being the incomparable of incomparables.

"Your mother does make a point, Althea. A young woman has only one way to carry on the honor of her family, and that is to ally her name with one that is equally illustrious. Since you were born I have tried to inspire in you the proper respect and reverence for the long and honorable tradition of the Beauchamps, and I am sure you intend to see to it that this tradition continues."

"Yes, Papa." Althea felt herself receding into the darkness. Was she a person to anyone but herself, she wondered? Did anyone wish to make her acquaintance or spend time with her because they appreciated who she was and not because of the fortune and connections she stood for?

The vision of a dark cynical face and scornful eyes raking over her rose before her. Well, there was one person at least who did not seem to care that she was the Season's most eligible young woman. It annoyed her intensely to be dismissed out of hand as she had been, to be judged before she was even acquainted, but it also intrigued her. Who was this Harwood whom her mother considered to be unfit for a properly brought up young woman, and why did he harbor such a disgust for Lady Althea Beauchamp? At least she could look forward to amusing herself at the next fashionable squeeze by trying to discover the answer to this riddle.

Chapter 4

Oddly enough, Althea was not alone in her wish to learn more about the person with whom she had briefly exchanged glances at the St. John's rout. Though he was not even aware of his desire to do so until he found himself surveying ballrooms for a beautiful face with a flawless complexion, sapphire eyes, and hair so dark it appeared shiny blue-black, Gareth too had been unable to forget the woman who caught his attention, unwilling though it was.

Gareth's mother, on the other hand, was fully conscious of her desire to see the sought-after Lady Althea Beauchamp again and make her acquaintance. In fact, an introduction to Lady Althea had become her major goal in attending the select events to which she dragged her son. Gareth still protested at the number and frequency of these functions, but if he seemed a little less resistant to the idea of escorting his mother than he had been previously, she was too intent on her quarry to remark upon it.

After observing Lady Althea at several of these fashionable gatherings, the marchioness was able to assure herself that at some point in the evening, Althea and her grandmother never failed to escape to the card room, and she laid her plans accordingly. The Marchioness of Harwood could not equal her son in his skill at cards—she had neither the wit nor the concentration for it—but she was no worse than most of those crowding around the tables and a good deal better than many.

She knew that her son, while faithful to his promise to accompany her, did try to limit the time he spent at *ton* affairs by leaving as early as possible, often seeking her out midway through the evening. Taking this into account, she carefully constructed her strategy.

"My dear Lavinia"—she fixed Lady Edgcumbe with a knowing eye as they sat together at Lady Nayland's annual ball—"you are such a sensitive creature. Surely your head aches as much as mine does from the heat and the crowd. Do let us repair to the peace and quiet of the card room."

Lady Edgcumbe glanced at her companion in some surprise, for usually the marchioness, who still retained some her former beauty, preferred to be as close as possible to the very center of activity and attention. But there was an insistence in Sally's voice that piqued her curiosity. "Very well." Smoothing out the ample skirt of her purple satin gown, Lady Edgcumbe rose in stately fashion and followed her friend in the direction of the card room.

They had only proceeded a few paces, however, when the marchioness grasped her arm and whispered loudly in her ear. "I do have rather a favor to ask of you, Lavinia. When Gareth approaches us, as he will fairly soon, no doubt, I beg you to think of some excuse to leave us."

Lady Edgcumbe loved intrigue as much as any other dowager who spent her evenings gossiping about the matrimonial prospects of those in their first Season and the indiscretions of young matrons who, having made their respectable alliances, were now intent on enjoying themselves, so she asked no questions, but smiled knowingly at her friend. The marchioness was an intrigant of the highest stature, and to watch her in action was worth the price of admission. Whatever her game was, it undoubtedly involved her son and money, two things that always seemed to be in short supply for the Marchioness of Harwood.

Gareth's mother had caught sight of Althea and her grandmother heading in the direction of the card room some time earlier, and she was relieved to discover that they had established themselves at a table with the Marchioness of Barlow and Lady Dalrymple, with whom she could claim some slight acquaintance.

Assuming an air of polite concern, she approached the table exclaiming, "My dear Lady Dalrymple, how glad I am to discover you here, for not five minutes ago I encountered your daughter and I must say, she does not look at all the thing. I suggested to her that I look for you, but she insisted it was nothing, a mere headache brought on by the closeness of the ballroom. I begged her to sit down by one of the windows and take some fresh air, for indeed, she was looking far from well."

Lady Dalrymple rose in some alarm. "In that case, I . . ."

"Do not distress yourself." The marchioness laid a comforting hand on the other lady's arm. "She assured me that she was not in the least need of assistance though she did appear to be remarkably pale."

By now Lady Dalrymple looked thoroughly alarmed and Gareth's mother, directing a meaningful look at Lady Edgcumbe, continued. "Well, if you insist on going to her, and I must say I think it is best, Lady Edgcumbe and I will take your places here at the table so as not to deprive your opponents of their game. No, my dear Marchioness, I do not blame you in the least for accompanying Lady Dalrymple. I am sure these ladies will excuse you, and Lady Edgcumbe and I will do our poor best to make up for your departure."

And with the most sympathetic and helpful expressions the Marchioness of Harwood neatly ousted the two women and took their places at the table with Althea and her grandmother. "I do beg your pardon for intruding, but as a fond mother myself, I know the agonies one suffers if one's child is unwell, even if that child is fully grown. I am delighted to see Your Grace looking so well. I remember, though I am sure you do not, being introduced to you my first Season. My mother pointed you out as someone whose dignified air and exquisite manners were well worth copying. 'A beautiful face can count for nothing,

Sally,' she told me, 'if one's manners are not equal to the distinction of one's countenance. And for manners you could do no better than to observe closely and emulate the Duchess of Clarendon's.'"

Too bemused by this unexpected effusiveness to react, Althea's grandmother could do nothing but nod graciously. Before she could even open her mouth to acknowledge her thanks, the marchioness rattled on. "And this must be your granddaughter, Lady Althea." Directing a conspiratorial smile at Althea, she lowered her voice to an intimate whisper. "A young woman whom I would not presume to embarrass by acknowledging as the incomparable of incomparables, except that it is a fact so widely known that everyone must acknowledge it. No, do not blush, my dear, for you certainly deserve such a reputation. Great beauty is a gift of the gods, but the notoriety it brings can be an enormous burden. No one knows that better than I, and I do sympathize, believe me. Now"—she laid a finger on her lips and smiled again—"I promise to keep silent and speak of nothing but the game."

And thus, with a skill that even Lady Edgcumbe was forced to admire, the marchioness not only succeeded in maneuvering the two of them into a game with the dowager duchess and her granddaughter, she managed to ingratiate herself with the two women as well.

It was some time later, and just as the marchioness had planned, that Gareth finally located his mother in the card room. They were in the middle of a game when the marchioness, who had been keeping close watch out of the corner of her eye, exclaimed, "And there is my Gareth now. Such an attentive son. I knew it would not be long before he came to see if his mama was in need of her shawl."

She glanced in a most pointed manner at Lady Edgcumbe who, immediately recognizing her cue, put a hand to her brow and sighed gently. "The air is so close in here. My dear Sally, I do feel the most vile headache coming on. If you all will forgive me, I believe I shall seek some fresh air." Smiling apologetically at Althea and her grandmother, she rose and hurried from the card room.

"Poor Lavinia. She is a perfect martyr to her dreadful headaches," the marchioness chirped brightly. "But no matter. Gareth can take her place. Can you not, my dear? Gareth is a superb player. It is said that he has won a fortune at cards, though his poor mama has yet to see any evidence of it." The acid tone of her voice was oddly at variance with the marchioness's fond greeting.

Althea, her gaze riveted to her cards, could not help darting a curious glance at the marchioness and her son. The bitter twist of the marchioness's rouged lips quickly smoothed into a doting smile as she presented her handsome son to her opponents, but not before Althea had seen her bitter look and wondered at it, as well as the angry tightening of the son's lips, an expression that was also quickly banished as he acknowledged the Dowager Duchess of Clarendon and her granddaughter.

In fact, Gareth was doing his best to hide the fury that had risen within him the moment he had discovered the identity of his mother's companions. The witch! As usual, she was bound and determined to have her own way. Not content with pointing out to him the most eligible young woman of the Season, she was forcing him into an introduction, and there was nothing, short of being brutally and inexcusably rude, that he could do to avoid it.

Gareth took his place in the fragile-looking gilt chair vacated by Lady Edgcumbe. Of course he could be brutally and inexcusably rude—he had been so before, and no doubt he would be again— but for some inexplicable reason, he did not wish to be so now. Picking up the cards Lady Edgcumbe had laid down he made a pretense of looking at them, but in truth he was examining the face opposite him. She was even more lovely up close than she was at a distance, and she refused to look at him.

Lady Althea sat proudly erect, her eyes riveted on her own hand, the beautifully sculpted face devoid of expression, any expression at all.

"We must deal over again." Althea's grandmother *was*

looking at him. "We certainly cannot expect Harwood to pick up in the middle of someone else's game."

"Thank you for your concern, but it is no matter." Gareth waved her objection aside. "I still hope to offer you a creditable challenge."

That got Althea's attention. The dark blue eyes fixed him with a measuring stare that quite took his breath away. They were her finest feature in a face full of fine features. As dark as the most priceless of sapphires and fringed with thick dark lashes that contrasted with the pale smoothness of a flawless complexion, they were deep enough for a man to drown in. But it was the expression in them that took him by surprise. There was not an ounce of coquetry, nor the slightest flicker of flirtation. And it dawned on him that Lady Althea Beauchamp was not the least bit interested in the Marquess of Harwood as a man. If she were interested in him at all, it was only as an opponent.

A rueful smile tugged at the corners of Gareth's mouth. Much as he hated to admit it, it was a rather lowering experience to be regarded in that light. He had become so accustomed to evading every feminine ploy, dampening matrimonial hopes in so many score of female breasts that, until this moment, he had begun to assume that he was irresistible to the entire sex.

Giving himself a mental shake, he stifled a grin and glanced back at his cards. If Lady Althea preferred a good opponent to a good catch, or even a good man, then, by God, she would not be disappointed. And ignoring the fact that he was breaking one of his cardinal rules—never cater to female expectations—he concentrated on giving her the best damn opponent she would ever have.

Chapter 5

I still hope to offer you a creditable challenge. In spite of her resolve to have nothing to do with the man, Althea could not help glancing up in surprise. The man was either a fool, a braggart of incredible proportions, or very, very good. But as she looked straight into those clear gray eyes that returned her gaze just as steadily and calmly as if he were taking aim at some target in Manton's Shooting Gallery, she could not detect even a hint of guile or unease.

Covertly, she studied the long, slender fingers clasping his cards, but could find no clue there either—not so much as a tremor or a nervous shuffling of his hand—that he was anything but supremely confident. Then, she concluded, and she did not know why it should have pleased her to arrive at this conclusion, he must be very good.

As the game wore on she was to amend that conclusion. The Marquess of Harwood was not only very good, he was very good indeed. Without betraying anything but the most casual interest in the game, he managed not only to hold his own against two practiced players, but rescued himself and his partner from several potentially disastrous blunders his partner had committed.

Oblivious to it all, the marchioness chattered on—London seemed particularly full of company this year, which was why it was especially plaguing that she was not ensconced in her own spacious town house in Berkeley

Square, but positively exiled to the most inconvenient lodgings in Hanover Square, which, her tone implied, was as far away from the truly fashionable enclaves as to seem like Timbuktu or the Americas.

"And it is also why we are being paid an exorbitant price for the use of a house in Berkeley Square with rooms too numerous and too grand for a widow who does no entertaining and her son who has quarters elsewhere." The marquess spoke so softly that for a moment Althea was not even certain he had responded, but the very softness of his low tone only added to its intensity.

His mother had sounded merely pettish and complaining, but he reacted in a way that suggested a far deeper and more serious antagonism, an antagonism that had been building for years. Althea recognized it in an instant as the response of someone who had been driven to it, someone who had been quietly putting up with a situation for years while resentment grew. She had suffered from that same slow, simmering resentment herself and was more than familiar with all its outward signs—the resentment of one whose interests were never recognized for they were considered unimportant or irrelevant in comparison to the desires of those who surrounded her, the resentment of someone who was not only expected to go along with these desires so totally contrary to her own, but to do so willingly and happily.

She stole another glance at the marquess, but the lean, angular features remained impassive. Only someone who knew what it was to stifle her own emotions time and again could detect the clenched muscles of his jaw and the tightening in the corners of his eyes that betrayed just how tightly he was holding his anger in check. It was another revelation to her. Until now, Althea had thought that it was only dutiful, unmarried daughters who suffered from the demands of rigid, self-centered parents, but apparently it was possible even for men, possessors of estates and ancient titles and considerable fortunes in their own right, who could be made to suffer as well, and she could not help smiling at the absurdity of it all.

It was the faintest of smiles, a mere tugging at the corners of her mouth, but it caught Gareth's attention in an instant. Good God. Could it be that the Ice Princess had actually deigned to smile at him?

He studied her curiously for a moment. Not only did she smile, but there appeared to be a glimmer of understanding in those magnificent eyes and a hint of sympathy in the gently curved lips. Disbelieving what he saw, he quirked one quizzical dark brow and, to his amazement, was rewarded with the faintest of nods and a ruefully sympathetic lift of the lady's own delicately arched brows.

Then she immediately focused her attention back on the cards in front of her and he was left to wonder if the silent communication had taken place at all or if he had just imagined it. However, Gareth de Vere was not given to flights of fancy where women were concerned and from what he had seen of this particular woman, she did not respond to anything unless she meant to.

And, he realized in some dismay, this woman and her partner had just taken the last three tricks. Taking himself severely to task for letting his concentration slip, even in such a trivial game as this, Gareth pushed all further speculations aside, tantalizing though they were, and concentrated on the game before him.

But it was slowly and unpleasantly borne in on him that wandering attention was not necessarily the reason for the three lost tricks, nor was it blind luck on the part of his opponent, he thought grimly as he surrendered yet another trick. Surprising as it seemed, the dowager and her granddaughter knew what they were about, or at least they knew enough not to give up the advantage of good hands easily.

Pay attention, Gareth admonished himself as he focused on the cards in his hand and rapidly reviewed in his mind as many of the tricks as he could remember being played. That done, he struggled to identify the method Lady Althea and her partner were using to signal each other as to which cards to play. It was certainly not the obvious one of leading a long suit.

This preoccupation cost him the game, which, as the cards were dealt out for the next, he grimly resolved would be the only one he would concede to the two ladies. His opponents might be better than average players, but there was no need to add to their sense of consequence by losing to them. It was time to stop handing them their tricks and play in earnest.

This was not so easily done, however. In the subsequent round the marquess was burdened with an extraordinarily poor hand and during the one following that his mother's increasingly provocative remarks to Lady Althea about her son's status as the Bachelor Marquess distracted him to such a degree that before he knew it, Gareth and his mother had lost the rubber.

Amazement gave way to interest in his opponents' success and Gareth soon became oblivious to anything but the cards. The lovely young woman across from him ceased to exist as anything but a strategist to be beaten. He cleared his mind and senses of all extraneous thoughts. His bored distaste for the fashionable crush around him vanished as the electricity of competition energized him. Here were opponents worthy of the name, opponents who changed this particular game from an enforced filial duty to a sport.

In fact, the intensity of the play was having the same energizing effect on other players at the table, all of them except the marchioness, whose constant flow of pleasantries began to dry up as it slowly dawned on her that no one was responding to them, or even listening. She surveyed her companions at the table in dismay. Here she had cleverly arranged an introduction between one of the *ton*'s most elusive yet eligible bachelors and the reigning incomparable of the Season, and for all the effect it was having she might as well have brought together two aged grandmothers. Her son and Lady Althea were completely oblivious to each other, oblivious to everything but the cards in their hands. The marchioness sighed audibly. Her rouged lips drooped in disappointment, but no one paid the least attention.

In truth Gareth had never concentrated so much on one woman in his life; he had certainly never spent so much time or effort trying to divine what she was thinking. This single-minded focus paid off, and during the next hand he was at least able to keep Althea and her grandmother from capturing all the tricks, though he suspected that his own handful of trump cards had as much to do with his success as anything else.

In the succeeding hand, however, rapid and careful calculations enabled him to capture the lead with a two of spades and he began to hope that he had recovered from the shock of being seriously challenged by females and had come into his own again. Gareth even allowed himself a tiny smile of triumph when Althea, caught off guard by such a bold move, glanced up at him with an expression of both admiration and dismay. Obviously Lady Althea Beauchamp was not accustomed to being bested at cards either.

This moment of inattention on her part cost Althea and her grandmother the game, or so Althea told herself. It would have been too annoying to believe anything else, but the marquess was certainly a skillful player and one who seemed to be as skilled as she was at remembering what cards had been played by whom and figuring the odds quickly.

As he captured the lead in another game, Althea even began to be concerned that she might lose. They battled on, neither one allowing the other to gain anything but the smallest lead, and what Gareth had intended to be only a hand or two of cards played to humor his mother into leaving the ball early turned into one rubber after another.

As the crowd in the card room began to thin, the marchioness allowed herself a small smile of satisfaction. She might not have succeeded in initiating any conversation between her son and the incomparable of incomparables, but at least she had maneuvered them into each other's company for a goodly amount of time and her son was no longer looking daggers at her for having done so.

In truth, the Marchioness of Harwood could not think of a time when she had managed to keep her son at a fashionable event for such a lengthy period of time. If only the Beauchamp girl would stop looking at her hand and concentrate on making herself agreeable to her handsome son.

Gareth's mother scrutinized Althea critically. The young woman was frowning meditatively at the cards in her hand without sparing a thought for what the wrinkles in her forehead did to her charming countenance. Any young lady who knew what she was about would have been smiling over her cards at the marquess and making a play with those exceptionally fine eyes. But the young woman in question did none of that. The marchioness shook her head sadly. Such imperviousness to her son's obvious attractions was almost unnatural. She was going to have her work cut out for her to bring these two together.

She cast a warm, approving smile in Althea's direction. "My dear, you play exceptionally well for one so young. I fear that means you have been buried in the country-side and away from company that can appreciate your beauty and charm for far too long a time. Is she not a most enchanting player, Gareth?"

"Too enchanting." Gareth raised a rueful eyebrow as he surrendered yet another trick to Althea and her grandmother.

"That is high praise indeed, my dear, for Gareth is a connoisseur of these things and very critical. We are quite honored that he deigned to play with us at all, are we not, Gareth?" She winked playfully at her son who, ignoring her completely, gathered up the trick and led the next one.

Realizing that all her efforts were fruitless at a table where the rest of the people insisted on playing cards, the marchioness eventually subsided and continued on with the game. But it had not been an entirely wasted evening. Her son and the Season's most eligible heiress had been introduced, and the next time she and Gareth encountered Lady Althea Beauchamp there would be no excuse for him not chatting or dancing with her. Then the Marchioness of Harwood could begin her campaign to repair her fallen fortunes and social standing in earnest.

Chapter 6

Surprisingly enough, both Gareth and Althea, if they had been asked, would have agreed with the marchioness. As two highly intelligent people who not only took card playing seriously, but appreciated the opportunity it offered to exercise that intelligence, they welcomed the test of competing against another person who possessed similar gifts. The discovery of such an equal was all the more surprising given the location—a ball where neither one had looked forward to anything more than social drudgery. But they were not allowed to ignore their larger surroundings by losing themselves in the game for long. Even though they had managed to play several rubbers, reality intruded all too quickly for both Gareth and Althea in the form of Althea's cousin, the Honorable Reginald Cathcart.

Beautiful to behold in a coat so exquisitely cut that it had cost his valet and a manservant considerable time and effort to help him into it, his cravat so intricately tied that it had taken the better part of two hours and a pile of rejected neck cloths to accomplish it, Reginald sauntered into the card room and strolled over to Althea's table.

His appearance in the card room was not in the least accidental. When commanded by the Duchess of Clarendon, as he had been, one obeyed as expeditiously as possible. Ordinarily, Reginald avoided his aunt whenever possible, for she always seemed to think of something for him to do the minute she laid eyes upon him.

He had come to associate an encounter with the Duchess of Clarendon with a considerable expenditure of effort, something Reginald did his best to avoid at all costs, unless it involved his tailor.

But he had allowed his attention to wander this evening as he had been critically surveying the latest crop of young misses through a slender gold quizzing glass. He knew he would have to pay the price for this lapse when he heard his name pronounced so close to his left shoulder that it was impossible to pretend not to have heard it.

"Reginald. Reginald, do pay attention."

"Aunt." Reginald had stifled a sigh as he turned to see the duchess moving purposefully toward him. "You never fail to look exquisite each time I see you." With a sinking heart he executed the graceful bow that had made him famous throughout the ballrooms of the *ton*. "You set an example of taste and style that makes you the despair of aspiring fashionables."

"Thank you, my dear. You always were the most discriminating of young men." The duchess glanced down with some satisfaction at the magnificent sapphire and diamond bracelets that matched her earrings, necklace, and the aigrette in her tocque à la Berri. "It is most fortunate that I encountered you, for you can be of great service to me at the moment."

"I am delighted. You have but to name it." Reginald cursed himself silently and thoroughly for not having kept a weather eye out for the duchess from the moment he had entered the ballroom.

"Althea and her grandmother have disappeared into the card room." The slight compression of the duchess's artfully tinted lips suggested that this was not the first time such a thing had occurred. "Dearest Althea is so solicitous of her grandmother that she forgets the purpose behind our presence here. Do be a dear boy and find her for me."

"Very well. I shall not return without her." The steely glint in the duchess's eye did not bode well for her daughter, and feeling like a traitor, Reginald headed off

in the direction of the card room. If Althea was not at
her mother's side, there was a good reason for it. She
must have escaped in order to protect herself from being
bullied into doing something she did not wish to do. Reginald had grown up with his cousin and knew that despite
being a person of decided opinions and fierce independence, she was no match for her strong-minded parents,
especially her mother.

He took his time as he threaded his way through the
crowd, stopping to compliment a preening dowager here,
a blushing young miss there, and generally making himself agreeable in the way that had earned him his reputation as a most affable young man about town.

Reaching the card room at last, Reginald paused in
the doorway to scan the tables for his cousin and her
grandmother. Finally locating them in the farthest, most
quiet corner of the room, he was beginning to make his
way toward them when his jaw dropped in astonishment,
or dropped as far as his high, starched collar points
would allow. His quiet, bluestocking of a cousin was playing cards with none other than the scourge of the
Brooks's card room, the misanthropic avoider of *ton*
functions, the Bachelor Marquess.

Faced with such a titillating bit of information, it was
almost impossible for Reginald to maintain his carefully cultivated air of blasé indifference. Indeed, it took
several deep breaths before he could muster the
strength to approach and deliver his message in an appropriately offhand manner. "Ah, Cousin, here you
are. My aunt has sent me to retrieve you from this
wasteland of chance and fortune and return you to
your proper sphere of admiring suitors where you are
sorely missed."

Althea scowled a most unladylike scowl and sighed
audibly. "Yes, Reginald. But I must finish this rubber
first."

Gareth quickly stifled a grin. No professional beauty
would have allowed herself to be caught dead with such
an unattractive expression on her face and he liked her
the better for it. As she deliberated longer and longer

over each play, he began to suspect that she was not a little reluctant to obey her cousin's summons and he could not help being intrigued. Perhaps there was more to this incomparable than met the eye. But whatever else she was, she was an angel with cards.

At last there was no avoiding it. Althea played her final card, captured the final trick, and won the rubber. As she rose to follow Reginald back to the ballroom she turned toward Gareth and his mother. "Thank you both for a most enjoyable game."

"We must play again soon, my dear." Quick to seize an opportunity to throw Lady Althea and her son together again, the marchioness smiled warmly and reached over to squeeze Althea's hand.

"I would like that." Althea smiled shyly back at the marchioness in a way that forced Gareth to reexamine his opinion of the Ice Princess yet again. Away from the watchful eye of the Duchess of Clarendon and free from her crowd of admirers, she seemed almost ingenuous. Could it be that she was reserved rather than cold, diffident rather than disdainful? It was such an interesting thought that Gareth found himself mulling it over and over again in his mind as he escorted his mother back to the detested rooms in Hanover Square and then made his way to Brooks's in search of more serious play.

Perhaps it was the fatigue of spending more than the usual amount of time with his mother; perhaps it was the constraint he had felt playing against females that now made him tired and stupid. Whatever the cause for it, Gareth found that the subsequent games he played at his club were decidedly inferior to those he had just experienced in Lady Nayland's card room.

For some reason the players at Brooks's that evening lacked the éclat and brilliance of true gamblers, or perhaps his fatigue was making him play mechanically and that was affecting both his partner and their opponents. Whatever it was, the play was decidedly flat and utterly lacking in challenge; despite his own lack of strategy he found himself taking trick after trick with such regularity that he became thoroughly bored with it all in a very short space of time. At last he laid down his cards in disgust and rose to go in search of more excitement.

"What? Leaving already, Harwood? The night is yet young." Lord Lincolnwood stretched his long legs in front of him and downed another glass of port.

Gareth stifled a yawn. "Devilish flat tonight, Linky. It is time for me to find some more enlivening diversion."

Lord Lincolnwood grinned. "We could triple the stakes, if you like. But perhaps that is not the sort of excitement you are seeking. Doubtless the lovely Maria Toscana can stir those jaded pulses more than the chance to win or lose a fortune at play. A passionate woman, Maria, if she is only half as electric in person as she is on stage."

Gareth shrugged. "Here I can do nothing but win. Where is the excitement in that? At least the lady's temper is more uncertain than the cards are tonight. I shall test my skills there and see how my luck holds after days of ignoring her."

"You are a devil, Gareth. If you do not have care you will lose her to a more constant cicisbeo."

"Not I. The beauteous Maria and I have a purely business relationship. I keep her liberally supplied with pin money and buy her whatever baubles her heart desires. These are the only expectations she has of me, and I only ask one thing from her in return—satisfaction. It is the best kind of relationship. The rules are well understood by both parties, and since they were clearly stated at the outset, there are no misunderstandings, no tears or tantrums."

"But you just said . . ."

"Every woman has her vanity, Linky; it is natural to the creatures. But Maria is a simple person, and her only worry when I ignore her is that I am dallying with another. She stands to lose significant income should I lose interest in her, a fear that can be quickly laid to rest by the presentation of another expensive trinket."

"Sounds like a damned cold-blooded relationship to me."

"On the contrary, it is extremely, ah, *ardent*. The Italian temperament is predisposed to lovemaking."

"Perhaps, but who wants a woman to look upon one as a mere banker?"

"Believe me, it is more pleasant than being what the world calls *loved*. Maria only asks money of me. That is easy to give. However, a woman who claims to love becomes jealous of one's time and attention. The object of her love is subjected to increasing demands; the expectations are as limitless and variable as the woman's state of mind, and the lover is supposed to be alive to all these variations all the time. I will take a woman who asks for my purse over the woman who demands my heart and soul any day."

"I tell you, Gareth, it ain't natural. At the end of a day every man wants a cozy little armful who cares about him."

"Not I. Give me freedom anytime. I prefer to live my own life to having it run for me by someone who does not understand me, but whose mere interest in me, for whatever reason—fortune, position, title—gives her the right to dictate my actions."

"Sounds damn lonely to me."

"But uncomplicated."

Gareth took his leave and headed toward the snug little villa in Marylebone that he had purchased for Maria some months before. The dancer had just arrived home herself after a most successful evening. Having been singled out by particular applause and numerous floral tributes, she was feeling quite pleased with herself. The long slender box that Gareth presented to her by way of apology for his absence only added to her sense of well-being.

"My lord," she exclaimed, lifting out the diamond bracelet and trying it on her slender wrist, "it is exquisite. You are so generous. But"—she wrapped her arms around his neck and pulled his head down to look up at him under seductively lowered lids as her tongue flicked over her full, red lower lip—"I can be generous too." Her mouth clung to his as she pressed herself into his arms.

Why, Gareth asked himself as his hands traced the ripe curves of her truly voluptuous figure, should he be thinking of a pair of startling blue eyes set under delicately arched brows when deep rich brown ones, warm with passionate invitation, were promising him a world of physical delights? He could not imagine why the image of another woman's delicate eyebrows frowning in concentration or her beautifully sculpted lips compressed in thought should intrude into his consciousness at this particular and most inopportune moment. Or why, he wondered, as his lips explored Maria's, should he be speculating on whether or not such passion could be aroused in an Ice Princess.

But Maria was far too skillful to allow a lover much time for wandering thoughts. Undoing the marquess's neck cloth as she pulled him toward the low damask sofa, she soon made Gareth forget everything but her long, firm dancer's legs and the hungry lips that claimed his.

Several hours later, a pleasantly exhausted Gareth slowly donned his clothes as he admired the picture she made, her nude body draped across the rich fabric of the sofa, the glow of the flickering firelight playing on her skin.

Maria raised her graceful arm to admire the sparkle of firelight in the diamonds on her wrist. "It is a lovely bracelet." She smiled with satisfaction at the picture it made on her bare arm.

"To make up for an absent lover and the warm welcome he received despite his absence."

"Why should I waste time sulking over his absence? The two things of most importance in my life are passion and money, and I savor them both—passion to be enjoyed for now, and money for when I am too old to enjoy passion."

Gareth glanced in the looking glass and gave his cravat a final tweak. "You are a practical woman, Maria, a rarity among your sex, believe me."

"What other way is there to be?" The dancer shrugged her elegant shoulders.

"What other way, indeed?" But Gareth found himself thinking not about the dancer's practicality, but the practical streak of someone so coolly self-possessed that she could ignore everything to beat him soundly at cards.

Chapter 7

The question of practicality was most definitely a concern the next morning in an elegant drawing room in Grosvenor Square where the young woman in question was trying desperately to convince herself that the inquiries she was posing to her cousin Reginald were motivated by purely pragmatic considerations.

His own curiosity piqued the previous evening by the sight of Althea playing whist with one of the *ton*'s most notorious gamblers, Reginald had made it his first priority, after consulting for the better part of the morning with his tailor, to call on his cousin and discover more about the particulars of the situation.

"My dear Althea, you are frequenting very select cardplaying circles indeed if you can convince Harwood to take a seat at your table, but are you sure you know what you are about? Do take care; he is dangerous company."

"Reginald, you *know* that I am always careful to a fault." Althea sighed. "I *never* do anything that is not perfectly becoming to the only child of the Duke of Clarendon. The Marchioness of Harwood was most gracious to Grandmama and me, befriending us and offering herself and her son as partners. In fact, she went so far as to say that we can count on seeing them regularly at all the functions Mama insists we attend. You know I find it uncomfortable to appear at these things where I know no one and Mama insists on thrusting me into the arms of one highly eligible young man after another, regardless of whether or not they can put two words together. The marchioness has been most cordial, which I cannot say of most people. She knows that Grandmama and I enjoy a game of whist, and the first time we played with her, she was so kind as to ask her son to take the place of her partner so that we could continue even when Lady Edgcumbe left because of a headache. I was not at all sure at the outset that her son was best pleased by this arrangement. He seems a rather formidable person, does he not?"

"Formidable! *Unbeatable* is more the word. My dear Althea, you have no idea! He has made a fortune at the tables. They say he never loses, and that he never wastes his time on a game where he does not stand to win at least ten thousand a sitting. The question is, what is he doing playing against you and your grandmother?"

"I told you, his mother asked him to take the place of her partner. And Grandmama and I are quite good, you know."

"Yes, I know you are, but Harwood is the *best*! He is a wizard with cards and no one has beaten him yet."

"Except me."

"You *what?*"

"I beat him. Well, Grandmama and I did. It was a very near thing, and he *is* certainly a very fine card player, but we beat him all the same."

Oblivious to the wrinkles he was making in his coat and his waistcoat, Reginald leaned forward eagerly, his boyish face flushed with enthusiasm. "I say, Allie, what was it like? It is common knowledge that no matter how much money you have to lose, he will only play against the best of the best; he says there's no point in it otherwise. I am longing to try my hand against him."

"No, Reggie."

"But, Allie, you know I have played . . ."

"Yes, but you have not established a reputation anywhere near to what you claim the Marquess of Harwood's to be."

"How can you say that? I have been playing since I was in short coats. I am a regular at Brooks's. I . . ."

"Because I have played against you, Reggie."

"Oh."

"And beaten your consistently." Althea could not help smiling at her cousin's crestfallen expression.

"Reggie, believe me, he is very, very good. You may have experience, but this man is brilliant, at cards anyway. It is quite obvious that he has a prodigious memory, a head for figures, and a talent for strategy. In fact, I have never seen better. However, they are just not equal to Grandmama's and mine. And," she added reluctantly, "his mother, though competent, was not an equal partner the way Grandmama and I are. If she had been, what a game it would have been." A reminiscent smile curved Althea's lips.

"All the more reason I should like to play against him."

"I warn you, Reggie, you will find yourself under the hatches in no time, and you cannot afford that. Even you must acknowledge that your talent for choosing a waistcoat or tying a cravat is far superior to your skill at cards."

"You sound just like Augustus. He too considers me a useless fribble."

His cousin's eyes softened. "No, Reggie. You are not a useless fribble. You have exquisite taste, which is no small accomplishment in itself, and you have winning manners. It just happens to be that your pompous brother cannot appreciate such things—not that he can appreciate anything beyond his hunters and that precious pile of stones he continues to call home, though any normal person would have moved out of that drafty abbey years ago. And it is not, as he claims, that your attics are to let because you *are* very clever about some things—people, for example. But you do not have the memory for figures or a head for mathematics. The marquess does, and so do I. Heaven knows it is not a particularly useful characteristic, and Mama is forever telling me that it is most unladylike, but there it is. And not having that is certainly no reflection on you."

"Well you must have whatever it is or Gareth de Vere would not waste his time playing cards with you at a ball.

They also say he refuses to play with women," Reginald concluded gloomily.

"Why ever not, if he is such a gambler?"

"Well, he is not just a gambler, at least not anymore. Now he only plays for the challenge of it, and he generally does not find competition stiff enough to be a challenge outside of Brooks's card room."

"Why 'not anymore'? What happened?"

Reginald glanced suspiciously at his cousin. It was unlike her to be so curious about a person. If the Marquess of Harwood had been a horse, her interest would have been understandable, for she infinitely preferred animals to people any day. But this particular person seemed to have caught her attention, for whatever reason. If he had not been so preoccupied with the enigma of Gareth de Vere playing cards with a female at a ball, Reggie might have speculated a good deal about his cousin's preoccupation with the man, but he still had not recovered from the initial shock of seeing the Marquess of Harwood at the card table with his cousin, nor could he accept the fact that Althea was warning him against playing cards with the man she had contrived to beat.

With a start Reggie realized that his cousin's eyes were still fixed questioningly on him. "What? Oh, er, why does the Marquess of Harwood no longer gamble? Well, he gambles, but only if the challenge is there. If he is certain to win, he will not play, no matter how high the stakes are—no sport in it. But there was a time when he would play for anything."

"When was that?"

"When his father died. He returned home from the Peninsula to find the family in dun territory. The estates were mortgaged to the hilt and most of the servants had left. He needed funds in a hurry and gaming was the only way, though gaming was the way his father had lost it all in the first place. Fortunately he was more successful than his father and it was not much more than a year before he was able to pay off the creditors and start on building his own fortune. Now they say he is rich as Croesus."

"He did play a very strong game with Grandmama and me, though we were not playing for high stakes."

"There is more to lose than money. Have care, Allie." His cousin looked puzzled.

"There is a reason that the matchmaking mamas are not flocking around one of the *ton*'s wealthiest, most eligible catches. He is known as the Bachelor Marquess, and it will do your reputation no good to be seen with him."

"Reputation, pooh. I could do with a little less reputation."

"It ain't a laughing matter, Allie. His name has never been coupled with a respectable woman's. And he lets it be known that he is not in the market for a wife—only women who ah, er . . . well, never mind, but being seen regularly with him, even if it is at card tables and even if you are accompanied by your grandmother, is bound to give rise to comment."

"And what is his aversion to marriage?" Not being in the least concerned about maintaining a reputation in a society for which she had very little use, Althea did not bother to respond to her cousin's warnings.

"Lord, Allie, how should I know? But it is not because he doesn't like women. I can tell you that he has got the nicest little, ah, er . . . Well, at any rate, he is very successful with certain kinds of women, but not the sort you should know."

"And what is—"

"That is all I am going to say, Allie," Reggie said, interrupting her. "Should not even had said that much. Not the sort of thing for a gently bred young lady to discuss."

"Nonsense, Reggie. I am more than seven, you know. I have spent my life in the country, where they do not put such a fine point on things. I hear the gossip among the servants."

"Well, you shouldn't listen to it. Ladies are not supposed to know such things."

"More fools they. They could spare themselves much disillusionment and heartache if they did. I wonder why he avoids all but 'certain kinds of women'?'' Althea stared ruminatively out the window at the branch of a beech tree whose buds were just beginning to open.

"I have not the least notion. But if I were you, Allie, I would forget the entire thing. Forget him. It ain't worth the risk."

"But, Reggie, you know that every good card player is accustomed to taking risks. And I am a very good card player."

"You cannot say I have not warned you." Shaking his head gloomily, Reggie rose and took his leave.

But his cousin sat for some time looking out the window at the square beyond and the lacy greenery of the trees softening what had been the stark branches of winter. Why was the Marquess of Harwood so averse to marriage, and what was it about the women of the *ton* that made him avoid them? Certainly his mother was eager enough for him to meet them. And she herself was all that was charming. She must have been a great beauty in her day.

Althea frowned thoughtfully. Her own mother had also been a great beauty, and Althea was well aware of the uncertain effects past glamorous reputations could have on present temperaments. Former beauties demanded a great deal from their children and everyone else around them. The more she considered it, the more she recalled the air of tension that appeared to exist between mother and son. Perhaps Lady Althea Beauchamp and the Marquess of Harwood had more in common than a head for figures and a proficiency at cards.

Chapter 8

*T*he marquess intruded into Althea's thoughts a good deal during the ensuing days, but it was not his relationship with his mother or with other women that attracted her attention. It was her cousin's revelation that the marquess had recouped his family's lost fortune at the gaming table. *He needed to find funds in a hurry and gaming was the only way,* Reggie had said.

What if she had a fortune all her own with no one—no father, no husband—holding the purse strings? The thought of such independence was dizzying. But perhaps now it was no longer an impossible dream. If the marquess had done it, and she had been able to beat the marquess, then surely, she too could win enough to purchase a snug little estate somewhere where she could live on her own, in control of her own life, far from those who sought to influence her every action, or to fashion her in their own images. The marquess apparently had won enough to pay off mortgages on large estates; all she needed to be comfortable was one small manor house. Surely that could not be too difficult?

"Do pay attention, Althea, and tell me if you prefer the Gloucester hat to the Leghorn bonnet." The Duchess of Clarendon's voice broke in on her daughter's reveries as they stood at the counter in one of Bond Street's most elegant establishments.

"It really makes no difference to me, Mama." Althea knew that the duchess would make her own decisions about her daughter's headgear as a matter of course despite any opinion that Althea might offer. It was simpler and easier to avoid all possibility of argument by letting her choose at the outset.

"Very well. We shall take the Leghorn." The duchess nodded at the hovering attendant. But once outside the shop and in their carriage, safely out of earshot, she reproved her daughter. "Do try for a little more interest in these things, Althea. A gentleman does not want a wife who is careless of her appearance."

"I do try, Mama. But both bonnets were comfortable and they were equally attractive."

"My dear, the difference between being an incomparable and being just anyone is the exquisite taste that distinguishes an incomparable from the hordes of young women trying to capture the attention of an eligible and appropriate gentleman."

"And I thought it was the Beauchamp name, excellent breeding, gracious manners, and immense fortune that made them seek me out."

"And how, pray tell, is any gentleman to discover anything about your breeding and manners if he is not first attracted to you by a decided air of fashion?" The duchess was too annoyed to hear the ironic note in her daughter's voice or notice the glint of humor in the depths of her blue eyes. But even if she had, she would not have approved. Cleverness in a young woman could be the kiss of death in the marriage mart, no matter how illustrious her family or how large her fortune. Men were not looking for wives who saw or understood too much, and they certainly did not want someone who was inclined to see the humor or absurdity in things. Women were supposed to enhance a man's sense of self-importance by being decorative, not threaten it by being too quick or too observant.

What the duchess did not understand was that cleverness and acute powers of observation could be as unwelcome to a woman as they were to a man, as uncomfortable for the observer as for the observed. Gliding around the brilliantly lit ballroom at Wroxleigh House that evening on the arm of Lord Foxworthy, Althea tried her best to ignore his frequent sidelong glances at her bosom, or the almost imperceptible squeezing of her hands.

Althea, who had no use for what fluttering eyelashes and coy smiles could win from a man, did not spend an inordinate amount of time examining her physiognomy or her figure in the looking glass, nor did she rate her own physical attractions very high, if she thought about them at all. But at the moment, she was uncomfortably aware that others in the room, including her partner, were of a different mind.

Happening to glance in the direction of the refreshment room, she caught sight of Lord Rupert leaning against a pillar and sniggering with his cronies as they ogled her through their quizzing glasses. And he was only one of a number of young bucks who stared pointedly at her and then leaned over to whisper a remark into a friend's ear.

Althea's spine stiffened. She loathed being the object of attention and speculation, and she detested even more the covetousness and lust she saw in men's eyes as they looked at her. It was not only in the eyes of this particular partner that she saw it, but any partner, every partner—or so it seemed to someone who simply longed for intelligent conversation, or even a friendly discussion. Whether it was desire for her body, or for the connections and fortune she would bring with her, did not much matter. Either way she was simply an object to these people, an object to be acquired, an object whose acquisition would confer glory and wealth on the fortunate gentleman who managed to capture it.

The room felt stifling. Her partner's hands were sweaty even through their gloves, and Althea wanted nothing more than to escape the lascivious glances and calculating looks for just one moment of peace and solitude. Desperately she willed the music to end, and then, with a barely muttered thank-you she hastily slipped behind a convenient nearby pillar to gather her wits before her partner could even think about returning her to her mother. Moving as unobtrusively as possible, and keep-

ing an eye out for the duchess, she glided from one pillar
to the next until she reached an inviting set of French
doors at the end of the ballroom.

The doors opened out onto a balcony. Glancing hurriedly around to make sure she was unobserved, Althea
carefully opened the doors and stole out, pulling them
gently closed behind her. The air was crisp and cool. She
gulped it in gratefully as, hugging the wall, she moved
as far out of sight as possible.

Tears of anger and frustration rose in her eyes as she
clung to one of the gnarled vines on the wall for support
and tried to steady her erratic breathing. It was not fair.
She had no wish to make a brilliant match, no wish to
be married at all, and yet she was on display to be observed and criticized by anyone and everyone—to be
stared at and commented on by men whom her parents
would never consider eligible, as well as by the very few
whom they would. She felt like a captive animal in some
menagerie instead of the much vaunted incomparable of
incomparables.

There was a click and a slight creak as the French
doors swung open. Althea pressed herself back into the
shadows, hoping desperately that she would not be discovered, a hope that dwindled rapidly as she heard footsteps moving purposefully toward her. Was she never
going to have peace from prying eyes?

"Are you all right?" Gareth could barely make out
her features in the darkness, but he was ready to swear
that the light filtering through the windows caught the
gleam of unshed tears in her eyes.

As always, he had been acutely aware of Althea's presence in the ballroom, and though he told himself that he
was just keeping an eye out to see if she went into the
card room, he knew deep in his heart that it was not just
the hope of matching wits against a very fine card player
that made him seek her out among the crowd. He was
still inexplicably and unwillingly attracted to her, and
that attraction had increased rather than lessened with
their acquaintance—a most unusual circumstance for a
man who more often than not had found that familiarity

with a woman bred contempt rather than a desire to know more about her.

He had observed Althea making her escape from the ballroom and been instantly intrigued. His first reaction had been to suspect her of an assignation, but when careful scrutiny had revealed no one else making his way to the French doors, he had decided that her furtiveness had been to secure the privacy of the balcony for herself.

"What are you doing here?"

It was not the response Gareth had expected. Usually women greeted him with pleasure, not barely concealed hostility. "I? Well, I saw you slip out of the ballroom, and you did it in such a way that you, ah . . . well . . . You seemed to be trying to escape something. So I came to see if you needed help."

"I was. Escaping, I mean. The crush, the heat. I just wanted to be alone."

Her voice quavered ever so slightly, and he could not tell whether it was from annoyance or distress. Whichever it was, it was abundantly clear that she wanted to be alone. The gentlemanly thing to do would be to leave her to regain her composure, but for some reason he could not fathom, Gareth found he could not. He was intrigued, and not a little touched, by a woman who, though clearly upset, was keeping her problem to herself. Anyone else would have made a play with wet lashes and heartfelt sighs designed to attract his attention and sympathy, but not Lady Althea Beauchamp. Could it be that she actually wanted to deal with whatever was troubling her on her own, solve her own problem? It was such a novel idea that Gareth found himself wanting to know more about a woman who did not appear to expect a man to take care of her and make all her difficulties disappear.

"Is there anything I can do?" What on earth possessed him? He had broken one of his cardinal rules, which was not to offer assistance to a woman unless absolutely forced to. The marquess knew from bitter experience how quickly and unpleasantly one could become entangled in a woman's affairs. His mother was amazingly

adept at embroiling people in all of her life's little complications before they even knew they had offered to
help her.

"No. Thank you. There is nothing wrong."

Her dismissal was firm and deliberate, but even at this
distance, he could see the tears welling in her eyes.

Althea blinked rapidly. How could she be such a nin-
nyhammer? If her exacting father had taught her nothing
else, he had taught her to exhibit majestic calm in the
most trying of situations, yet here she was on the verge
of tears. *Beauchamps are always in command of every
situation,* he had constantly intoned at the most trying
moments of her life. She had been expected to remain
composed when she had fallen off her pony at the age
of three, or lost her favorite doll, scraped her knee, or
found a dead bird. Nothing, not even the death of that
first pony was to affect her. Yet here she was now, dis-
solving into a watering pot because some stranger in-
quired after her well-being.

"Forgive me, but that is clearly not so."

Not trusting herself to speak, Althea shook her head.
But he drew closer. Long, lean fingers tilted her chin up
to face into compelling gray eyes.

"Surely we have played enough against each other at
cards for you to know that I am not a fool."

"Yes, but at the moment I am." Althea gulped down
the sob that rose up from nowhere.

He was completely disarmed by this unladylike noise.
"My dear girl, whatever is amiss?" Letting go of her
chin, he gently grasped the hands that were clenching
and unclenching at her sides and pulled her toward him.
"I have pitted my wits against yours enough to know
that you can risk everything without blinking an eye. If
you are as agitated as this, something is seriously wrong."

"No. I am just being foolish. That is all. It is simply
fatigue."

"Nonsense."

The gray eyes bored into her as though looking into
the innermost depths of her soul. It was useless to pre-
varicate. "I . . . It is nothing. I mean, it is quite absurd,

really. I just feel as though I am constantly on display like some trinket in a shop, an object in a museum, a picture at a exhibition."

"And you are. But is not that the sum total of what all young ladies aspire to? Especially if they are being displayed in such exclusive circles and to such acclaim?"

"I loathe it."

She spoke so softly that he had to bend his head to catch her words, and even then he was not entirely certain that he had heard correctly. "But why? You are the incomparable of incomparables, the envy of every woman in the *ton,* young or old."

"But it is not I they are seeing when they stare at me. I see them, everyone, dissecting every detail of my appearance. The woman are looking for every flaw, the men . . ." She shuddered, and the tears that had been threatening to flow now spilled over and ran down her cheeks. "I am utterly alone, isolated by being on display, and I feel like a freak in a traveling show. It is not necessarily that I dislike being alone or that I long for friends, but these people do not care who I am. They are judging me on my appearance alone, not my character. And it is an appearance I have very little to do with. I was born looking as I do. I see the envy in their eyes, the greed. I feel as though I am being poked and prodded and examined like some piece of livestock at a fair. I have no protection from it. I cannot escape it." She bowed her head and covered her face with her hands.

"My poor girl." Aching for the anguish he read in her eyes and heard in her voice, Gareth pulled her close, gently stroking the dark hair until the violent trembling that overcame her ceased.

He had never stopped to think about the *ton* in such terms, at least where women were concerned. He had simply assumed that all women were like his mother, that they flourished on public display and admiration. But the more he considered it, the more he supposed that it was logical to assume that if he despised being the object of marriage-mad misses' schemes, then a young woman might very well feel the same way he did, especially a young woman of the sort that Lady Althea Beauchamp was proving to be.

Althea raised her head and shook it ruefully. "I do beg your pardon. I do not now what came over me. I assure you that I am not usually such a watering pot. But I have been squeezed and ogled to such a degree tonight that I was frantic to get away."

Chapter 9

Gareth stared down into the dark blue eyes swimming in the tears that continued to well up. The tears clinging to her long dark lashes glittered like diamonds in the faint light cast from the ballroom's enormous chandeliers. He had the maddest impulse to kiss her drooping lips into a smile. His heart went out to her, yet he was utterly powerless to change the situation, to save her from the time-honored rituals of the *ton*. "I wish there were something I could do to help you," his heart volunteered before his mind could react.

Althea tilted her head to stare gravely up at him. "Actually, there *is* something you could do for me."

The stab of disappointment was so strong that it physically hurt him. So she was no better than the others after all, just more clever. She too was trying to trap him into doing something for her, only she was doing it with a great deal more subtlety and strategy than the others—like the master card player she was.

"You must tell me what it is."

Althea frowned thoughtfully. "No. It is nothing, really. You are too kind. I thank you for your concern." Brought back to her senses by the wary expression in his eyes and flatness in his voice, Althea turned away from him toward the ballroom. His words had offered help, but his conventionally polite tone told her that he was only doing so because he felt he had no choice.

He caught her hand as she moved away from him. "No. Please. I *do* wish to help you." He was correct in thinking that she was cleverer than the others; she was also more sensitive than they were, reading his reaction in an instant. And oddly enough, he did want to help someone like that. Besides, now his curiosity was getting the better of him. "Tell me what it is you wish me to do."

He meant it this time. There was a sincerity in his eyes and a conviction in his voice that had not been there before. For the first time in her life, Althea felt as though someone was actually paying attention to her, not Lady Althea Beauchamp, dutiful daughter and eligible heiress, but just Althea. "Well, if it would not be too much trouble, I should like very much to have you teach me to win at cards."

"You what?"

His thunderstruck expression was so absurd and unexpected that she could not help chuckling.

"But you already play cards too well for my comfort. What could *I* possibly teach *you*?"

"How to win a fortune. Reggie, I mean my cousin Reginald, says that you were able to win a fortune at cards."

"That was because I had to."

"So do I."

"You? Whatever for?"

"So I can live my life the way I wish to."

"Surely with your fortune, your expectations . . ."

"They are not *my* expectations, and it is not *my* fortune. They are my parents' expectations and my family's fortune. I have nothing of my own until I marry a man selected by them, and then it will belong to my husband, who will have his own expectations. And believe me, any husband my parents choose for me will not have the same expectations of life that I do."

The conversation was growing more and more amazing by turns. Gareth did not have the slightest idea what this astounding young woman was going to say next, but he was desperate to find out. Ordinarily, the more he discovered about a person, a woman especially, the more disappointed he was to learn that no matter how intriguing the exterior, the interior was inutterably banal. This young lady, however, was quite different.

"And what are these expectations that the husband your parents choose for you will not share?"

"Mine? I should like to have a small place of my own in the country where I could have a garden and enough livestock or crops to support myself. Then I would spend my day tending it, taking long walks, and reading." Althea smiled apologetically. "Actually, when I describe it, it does sound rather dull, does it not? But to me, especially at this moment, it sounds like a veritable heaven on earth."

"Then we shall have to see what we can do to get you this heaven of yours."

"You will help me? Oh, thank you ever so much."

He was no proof against her gratitude. The light that gleamed in those amazing sapphire eyes at the prospect of living a peaceful, rustic existence made him want, for the second time that evening, to pull her into his arms and kiss her. And something akin to a feeling of chivalry made him want to do everything in his power to make her dreams come true.

The very fact that she longed for such simple things—peace and solitude—made Gareth wonder what sort of life she had had to endure to this point. Outwardly she seemed blessed with all that a young woman could wish for, but something had caused the somberness at the back of her eyes, the serious expression her face habitually wore. He recognized those signs himself. They came from the feeling of being utterly alone in a world of vanity and greed, shallowness and indifference.

"But . . ."

Gareth looked down at her. The sparkle had vanished from her eyes. "But what?"

"I . . . Well, I have no way to repay you, at least not at the moment. Of course, I shall be able to repay you when I win my fortune—if I win my fortune."

"My dear girl, you have no need to repay me. I shall help you for the sport of it, for the sheer pleasure of seeing you win your fortune and your heart's desire from a pack of pleasure-seeking fools."

"I only hope it is possible. As a woman, I shall not be

able to play with the true gamblers who bet vast sums on the turn of a card, but I do think I can hold my own against females, and some of them wager almost as much as most men."

Gareth snorted. "Believe me, you can win against anyone. After all, you beat my mother most handily. She may appear to be a very silly, frivolous woman, but, believe me, where her own interests are concerned, she is very serious indeed, and she can be as clever and as ruthless as anyone I have ever encountered. The game you played against her is a fair representation of the stiffest competition you are likely to encounter. And the more you win, the more formidable your reputation, the more people will wish to play against you, and the greater sums they will risk when they do so."

Althea was silent for a moment, considering his words. "I suspect you are right." She nodded thoughtfully. But at the moment, she was thinking more about the speaker than his words. What had his mother done to him to bring that bitter edge to his voice whenever he spoke of her? Behind that cynical attitude, to his mother in particular and the world in general, must lie a great deal of suffering. Odd to think that a man born to inherit a title and estates, a man born to control his fate and the fate of all those working for him, could have suffered anything. She forced these distracting speculations from her mind to concentrate on the matter at hand, "Well, I shall be grateful for anything you can teach me and any advice you can give me."

"As I told you before, I am not sure that there is much I can teach you about card playing that you have not already learned. You are very good, you know."

"Thank you. Coming from you, that is praise indeed."

Gareth watched in fascination as a blush rose in her cheeks and her lips curved into a shy smile. The genuine pleasure she seemed to derive from such a mild compliment was astonishing. For a moment she was transformed from a serious, self-contained lady into a charming young woman. The change made him wonder about the parents whose expectations she was supposed to fulfill. Had it been these expectations concerning who and what Lady Althea Beauchamp was supposed to be that had turned her into the coldly perfect incomparable who had caught his attention the first night he saw her. "I may not be able to teach you anything more about card playing, but I can teach you the most effective way to win a fortune."

"That is very kind of you, for there is no earthly reason you should help someone you are barely acquainted with simply because she asks it of you. But I am exceedingly grateful that you will."

"I do, however, have to tell you in all honesty that the quickest way to acquire a fortune is to marry it."

She grimaced in a way that was so natural, so unlike the behavior of a rigidly proper young lady of fashion that he found it enchanting. "The quickest, perhaps, but not the easiest, for it requires one to give over one's life to another person."

"You are entirely correct on that count. Yet most young ladies are hell-bent on doing just that, finding someone who will manage their lives for them. And the richer the manager, the better. To many of them it is a way to gain freedom—freedom from their families, freedom from the constraints that society puts on the behavior of its unmarried young ladies. There are a number of advantages to be gained. Are you sure you do not wish to marry?"

"Quite sure."

Terse as the answer was, it was delivered with such a wealth of conviction that Gareth was struck by the purposeful tone in her voice and the sparkle of determination in her eyes. Everything about her—the proud lift of the chin, the firm set of her shoulders—spoke of an intense resolve to manage her own life. He could not help admiring her for it and wanting to help her achieve it. "Very well, then, I shall be happy to teach you all that I know. But how are we to accomplish this?" Even as he asked, he felt reasonably certain that such a determined young woman had already thought of a way to eliminate the difficulties involved in pursuing such a project.

She had. "I shall be extremely agreeable this week and allow Mama to drag me to all the establishments on Bond Street so that on the day you and I agree to meet it will be only natural for me to develop a headache and be unable to accompany her on her calls. Papa is always at his club in the afternoon so I shall be able to slip out with my maid undetected. If you will but give me your direction, I can then call on you."

"Call on me? Are you not concerned for your reputation? Why, if even a hint of such a thing were to reach anyone's ears you would be ruined."

Althea cocked her head to one side as she considered this. "I realize that, but I see no way for me to meet you that would not cause comment. And besides,"—a mischievous smile tugged at the corners of her mouth— "if my reputation were ruined, then no one would want me as a wife and I should be packed off to the country where I wished to be left in the first place. So no matter what happens, I am likely to be better off than I am now."

An answering smile twisted his own lips as Gareth shook his head. "Almost, I feel sorry for your parents. Dutiful you may appear to be, but I can see that your strategist's mind is not confined to the card room."

"Believe me, it is the only way. For years I have begged them to leave me at Clarendon. I can manage the household quite as well as Mama, and the estate as well as Papa's own agent, but they would have none of it. 'A Beauchamp's duty is to bring glory to the name.'"

Listening to her, Gareth had no doubt that this maxim had been drummed into her head since the cradle, and he could not decide which was worse—to be ignored by parents who were intent on pursuing their own wasteful and destructive pleasures, or to be continually prodded and shaped into becoming the living, breathing expression of centuries of familial ambitions. Either way, one was not given much credit for being a person in one's own right, and either way, one's own hopes and dreams were utterly ignored.

"Very well. I shall arrange to be at home in my rooms

in Curzon Street every afternoon this week." Ruthlessly Gareth stifled the little voice inside telling him that he must be completely mad to commit himself to such a course of action. After years of successfully avoiding the most rapacious of matchmaking mamas and eluding even the cleverest schemes designed to deprive him of his cherished bachelor status, was he now falling victim to the cleverest scheme of all? He gazed down into the eyes looking up at him and saw nothing but profound gratitude in their sapphire depths.

"Again, I must say that I do not know why you are being so kind to me, other than that I asked it of you, but thank you. I promise you, I shall not disappoint you."

A brief, shy smile, and then she was gone, slipping back into the golden light of the ballroom, leaving him to a wealth of confusing thoughts and emotions. Why did he want to help this one particular young woman, a woman whom he had detested at first sight as being the epitome of all he disliked—a cold, calculating beauty? And even now, he was not entirely certain that he had not been made a victim of it.

But then Gareth recalled the expression in her eyes and the firmness in her voice as she had promised not to disappoint him. It had been more than a promise; it had been a pledge. No one in his entire life had promised him anything. And, with the exception of the men in his cavalry regiment who shared an unspoken responsibility for one another's lives, no one in his entire life had ever felt they owed him anything—not even friendship. Yet somehow he believed that this inexperienced young woman, a girl really, was someone he could trust. His mind told him that this was a wildly irrational conviction inspired by his unwanted physical attraction to an exquisite face and figure, but his heart told him that it was something more than that.

Chapter 10

Several days later, as she followed her mother into yet another fashionable Bond Street establishment, Althea was beginning to wonder if anything the Marquess of Harwood could teach her was worth such penance. Her head truly did ache after being forced to examine and select from a dizzying array of gloves, bonnets, ribbons, shawls, and all the other accoutrements of a young lady of fashion.

"Do try for a more pleasing expression, Althea. Anyone who looked at you would think you were suffering from the megrims."

"But I do have a dreadful headache, Mama."

"Ridiculous. No properly brought up young woman contracts a headache from a simple shopping expedition. And she would certainly not let on if she did."

"Yes, Mama." Althea followed her mother out to the carriage and sank gratefully onto the velvet seat. Ordinarily she considered that the disadvantages of being a duke's daughter far outweighed the advantages, but being able to retreat into a well-sprung carriage was one of the few perquisites of wealth and privilege that she could say she truly appreciated.

The duchess was not alone in her low opinion of people who succumbed to such weaknesses as headaches. When they arrived home to encounter the duke leaving for the more congenial company at White's, he took one glance at his drooping daughter, frowned, and shook his head. "You do not look at all the thing, Althea. I would not have thought that you would be overset by such a trifling excursion."

"I am sorry, Papa." Althea undid the ribbons and removed her bonnet that was now beginning to feel like a vise clamped on her head. "Perhaps it is the heat. The sun is quite bright today and . . ."

"Nonsense, my girl. Beauchamps never pay attention to such minor discomforts. Or, if they are aware of them at all, they simply ignore them." Without a backward glance, the duke took his hat from the footman and proceeded briskly down the marble steps.

"Yes, Papa. Of course, Papa. If you will excuse me, Mama, I believe I shall retire to my bedchamber."

The duchess, already involved in giving instructions to the butler, nodded vaguely as her daughter escaped upstairs to the cool, serene surroundings of her blue damask bedchamber. There she gratefully accepted a cloth soaked in lavender water handed to her by her maid and pressed it against her throbbing forehead. Away from the pressure of her parents' critical eyes, she let out a gentle sigh of relief and sank back into a chair, her eyes closed, her mind racing.

After some minutes like this, she rose, handed the cloth back to her maid, sat down at a delicate rosewood escritoire by the window, scribbled a hasty note, and addressed it to the Marquess of Harwood in Curzon Street.

"Jenny, would you be so good as to give this to Jem and ask him to deliver it for me? And instruct him to wash his face and hands before he goes."

The maid directed a curious glance at her mistress, but took the note without comment. As far as Jenny knew, her lady was acquainted with no one in London, poor thing. In fact, she was allowed few friends in either the country or the city, her parents being such high sticklers as far as mingling with those of inferior station, "which is just about everyone," the maid muttered to herself as she hurried down the stairs and out to the stables.

Jem was a sharpish looking lad with a twisted foot and a wizened face far too old for his sixteen years. The stable boy was a special protégé of Althea's, for she had discovered him cold and starving one morning huddling in a ditch where his father, a tinker, had left him. Jem had fallen and broken his ankle, and his father, already tired of having an extra mouth to feed, had used this infirmity as an excuse to cast off the burden he had been forced to bear since Jem's mother had died the previous spring.

Althea had taken the lad home and seen to it that he was fed and given a place to sleep in the stables until suitable employment was found. But the lad had found his own employment by demonstrating such an affinity with the horses who shared his quarters and such a willingness to put his hand to any task that the coachman and the grooms could find for him that they began to wonder how they had ever functioned without him. As for Jem, he considered himself to be in paradise and Lady Althea to be the angel who had put him there. There was nothing he would not do for her. Even being forced to wash his face and hands before hastening to Curzon Street was not too big a price to pay to be of service to his angel and deliverer.

Perusing Althea's note, Gareth again asked himself if he were being made a bigger dupe than all the other poor fools he had scorned for selling their souls to please a pretty face. Did the lady in question truly wish to learn how to win a fortune, or was she cleverly maneuvering him into a compromising situation?

As he penned his reply, Gareth told himself that the risk he was taking added a little spice to a life that was threatening to become flat now that he had reestablished the family finances. Certainly nothing else besides the challenge of it was responsible for his agreeing to see the young lady, not her lovely face, her clever mind, or the intriguingly different personality he had been allowed to glimpse beneath the exquisite exterior of the *ton*'s latest incomparable.

Welcoming Althea into his mahogany-paneled library some hours later, Gareth scrutinized her carefully as Ibthorp, his butler, valet, and general factotum, took her blush-colored spencer and matching bonnet. But there was not an ounce of guile in the grateful smile she gave him as she took the chair he held for her at the small table he had set up.

"I wish to thank you again, my lord, for agreeing to help me, and for allowing yourself to be put out at a moment's notice. I cannot think where I came by the brazen effrontery to ask you for your assistance. It must have been desperation. I did take all precautions to ensure that no one knew of my destination, but I thought it best to bring Jenny, here, along with me, so if by some unlikely chance it should be discovered that I visited you at your lodgings you would not be compromised."

Gareth glanced at her in some surprise and the corners of his mouth twisted into the hint of a smile. The woman had read his thoughts to perfection. Such omniscience in a card player was dangerous indeed. Undoubtedly that was why she was already a formidable opponent, though she was naive in the extreme to believe that bringing a maid would protect the reputations of young ladies who visited gentlemen in their rooms.

"You appear to have thought of everything, Lady Althea. Now"—he seated himself opposite her and dealt out four hands—"I thought I would go through one game, playing each one of the hands in turn and explain as I go. From playing against you, I know that you are already aware that winning is merely a matter of memory and mathematics. Remembering what cards have been played, deducing from that the cards remaining, and figuring on the possible combinations of those remaining cards is the essence of the game. What you may not possess, and what I hope I can help you with, is a larger strategy for winning the sums you wish to win. The key to all of it, however, is never to put your opponents on their guard and never to betray, by so much as the flicker of an eyelid, what you have in your hand. I am sure you have heard that the true gamesters wear broad-brimmed straw hats, not only to shade their eyes from the light during long hours of play, but to hide their expressions from the rest of the players at the table."

"And what of this 'larger strategy'? How did you develop it?" Her eyes fixed on the marquess, Althea leaned forward, listening intently.

Gareth could not help smiling at the picture she made. In her eagerness to learn everything, she had so far forgotten herself as to prop her elbows on the table and rest her chin in her hands so that she looked like a little girl begging to be told a fairy tale. And he had the oddest, almost uncomfortable urge to gather her in his arms, hold her close, and pour out his life's story to her: the lonely upbringing isolated on the estate near Newmarket while his parents pursued their separate amusements in London, his disgust with their vain and useless lives, his enlistment in the cavalry that brought with it the glories and horror of war in the Peninsula, being forced to sell out and return home when his father died a ruined man, the struggle to keep his home from falling into total disrepair while he risked every spare guinea he had to win a fortune, and all the while being forced to endure the endless complaints of a mother he had always despised for her monumental selfishness.

"Ah, er, what?" He came to with a start as he realized that she was waiting for an answer.

"I asked you about your 'larger strategy,'" Althea prompted him as she cocked her head to study his long angular face with its thick, dark brows, high, bridged nose, and prominent cheekbones. It was the face of a man tested by experience, a face full of character. At the moment, however, he was looking at her in the oddest way, a half smile on his lips and a faraway, almost dreamy expression in his eyes. What was going on in that quick, intelligent mind of his? Was he doing as he had instructed her to do, hiding his thoughts behind a vague expression?

"Oh, yes, my strategy."

Althea's eyes narrowed. If she did not know better, if Reggie had not told her of the man's steely self-control in even the most highly charged moments at the gaming table, she would have said that a self-conscious flush stole across his lean face.

"Well, er, my strategy for the most part has been to

retain as much control of every situation as possible, beginning with a modest amount of risk and then accumulating my winnings slowly and steadily."

"But Reggie says that you are known to wager fabulous sums on the turn of a card without even blinking an eye."

"Reggie says?"

It was Althea's turn to blush as he cocked a quizzical eyebrow at her. "Yes. He says that it is common knowledge that you are a very cool customer, indeed, and that you do not possess a nerve in your body. A man does not gain a reputation like that by taking only modest risks."

Gareth was unprepared for the warm sense of gratification her words brought him. So she had been discussing him at some length with her cousin, had she? Good. Lady Althea Beauchamp had lately been occupying far too large a place in his thoughts for his own comfort, and it would have been most disconcerting to think that he had made any less an impression on her.

"Yes. Reggie has told me about some of your wagers."

"Ah, but those were after I had gained a reputation and a fortune. I could afford to lose, and my reputation had become such that people wagered foolishly against me just to be able to claim that they had. But when I could not afford to lose, I assure you I was as meek and quiet as a lamb."

The picture of the cynical Marquess of Harwood as a mild, biddable creature was too much. Althea struggled to stifle a burst of laughter, which only ended in a most unladylike fit of coughing.

"Is that so unbelievable?" Gareth had never actually seen a lady laugh heartily before, or even struggle not to, and he found her naturalness more charming than the most seductive glances of the most practiced ladies he consorted with. There was something utterly endearing about her unaffected reaction and it made him suddenly wish to have Lady Althea Beauchamp as his friend. *And perhaps as something more,* an unbidden voice whispered to him. Ruthlessly he ignored it as he struggled to stifle an answering grin.

"Well, yes. You are rather daunting, you know. When I first . . ." Althea shut her mouth with a snap as she realized that she was about to reveal her consciousness of his presence from the moment he had entered the ballroom at Lady St. John's rout.

" 'When I first' . . . When you first what?" This was even more intriguing than her discussions with her cousin. After all, anyone who knew Gareth, or knew of him, would have been astonished to see him wasting his time on a card game with a young lady and her grandmother, so it was not unusual for Reggie to remark upon it to his cousin, who also happened to be the young lady in question. But it was obvious that Reggie's cousin had been as aware and as conscious of the Marquess of Harwood as he had been of her from the very beginning.

A triumphant smile hovered at the corner of Gareth's mouth. He was glad. The irresistible attraction that had drawn him to Lady Althea Beauchamp in the first place had been as unnerving as it was unusual, and it was reassuring now to discover that this awareness of her presence had at least not all been one-sided.

Althea gulped and straightened her shoulders. Beauchamps never hesitated. They never avoided an opponent, an unpleasant truth, or a problem, but tackled them head on. "*When I first saw you at Lady St. John's rout,* was what I started to say. You entered the ballroom and looked straight at me as though I were the most despicable sort of worm."

It was Gareth's turn to chuckle. If the Marquess of Harwood as a lamb was difficult to picture, Lady Althea Beauchamp as a lowly invertebrate was even more absurd. But along with the chuckle came a most uneasy feeling that after years of despising the mating rituals of the *ton,* and cultivating a bored indifference to every beautiful new face or every clever ploy for his attention, he had failed to stifle his immediate response to one lovely face in particular, to one female who had done nothing to try to draw his attention to her. His mask of boredom had slipped and she had caught a glimpse of the person inside. There was little new that he could teach Lady Althea Beauchamp about reading an opponent's expression; she had already charmed him into revealing too much about himself as it was.

Chapter 11

"You are no more a worm than I am a lamb; far from it. Judging by the disdainful expression I observed on your face at Lady St. John's, I would say that it was the rest of us who were worms and you the goddess who deigned to notice a lucky few."

"What? I?" Stunned, Althea tried to remember that night beyond the scornful look cast in her direction by the Marquess of Harwood. "All I was thinking of was escape."

"Perhaps, but you stood there cold and aloof as though you had not the slightest interest in or concern for the poor supplicants clustered around you dying for one word from the incomparable's lips."

"Incomparable? I?" She seemed genuinely astounded. "No, it is only my fortune and my family that are incomparable. As to the rest of it, you are entirely correct, I was trying not to think of them, trying desperately to ignore their ogling eyes, their greedy expressions. I could have been a half-wit and they still would have clustered around me. To them I was not a person; I was a chance at a fortune and family connections. Why should I not act scornful? I scorn their motives and I scorn them for having those motives."

The blue eyes blazed and her voice shook with passion. Gareth could not help feeling slightly ashamed at his gross misreading of the situation. His only excuse was that he had never before encountered a woman who did not look upon men as her playthings, to be enslaved by her beauty, used, and then tossed aside. Yet this woman seemed unconscious of her stunning physical appearance. Most women would have said *I could have been ugly or I could have had a squint and they would have clustered around me,* as though not being thought beautiful were the worst fate that could befall a woman. But Althea had protested *I could have been a half-wit.* Gareth hardly knew any men who considered it important to be clever, much less women, but it was obviously important to her. He found it not only unusual, but strangely attractive.

"I stand corrected, Lady Althea, and offer you my humblest apologies for completely underestimating you."

Althea heard his words, but mostly she was struck by the discovery that when he smiled, the Marquess of Harwood was a singularly attractive man. The smile softened his haughty features and warmed the cynical glint in his cool gray eyes, revealing an unexpected intimacy in his otherwise distant expression.

"*Underestimating* me or *misunderstanding* me, my lord?"

Gareth shook his head ruefully. Lord, the woman was quick. Her eyes were still wary. Obviously she had as little reason to trust as he did. "*Misunderstanding* you, is what I mean. You see, I have never known a woman who did not wish to use her beauty to its best advantage to establish control over men and their fortunes. And though I scorn those men who care only for a lovely face and nothing for the person beneath it, I pity them, poor fools, for falling into the traps that are set for them by the females of this world."

In his eagerness to explain himself, he allowed his expression to betray far more than he had intended. There was no mistaking the bitterness in his voice. At some point in his life, the Marquess of Harwood had been badly mistreated by someone. "Females, my lord, or one female in particular?" Althea had no idea where this bold curiosity came from. Ordinarily the most reserved of mortals, she protected her personal thoughts and feelings with a quiet, impenetrable dignity, and she respected that in others. But there was something about this man

that seemed to reach out to her. She recognized his cold-
ness and his cynicism as being much like her own, shields
against the petty inquisitiveness and spiteful gossip that
was the lifeblood of the *ton*. She too was an unwilling
participant in the fashionable world, and aloofness and
indifference were the only protection she had.

Gareth looked up in surprise. Her blue eyes were
softer now, alight with sympathy and understanding.
Compelled by an insatiable urge to confide in her, he
nodded slowly. "One female in particular. Someone who
at her very first ball in her very first Season attracted the
attention of a wealthy, impressionable young man and
eventually, through her selfishness and extravagance, ruined him. He was an amiable young fellow, from an ancient and highly respected family, sociable, with excellent
manners, but very little as far as intelligence goes. She
was a girl of modest family and fortune, but she soon
saw that he was utterly infatuated with her and she married him promptly, in a wedding designed to establish her
firmly in the very exclusive circles to which she aspired.

"Once she became the young man's wife she ignored
him completely as she devoted her energies to creating
herself an image as a leader of fashion. Her taste was
exquisite and extravagant, and it was not long before she
was spending far beyond her means. Her husband's fortune was substantial, but it did not compare to the limitless wealth of those to whom she compared herself, and
she soon found herself in dun territory to such a degree
that she was forced to confess all to her husband.

"He was a heedless young man himself who had never
spared a thought for where his fortune came from. He
had never been forced to consider it before, but now he
was, and it alarmed him. However, he could deny her
nothing, so instead of telling her that he could ill afford
her expensive habits, he struggled to procure the means
to support them the only way he knew how—by mortgag-
ing the family estates.

"Now the moment of confession had forced the young
wife to use all her charms on her husband with the expected results; she soon found herself pregnant. The hus-

band was genuinely pleased at the prospect as well as relieved by the thought that motherhood might curtail her thoughtlessly expensive existence and her restless desire to become the high priestess of fashion. However, it did not. Her confinement only brought discontent and a renewed resolve to reign supreme in the Upper Ten Thousand."

"The moment the baby was born, she handed it over to the nurse and returned to her life in London, leaving her husband behind in the country with no one but a squalling infant and a houseful of servants to keep him company. Restless and bored himself, and dimly aware that the world considered him to be the foolish dupe of his wife, he too returned to the metropolis and sought excitement at the gaming tables of White's.

"Not being particularly clever, he arose a loser far more often than he arose a winner, and thus was eventually forced to seek out less exclusive but more risky games of chance in the gambling hells of St. James and Pall Mall, where the company was less nice and he almost never won.

"Preoccupied with their own pursuits, both parents left their son to be raised by a series of servants and tutors until he was old enough to be sent to school where, unaccustomed to having any friends, he was lost and lonely. Not knowing what to do with himself or how to behave, he devoted himself to his studies and strengthened his resolve never to be a guileless fool like his father.

"Gradually he discovered among the boys a few like-minded lads and he developed some tentative friendships. But all his lonely hours of observation from outside of the group had brought him to the conclusion that he wanted a life where he could do something of value, not bungle through an empty, pointless existence like his parents. So after finishing university, and unaware of the family's precarious financial situation, he asked his father to buy him a commission in the Royal Horse Guards and left for the Peninsula, putting as much distance between himself and a father who paid more attention to games of chance than to his son and a mother who disliked

him for being the constant reminder that she was no
longer young.

"It was only a few years after his departure for the
Peninsula that his father died and the young captain was
called to take up his duties as head of the family. It was
not until that moment that he became aware of their dire
financial situation.

"Not only was the estate heavily mortgaged, but his
father had been in debt to every tradesman in London
as well as in the country. His mother, who put the entire
blame upon his father, refused to accept the unhappy
reality that her son was left to repair their fortunes as
best he could, and the stringent economies he was forced
to practice only brought bitter recriminations from a
woman who considered the luxuries of the latest in fashionable attire to be her prerogative. There was no way
to recoup their finances with the income from the estate,
so he was forced to look to some other way to earn
money.

"He sold his commission and with what he raised from
that, set out to win as steadily as his father had lost at
the gambling tables on the *ton*. But in the meantime, in
order to survive and keep his estate from falling into
utter and irreparable ruin, he was forced to remove himself and his mother from their mansion in Berkeley
Square in order to derive some income from renting it
out. They eventually took up residence in some rooms
in Hanover Square, where it was slowly born in on him
what his father's existence must have been like—one
long, continuous effort to satisfy the demands of a
woman whose entire life was devoted to proving herself
to be more fashionable than her acquaintances.

"The gambling fever that had gripped his father had
been a weak man's response to these incessant demands." Gareth paused to smile ironically. "At first, the
son's response to these dire financial straits appeared to
be no different than his father's. He used the proceeds
from the sale of his commission to set up a faro bank
and then, when the worst of the debts had been paid
with the winnings from that, he devoted himself to the

gaming table. In fact, at this point, the only ostensible difference between father and son was that the son arose a winner as consistently as his father had been a loser, but that was to change. Instead of pouring all his winnings into games of chance, the son set about repaying debts and restoring the family estate.

"Eventually the debts were paid and repairs begun on the estate, while the unhappy widow continued to accuse her son of stealing from her nonexistent widow's jointure. But I have said far more than I should have. I am sure it is a common enough tale." Gareth broke off abruptly and stared unseeingly at the cards in front of him.

Appalled by his story, Althea sat silent as she struggled to reconcile the image of the fluffy-haired, charming Marchioness of Harwood with the determinedly selfish woman of her son's tale.

Absorbed in his own bitter thoughts, Gareth seemed to forget his visitor for a moment. Then he looked up, his lips twisting into a self-mocking smile. "Forgive me, I cannot think why I told you all this."

"Because I asked you." Althea laid a sympathetic hand on his arm. "Do not apologize. I am glad you did. It makes you. . . Well, I am flattered that you trusted me with your confidence."

"It makes me what?"

She flushed self-consciously. "Well, ordinarily you seem so self-assured, so unruffled by anything, so scornful of the rest of us poor mortals." Althea paused as she cast about for just the right words. "Well, it makes you human after all," she concluded smiling shyly at him, and he could not help smiling back.

"All too human, I am afraid. If I were not, I should be able to ignore it all and keep myself from being annoyed and angry."

Althea nodded. "But she seems so charming, so . . ."

He stiffened, and the gray eyes that had been warm with the intimacy of shared experience grew dark and cold as slate.

"I mean"—Althea hastened to retrieve herself—"at least she *seems* to be charming and interested in one. My mother does not even pretend to be concerned with anyone but herself."

"Perhaps she is the more honest of the two."

It was a concession. The bleak, angry lines of his face softened a little, but Althea could see that her remark had cost her his openness and some of his trust. He looked so aloof and alone that her heart ached for him as she thought of the little boy abandoned and ignored, now grown up who, despite his years and sophistication, still suffered from that abandonment.

She rose and held out her hand. "I have taken enough of your time, my lord. I thank you for taking an interest in me and helping me."

Gareth had been annoyed at her for not understanding him completely, for doubting him even the slightest bit. Her remark about his mother's charm had hurt him, for he had felt just the slightest bit betrayed by her inability to recognize the utter falseness that lay beneath it. This had made him draw back from her. But now that she sensed that withdrawal, now that she was leaving, he wanted her to stay, though he could not let himself admit it. Nor could he admit to himself how desperately he wanted her to be on his side, utterly and completely. "It was an honor to be of service to you, Lady Althea."

The formality of his words chilled her. She longed to retrieve the intimacy of a few minutes before, but she did not know how. "I cannot begin to say how much . . . Well, thank you," she muttered awkwardly as she rose, nodded to her maid, gathered her bonnet, gloves, and spencer, and hurried from the room.

Althea descended the stairs with unladylike haste, not even pausing to acknowledge Ibthorp who had hastened ahead to open the door for her. She did not slow her pace until she reached the street, where she paused, drew a few deep breaths, and tried to collect her thoughts as best she could.

Her seemingly innocuous remark concerning his mother's charm had destroyed the fragile bond they shared, and it hurt her more than she cared to admit to acknowledge it. Somehow, she was going to have to overcome that unfortunate remark and prove to him that he could trust her with his confidence, though how she was going to do so she could not imagine.

Chapter 12

The opportunity to repair her relationship with the Marquess of Harwood presented itself sooner than Althea could have hoped and oddly enough, it was engineered by the cause of the rift in the first place—the Marchioness of Harwood herself.

On the pretext of introducing her granddaughter to the grandson of an old acquaintance, the Dowager Duchess of Clarendon was leading Althea in the direction of the card room at the Countess of Hartington's opulent mansion in Berkeley Square when they found themselves face-to-face with Gareth's mother.

"How delightful to encounter the two of you without a card table separating us. So much more conducive to conversation, do you not agree? Do let us take a seat in that alcove and have a comfortable coze." And without giving Althea or her grandmother a moment to think, the marchioness slipped between the two of them, linked arms with both of them, bestowed a charming smile on each one, and led them to a group of delicate gilt chairs conveniently arranged in a corner for those who wished to watch the dancing or exchange the latest *on dits*.

"Now"—the marchioness gracefully deposited herself on the middle chair and waved to them to take the ones on either side of her—"do tell me, Lady Althea, how you are enjoying your introduction to the *ton*. I already know that it is enjoying its introduction to you very much, for one hears your name on everyone's lips. But I know that it can be just the tiniest bit overwhelming.

The lot of an incomparable is a difficult one. There are so many people waiting to catch you in a faux pas, so many people who make spiteful remarks. The world is a very jealous place where someone as lovely as you is concerned."

The smile she directed at Althea was so warm and sympathetic that Althea could not help smiling in return. "Indeed it is, my lady. And to tell the truth, I am longing to return to the peace and quiet of the country."

"Oh no!" The marchioness raised a dainty hand to her mouth in horror. "You may believe that, but you must *never* admit to such a thing in public, my dear, no matter how strongly you feel, or you will become a laughing-stock. No one, no matter how much they may criticize the metropolis for being a vain and frivolous place, wishes to be thought ridiculous. Why, that is even worse than being labeled a bluestocking!"

Privately, Althea thought she would rather be labeled a bluestocking than an incomparable. No one would waste a second thought on a bluestocking, but everyone's attention was focused on an incomparable.

The marchioness leaned forward to whisper behind her fan. "I quite agree with you that London is a very noisy and dirty place, but if one wants to be acquainted with the most charming, most fascinating people, one simply *must* journey to the metropolis."

Althea nodded thoughtfully as she recalled the stultifying conversation of the squire's wife and his two vapid daughters back at Clarendon. The marchioness did have a point; there was certainly greater variety to be found in town. Perhaps the marquess had been mistaken about his mother; perhaps she had not been so vain and frivolous as she had been lonely in the country.

"It may be rather overwhelming at first, but in time, I assure you, you will come to feel as comfortable here as you do in the country." The marchioness reached over to pat Althea's hand in a kindly fashion. "But keeping up with the *ton* can be fatiguing if one is not accustomed to such a hectic existence, and being the cynosure of all eyes is wearing in the extreme. Even my Gareth complains of it, and as a gentleman, he is not subjected to the scrutiny that a young woman is. Not that he does not cut a most dashing figure, but gentlemen's fashions are so much simpler than ours; do you not think so? And it takes so much less effort on their part to stay à la mode."

Althea, who had wished countless times as she was being decked out for yet another function that she were the son her father longed for, nodded emphatically.

"Good. I am glad that we are in agreement. But it can be difficult even for gentlemen. Gareth here . . ." Catching sight of a tall figure not far away from them, the marchioness beckoned to her son in a way that could not be ignored. "Gareth hardly dances at all at these things, and I know it is simply that having suffered from excessive reserve as a boy he finds it difficult to intrude on others even as a grown man. Gareth, my dear, I know that Lady Althea is absolutely longing to dance, but the young men are all so concerned with cutting a dash themselves they do not stop to think for a moment about the young ladies. You have inherited your dear father's grace on the dance floor and will make her a most pleasing partner." The marchioness turned to a miserably self-conscious Althea. "I know that you waltz, my dear, for I have seen you do it quite beautifully times out of mind."

Gareth was left with no alternative but to bow with as good grace as he could muster, offer Althea his arm, and lead her to the floor. "Now you have had your own opportunity to experience my mother's infinite capacity for making others do her bidding," he remarked cynically as they joined the other couples on the floor.

"She was only being kind, my lord. She *did* seem to understand what it is like to be the object of all eyes, the subject of hundreds of comments. I found her to be surprisingly sympathetic."

"Because she wished to be." Even to his own ears, Gareth's voice grated harshly. "I know you think I am being overly critical, but did it occur to you why she wished for you to be my partner?"

"She said as much, that you, that I . . ."

"Yes, what did she say about the son she hardly ever spent any time with?" His gray eyes bored into her.

"She said exactly what you said about yourself. That you were reserved as a boy and therefore do not like to intrude on others." Althea thrust out her chin defiantly.

A bitter laugh escaped him. "A masterful stroke. No, I have told her many times that I do not dance because I have no desire to make idle chatter with some silly miss who only wishes to attach my interest in order to cut a dash or to lure me into making her an offer. No, my mother wished me to dance with you, not out of concern for you or for me. She wished for me to dance with you because she wants more pin money."

"Wants more pin money?"

Annoyed as he was, Gareth could not help chuckling at the confused expression on his partner's face. "You are an incomparable, Lady Althea, I will grant you that, but you are not the only incomparable in the room."

"I quite agree. Mama is forever telling me that I should exert myself to have manners as captivating as Lady Mary Sotherton's, and that gentlemen prefer a woman who is fashionably fair and always exquisitely turned out like Miss de Villiers."

"Exactly." He found her utter lack of envy toward these two potential rivals dangerously endearing. Casting back in his memory Gareth could not recall ever meeting a single woman so utterly unimpressed by her own charms as Lady Althea Beauchamp. "What distinguishes you from these other two young ladies, if you will forgive me for saying it, is your immense fortune. I apologize for putting it so bluntly, but as you yourself have often alluded to it, you have no illusions as to its attractions."

"No." Althea stared off over his shoulder as she considered this argument. It was true that Lady Mary and Miss de Villiers were more conventionally beautiful, and they were charmingly coquettish in a way that, according to the Duchess of Clarendon, men found impossible to resist, but they did not attract the crowds of admirers Althea did.

As they whirled around the floor, Althea caught a

glimpse of the Marchioness of Harwood watching them closely, a triumphant smile curling her lips. An unpleasant shiver of recognition ran up Althea's spine. Her partner was right. There was no mistaking the expression on the marchioness's face. It was not pride at the handsome figure her son and his partner cut on the dance floor. It was not pleasure in the fact that she had matched him up with someone he could enjoy conversing with. It was greed, pure and simple. Althea had seen the same expression on the faces of her own admirers too many times not to recognize it for what it was.

The familiar ache of disappointment swept over her as she realized that once again she had hoped for more from someone she was beginning to think of as a friend, or at least a pleasant acquaintance. Once again she represented nothing more than wealth and connection to a person who had seemed genuinely interested in her welfare. But this time the disappointment was tempered by the knowledge that the marquess, who must have suffered such disappointments a hundred times over, had been telling her the truth.

At least, Althea thought, her parents had never deceived her. They had been nothing if not forthcoming about their plans for their daughter's future, and no matter how strongly she disagreed with those plans, no matter how powerless she might feel, Althea did not feel like a dupe. The marquess, however, must have felt duped and betrayed many times through the years, as duped as his father had been before him.

"You, you, are . . . I apologize for having doubted . . ." Shock, disgust, and disappointment clogged Althea's throat to such a degree that it was more a croak than an apology.

Gareth glanced down at her and, much to his surprise, saw the faint sparkle of tears in her eyes. His anger and frustration evaporated in an instant. He wanted to hug her to him and laugh triumphantly. For the first time in his life, it seemed, someone had believed him instead of his mother. He was unprepared for the tremendous sense of vindication it brought, along with something else, something stronger and more compelling, something that warmed him through and through as he realized what it was like to have another person understand and sympathize with him.

But as he looked down at Althea, the sympathetic expression faded, and a faint, almost crafty smile tugged at the corner of her mouth. Gareth held his breath. Surely he had not been mistaken in thinking she understood. Please let him not be mistaken.

"And now, I think it is high time you return the favor."

"What?" If Althea had looked confused a few minutes earlier, Gareth looked even more confused.

"If your mother is trying to marry you off to a fortune, why do you not do the same to her?"

"But I do not wish to marry."

'No, not you." She chuckled indulgently, almost as though she were addressing a young child or a simpleton. 'Your mother. If your mother wants a fortune, then let *her* marry a fortune, not you."

It was so simple, so obvious that he could not believe he had not thought of it before, or, more surprisingly, that his mother had not.

"Your mother is still an attractive woman. There must be many, or at least some wealthy widowers who would like a wife to take them in hand."

"I do not know. I have never thought . . ." Gareth tried desperately to gather his wits, wits that he had thought served him well all these years until a mere slip of a girl had lately begun to outwit him at every turn.

"Grandmama will know some. She still has many friends in London and maintains a constant correspondence with many others across the country. She will know someone of wealth and rank who needs a wife or a hostess to run his establishment. In the meantime, we can keep our own eyes out for such a person here and we can check with each other regularly. That will keep your mother happy because she will see us together and think you are making great strides with an heiress. And my mother will think I have attracted the interest of an eligible bachelor."

"How gratifying.'

"Well, she has warned me against you as someone who has never distinguished anyone with serious interest, and certainly she would prefer a duke, while my father would rather have someone more useful politically, but you are better than nothing."

"You are too kind." He laughed. The wickedly teasing smile and the impish gleam in her eyes made the Ice Princess look like a naughty ten-year-old. He could not help wondering if the serious and perfect Lady Althea Beauchamp had ever been allowed to be a naughty ten-year-old, or six- or five-year-old, for that matter. Had she ever been allowed to be a little girl by those rigid, exacting parents of hers?

Chapter 13

Inspired by a plan that would not only help free the marquess from his mother's interference in his life, but would serve to distract her from her own worries about her future and give her grandmother something to put her mind to, Althea sought out the Dowager Duchess of Clarendon in her chambers the very next morning.

A spritely, energetic lady, the dowager duchess rose at dawn every morning, but, to ensure uninterrupted privacy, she allowed her son and daughter-in-law to believe that her age made her a much later riser. Since the duchess herself would never have been so unfashionable as to rise before noon, this gave Althea and her grandmother plenty of time to enjoy lively discussions of the previous evening's card game or the most recent articles in *Blackwood's* and the *Edinburgh Review,* copies of which could be found littering the dowager's desk. Her bookcase was already crammed too full to afford any extra space for them.

Grandmama, I have a project for us," Althea announced as, pushing aside yesterday's edition of the *Times,* she cleared a space for herself on a small settee near the fire.

"Oh?" The dowager had not seen her granddaughter looking this energetic or interested since they had left Clarendon.

"Yes, and I shall need your help." Briefly Althea related Gareth's history and outlined her plan.

As she listened, the dowager duchess grew thoughtful.

Her granddaughter was always the soul of kindness, beloved by everyone at Clarendon for her warmth and interest, but she generally reserved her real concern and attention for the animals on the family estate. With the exception of Jem, it was not like her to become so involved in helping a human, especially a man of the *ton*. She usually reserved her efforts for those weaker and more unfortunate than she. There was more to this than met the eye, and the dowager duchess felt her own interest and energy rising.

"Do you know any such men?"

"Lord yes, child. There are plenty of vain, foolish old men who would be more than happy to support the expensive tastes of a vain foolish women who is still lovely enough and à la mode enough to add to their consequence. Sir Digby Cricklade is just such a one. He has spent a lifetime hanging around the incomparables of twenty Seasons without ever having caught one. Undoubtedly he would be willing to invest a great deal for the chance to squire around a diamond of the first water even though her reputation was gained years before you were born. And then, of course, there is Cuthbert. You remember Lord Battisford, an even bigger fool than Sir Digby, and even plumper in the pocket. He has no mind of his own, and since that harridan of a wife died, he has been in desperate need of someone to lead him around by the nose. Your marquess's mother may be too indirect in her methods, for Cuthbert is clearly comfortable with only the most imperious of women. However, we may be able to do the trick with one or the other of them I should think."

"Thank you, Grandmama. Will you help arrange introductions?"

"Certainly, I shall. Of course, both of them are too stupid to be of any use in the card room so we shall have to confine our strategies to the ballroom."

They initiated their campaign that very evening among the select crowd patronizing that most exclusive of gathering places, Almack's. Althea actually found herself looking forward to the evening though ordinarily she loathed the Wednesday gathering above all others, for the intensity of observation and speculation was almost palpable among those lucky enough to attend. The plainness of the ballroom itself, the mediocre quality of the suppers, and the low stakes at cards meant that there was nothing to distract anyone from the major function of the place which was to serve as the premier center of the marriage mart and hotbed of gossip.

But their project took her mind off this, and it was with a mingled sense of relief and anticipation that she identified the Marchioness of Harwood in a tête-à-tête with her constant cronies, the Countess of Rothsay and Lady Edgcumbe at the very moment that her grandmother murmured in her ear, "We are in luck. Sir Digby and Lord Battisford are both here, though I supposed it is hardly a surprise since both of them would rather die than miss being seen in these hallowed halls. Now we must contrive to fall into conversation with them. Come."

They had been standing not too far from the entrance to the ballroom, the duchess on one side of Althea, and her grandmother on the other. It was left to the dowager not only to manage a casual encounter with their quarry, but to come up with a compelling reason to detach her granddaughter from her daughter-in-law.

Glancing quickly around the room Althea's grandmother searched for acquaintances who possessed eligible sons or grandsons. "Ah, there is Lady Carstairs, whose mother was at school with me. Eugenia is now too frail to leave the country, but she writes to me regularly. Her letters continually bemoan the fact that her grandson still has not found someone possessing the qualifications he considers necessary in a wife. Perhaps Althea does. Come, Althea."

Before her daughter-in-law had a moment to respond, the dowager steered her granddaughter toward a handsome, dark-haired matron wearing a strikingly elegant robe of black satin over a white petticoat.

"But, Grandmama, there is really no need for me to meet another eligible suitor," Althea protested as they threaded their way across the floor.

"There is, if the mother of one is standing next to Lord Battisford. Besides, your mother would question any other reason for deserting her. And you have no cause to worry, for Eugenia's grandson is a complete misogynist and even more of a confirmed bachelor than the Marquess of Harwood is reputed to be."

Althea was too busy inspecting the foppish older gentleman standing next to Lady Carstairs to notice her grandmother's sharp eyes focused on her cheeks where the faintest tinge of color appeared at the mention of the Marquess of Harwood. Presumably this man in absurdly tight satin knee breeches, shirt points so high he could not turn his head, and an enormous emerald ring was the Lord Battisford they hoped to introduce to the marchioness.

"Your Grace." Lady Carstairs smiled at them as they approached. "I am delighted to see you. Mama will be so glad to hear that we met. And of course, everyone who is anyone has heard your granddaughter's praises sung everywhere. I only wish my George were here to make your acquaintance, but . . . ." Lady Carstairs shrugged with all the resignation of a mother who had tried unsuccessfully to interest her son in the beauties of a score of Seasons.

"And how does your mother go along?" The dowager shifted ever so slightly so that her words carried easily to the plump man Althea had already identified as their quarry.

"She is well enough, thank you, though she tires very easily, and finds herself prostrated by even the slightest excitement."

"I miss her company sadly. There are so few old friends left. I am glad to see the Marchioness of Harwood over there. Of course she is a good deal younger than I, but her mother-in-law was also at school with me. It hardly seems any time at all that she was taking the town by storm, yet now she is the mother of a grown man and a widow. It is good to see her here, for she is far too lovely and charming to bury herself in the country. And I am sure it will be no time at all before men are fighting to pay her their addresses again—such style, such elegance, and, if I recall, one of the most graceful dancers Almack's has ever seen. The man who wins her will be the envy of everyone, I am sure." The dowager smiled slyly as the plump white hand of the man next to her groped for the ornate quizzing glass hanging around his neck and stared through it at the marchioness.

"But now you must excuse us, for I see my daughter-in-law looking to see where we have gotten to. Do give my regards to your mother." The dowager smiled at Lady Carstairs and began a slow stately progress back toward Althea's mother.

"Grandmama, I had no idea you knew the Marchioness of Harwood's mama-in-law."

"I did not know her; I said that she was at school with me. Just because I do not seek to, er, *influence* people the way your Mama does, does not mean that I am not perfectly capable of it when called upon to do so. Now, if I do not miss my guess, Lord Battisford is already seeking out someone who can introduce him to the marchioness. And where he goes, Sir Digby Cricklade is sure to follow, for there is enormous competition between the two of them. Neither one can bear to let the other steal a march on him. There. See. What did I tell you? The tall, thin man over there looking daggers at Lord Battisford is Sir Digby."

Althea glanced out of the corner of her eye to see Lord Battisford accompanying a hatchet-faced dowager in purple satin in the direction of the marchioness. "Grandmama, do let us stop and see what happens."

"Your mother will wonder what has become of us, but mark my words, Lord Battisford, who considers himself a veritable caper merchant, will be leading the Marchioness of Harwood to the floor in no time."

Althea paused as they approached a knot of people in animated conversation, and using them to screen her from the duchess's view, watched gleefully as her grandmother's predictions came true. "You are absolutely correct, Grandmama. I could positively hug you."

"But pray do not or your Mama will accuse me of

being a bad influence on you—encouraging undignified behavior." The dowager's black eyes twinkled. "Though I must admit that I myself have never enjoyed an evening at Almack's half so much. Perhaps there is something to this marriage mart notion after all. It is rather amusing, is it not?"

"Only if you are the matchmaker and not the match. It is all very well for those women who would like nothing better than to have a man look after them. But I would rather look after myself."

"I know you would, dear, but truly, it isn't at all practical. A young woman cannot live alone."

"Perhaps not, but she could live with a companion." Althea fixed her grandmother with a speculative look. "You are not all that happy being under Papa's thumb."

"I would not say that, child. He is a most dutiful son who provides me with all the comforts . . ."

"But he is an old stick who does not pay the least attention to what would make you happy. If he did, you would be at home in your garden now instead of accompanying us from one ball to another."

"But he is entirely correct in maintaining that it is my duty to see you well established," her grandmother acknowledged with a look that Althea could only characterize as self-conscious.

"He has Mama to do that. There is not the least need to drag you all over London. You dislike the crowds and the noise as much as I do, and you miss the gardens at Clarendon as much as I miss the horses, the dogs, the sheep, and oh, all the animals. And even though you have your garden at home, you know you would be happier living in a simple cottage rather than the stuffy formality of Clarendon, but Papa simply could not bear to have a Beauchamp living an existence that some might label eccentric."

"Your papa has a very strong sense of family pride." It was a weak defense, and they both knew it.

"Somehow I shall fix it, I promise you. And it will not be because I marry some duke," Althea vowed fiercely.

"That would be a pity, dear."

"Surely *you* do not want me to marry someone who will increase the glory and the consequence of the Beauchamps?"

"Not necessarily, but I would like you to find someone whom you could truly love, who would love you and appreciate you in return, someone who could share your life and enrich it."

"The way Mama loves what Papa's fortune and family did to establish her as a leader of the *ton*, or what Mama's beauty and elegance did to make Papa the envy of everyone?"

"No!" Even Althea was surprised at the emphatic note in her grandmother's voice. Until this moment Althea had not really considered that the Duke of Clarendon's coldly formal relationship with his wife might be a source of disappointment to his mother. "*Not* like that. You never knew your grandfather." The dowager smiled reminiscently and a tender expression softened the strong lines of her aristocratic countenance. "Harry was a wild harum-scarum lad, ripe for any sort of mischief. How he could have produced a son like . . . Well, that is beside the point. We must get back to your mother." The dowager looked across the floor to where the Marchioness of Harwood and Lord Battisford were gracefully executing the figures of a quadrille. "At least we can say that we have done some good work this evening."

"Yes." Althea only wished that the Marchioness of Harwood's son were here to witness the success of their scheme. She had told herself that a cynical bachelor such as the marquess would avoid Almack's as if his life depended on it, but that still did not keep her from scanning the crowd for the tall athletic figure of a scornful observer surveying the scene with the cynical detachment of one who was more than familiar with the follies of mankind in general and the *ton* in particular.

Chapter 14

She would never know how much it had cost him not to go to Almack's. As a matter of fact, Gareth himself could not believe that the first thing he thought of when his eye caught the date at the top of the *Times* as he drank his morning coffee was that it was Wednesday, a day no incomparable would be anywhere but Almack's.

He grinned as he remembered his last conversation with Althea and the teasing twinkle in her eyes. Did she ever look that way with anyone else? Surely not, or she would never have earned her nickname, the Ice Princess. And what was the Ice Princess doing now? Had she confided her absurd plan to her grandmother? Not that he objected to having his mother married off. To have another man catering to her whims and incessant demands for money and attention would virtually solve all his problems, but Gareth seriously doubted that there was a man in Christendom foolish enough or long-suffering enough to put up with the Marchioness of Harwood.

As the clock struck eleven that evening, he actually considered, for one crazed moment, donning knee breeches and going. The thought that his mother and several other determined matchmakers would suffer apoplectic fits if they saw the Bachelor Marquess entering those sacred portals made it almost attractive enough for him to succumb to temptation, but reason rapidly reasserted itself and he sauntered off to Brooks's instead.

The card room was relatively thin of company, which was just the way he liked it. Those crowding around the green baize tables were the dedicated card players who could not be lured away by more convivial forms of entertainment. Gareth was lucky enough to arrive just as someone left the Duke of Portland's table, but even faced with that formidable adversary he still found the play flat and the competition tepid. And despite the fact that he arose one thousand pounds richer, he found it all completely uninteresting. Stifling a yawn, he nodded to the rest of the company and sauntered home.

Perhaps he had been mistaken. Perhaps an evening at Almack's would have been more enlivening after all. He wondered if that determined matchmaker, the Duchess of Clarendon, had allowed her daughter to escape to the card room or if she had kept her dancing with eligible partners the entire evening.

Poor Althea. He really did sympathize with her. Irritating as his own mother was, she never actually dared to order him around in public as he had occasionally observed the duchess doing. His mother cajoled and sighed dramatically, but his word, when he chose to assert it, was still law. The consequences of ignoring his mother's wishes could be unpleasant, but he did have more control over his own life than Althea did. Small wonder that she wished to win a fortune and take control of her own destiny. Not for the first time that day, he wondered how she was faring with her schemes.

Though he did not go so far as to appear at Almack's, Gareth did seize the first opportunity to catch a glimpse of Althea at the Countess of Carmarthen's rout. Carmarthen House in Pall Mall was as impressive a structure as York House or any of the others along the broad avenue. Though it could not compare in magnificence with the nearby Carlton House, it was a certainty that all the fashionable world would be beating a path to the splendid residence of the popular countess. In fact, Gareth was rather surprised that his mother had not demanded his escort to such an important function, but he soon forgot this odd departure from her usual routine when he entered the brilliantly lit ballroom. Even Althea, striking as she was, would not stand out in a crowd of such magnitude.

Keeping his eyes fixed on the dance floor in the center, Gareth slowly made his way around the perimeter of the ballroom looking in vain for a tall, slender figure surrounded by a crowd of admirers, but he had no success. Had she already escaped to the card room?

He was about to press in that direction when his eye fell on another woman flanked by admirers. His jaw dropped for the briefest of moments before a slow grin spread across his face. Clever girl. She had managed it. Gareth had no doubt that the knot of elderly gentlemen vying with one another to capture his mother's attention were all somehow acquainted with the Dowager Duchess of Clarendon. He recognized the chief competitors, Sir Digby Cricklade and Lord Battisford, who stood in the favored position at the marchioness's right hand. So, Lord Battisford was the reason that Gareth was free to come and go as he pleased without having his mother dragging on his arm as she pointed out this heiress or that highly eligible young lady.

There was no doubt about it, Lady Althea Beauchamp was a woman of her word. She had taken his mother off his hands as she had said she would. How successful would she be at freeing herself from her own parental interference? Gareth paused on the threshold of the card room and let out a sigh of relief as he caught sight of a dark head, the simply arranged braid threaded with pearls, at one of the tables in the room. She was here after all.

Then he stiffened as he recognized the identity of the man lounging negligently in the chair across from her, a wolfish smile twisting his lips as he languidly surveyed the cards in his hand. It was Sir Montague Rochfort.

A frisson of disgust ran down Gareth's spine. He should have known that sooner or later that noted plucker of innocent pigeons would appear once Althea had established her reputation as a card player of some skill. Gareth frowned as he eyed the man. Cheating rustics in the hells of St. James and Pall Mall was one thing, but would he be bold enough to try it in this company?

Gareth made his way around the room toward the table

as unobtrusively as he could, taking his place in a shadowy corner where he could observe the play without being seen. He could not ever remember feeling so tense or so helpless as he did now. There was no way to warn Althea, and one could not call a man a Captain Sharp without ample proof. Even then, it was grounds for a duel.

Others were as fascinated by the contest as he was, and Gareth heard something about ten thousand whispered somewhere in the background. Ten thousand! She must have been mad, or desperate. Yet she and her grandmother sat at the table as calmly as though they were playing Pope Joan or Speculation in the schoolroom.

The tricks were fairly evenly divided and Gareth could feel the tension growing among the spectators. Still, it seemed to him as though the advantage was on the side of Althea and her grandmother. He scrutinized Sir Montague suspiciously. To the casual observer the man appeared suavely confident, but to the experienced eye of a dedicated gambler who saw the sheen of sweat on his upper lip and the awkward way he held his cards, it was obvious that Sir Montague was extremely nervous. And so he should be given his opposition, Gareth thought.

Gareth glanced over again. He could have sworn that there was a card tucked into the cuff of the man's sleeve, but it was so discreetly done he could not be sure enough to comment or do anything. Hoping to catch Althea's eye, he stepped out of the shadows to try to signal her in some way, but there was no distracting her. She sat erect, eyes focused on her cards, her lower lip gripped in her teeth, a frown of concentration wrinkling her brow. It was an expression that Gareth always found upsettingly endearing, and he found it even more so now.

He stifled the hot flash of jealousy stabbing him that anyone else should see her in this unself-conscious state. Somehow her obliviousness to everyone and everything made her seem oddly vulnerable, and he felt the strongest urge to rush in brandishing a sword to protect her. But there was nothing clever or resourceful that he could do to save her. The Marquess of Harwood had never felt so helpless in his life.

Althea and her grandmother took another trick and Gareth saw Sir Montague's lips tighten. Surely that was the last one he was going to allow them to take.

Spades were led. As Althea's grandmother played the queen, Gareth, whose eyes were glued on Sir Montague, thought he saw the man's eyelids flicker as his partner sighed, shook his head, and laid down a heart. Althea, also shaking her head, offered up a diamond, remarking quietly, "I believe that you have forced the knave out of hiding, Grandmama."

Sir Montague blanched, coughed, and so discreetly that no one realized what he was doing, pulled out the knave that he had been holding in reserve in his sleeve.

Althea's eyes, which had been fixed fiercely on her opponent, never wavered as he laid down the card. "Then I believe this will be our game."

Sir Montague turned a ghastly shade of gray as he struggled to sound appropriately nonchalant. "But my dear young lady, there are more tricks yet to be played."

"Of course. You are right, Sir Montague, there are more tricks, but I believe you will find that I am correct in saying that it is our game." The words were spoken quietly enough, but to Gareth, at least, the menace in her tone was abundantly clear. He let out the breath he had been holding unconsciously and slumped against the wall from the sheer relief of it. She knew, had known perhaps even longer than he had, that Sir Montague was cheating. Lady Althea Beauchamp was as brilliant as she was fearless. Gareth wanted to shout and call all the world's attention to it. He wanted to laugh and hug and kiss her until they were both breathless, and he wanted to do it now.

The four of them continued to play it out, but Althea was right, and she and her grandmother rose the victors. "I thank you for the game."

Sir Montague gnawed his lip uncomfortably as he replied. "I shall send my man over with your winnings."

Althea nodded and without further ado, swept toward the door, every inch the Ice Princess, not betraying by so much as a flicker of an eyelash that she had beaten a cheater at his own game and won a small fortune from him.

Gareth caught up with Althea and her grandmother as they reached the door to the card room. "Lady Althea." He desperately racked his brains for a way to steal a moment alone with her. Over her shoulder he spied a French door at the end of the ballroom just as the orchestra conveniently struck up a waltz. "May I have this dance?"

"My mother, I must . . .", she stammered, made wary by the oddly intent expression in his eyes and unable to interpret the urgent tone in his voice.

"I feel certain that if your mother knows you are dancing with an eligible partner she will forgive your deserting her. Do you not agree, Your Grace?" He winked at the dowager.

"I feel certain that you are correct in that assumption, Lord Harwood." The man was a scamp, the dowager reflected, much like her Harry had been. Her granddaughter needed a man like that, not some stiff-rump, prosy old bore like her own son. How she and Harry had come to produce a child like that there was no telling, though Harry's mother had been a Featherstonaugh, and the Featherstonaughs were known for being as prosy as Methodists.

"If you insist, my lord. Grandmama, will you tell Mama where I am?"

"I shall be delighted to, child." The dowager winked back at the marquess as he led her Althea to the floor. It was clear that the man wanted something besides a dance with her granddaughter. She had seen him watching them like a hawk as they sat at the gaming table and she could have sworn he had looked worried. Of course Rochfort was a scoundrel of the worst sort; anyone with their wits about them could see that, but no one was a match for Althea. The dowager knew that, and she also knew that the Marquess of Harwood had desperately wanted to believe it too as he stood watching them take trick after trick. But the frown wrinkling his forehead had been the frown of a worried parent. Odd that a man

notoriously skittish where any connection with a lady of
quality was concerned should interest himself in one who
had obviously been brought to London to contract an
eligible alliance.

The dowager's black eyes gleamed with suppressed
amusement as she went in search of her daughter-in-law.
The Marquess of Harwood was undoubtedly an eligible
parti of the highest order, but not one likely to raise any
hopes in the Duchess of Clarendon's breast. She liked
her men to be biddable, and there was nothing biddable
about Gareth de Vere. From the fierce gray eyes under
straight black brows to the hawklike nose and firm, un-
yielding mouth, from broad shoulders to narrow waist
and long legs, he was a man born to command, a man
who knew what he wanted and got it.

And at that moment, he apparently wanted her granddaughter. The dowager hoped she knew what he wanted
Althea for. There was something between the two of
them, an electricity that only someone close to either one
or both of them could see.

Meanwhile, on the terrace, beyond the reach of prying
eyes, Gareth was explaining to Althea precisely why he
had asked her to dance—to give her a good scolding.
"What were you thinking? Were you mad? Rochfort is
the worst sort of a knave, a Captain Sharp as dangerous
as any that haunt the hells waiting to pluck rich young
pigeons. Just because he bears an ancient name does not
mean he is any less likely to cheat you."

"I know that."

"You what?" Even though he had just witnessed her
fleecing one of the most notorious gamblers in London,
Gareth was still thunderstruck by her admission.

"Even if I had not mistrusted him from the very first,
I would have the moment he staked ten thousand for a
game of whist with an heiress from the country. It was
quite obvious the man was up to no good, and I am no
fool, my lord."

"I know that. You are quite the opposite, as I have
discovered, to my chagrin. But being clever at figures
and cards isn't the same as being wise to the ways of the

world. And an incomparable in her first Season, even an incomparable of incomparables, is no match for a man who has been swindling young bucks since before you were born. It is only the man's consummate skill that keeps him from being caught and refused admittance to respectable gatherings."

Althea's chin, which had lifted defiantly at his characterization of her as "an incomparable in her first Season" now rose a fraction higher. "My lord, an 'incomparable of incomparables,' as you insist on calling me, is accustomed to deception and trickery in things far more serious than cards. Believe me, I can recognize a *bad* 'un, as John Coachman calls it, with greater facility than you obviously credit me with."

The angry sparkle in her eyes warned him that he had already gone too far, but he could not help himself. "Perhaps. But Sir Montague is an ugly customer, a very ugly customer indeed, and I cannot believe that you have encountered men of his stamp before."

Althea drew a deep, steadying breath. "It is very kind of you to concern yourself over my welfare, my lord. I may not have your worldly experience, but I have enough people concerning themselves over my welfare as it is. I bid you good evening."

He caught her wrist as she turned to go. "No. Althea, I mean, forgive me. I know I may sound patronizing, but . . ."

"You do."

"But it is just that I am worried for you. No, do not frown at me so. It is not that I worry you will be deceived or even that you will fail. Believe me, I have too much respect for your talents and abilities to do that. It is just that I want so much for you to succeed that I . . ." He let go of her wrists to clasp her hands in his. "Have you not wished for something so much that you were afraid it could not possibly happen simply because you wished for it too much?"

She nodded slowly, mesmerized by the look in his eyes.

"Well, that is what I mean when I say I am worried for you. I want so much for you to win your heart's desire that I cannot bear for anything to stand in your way." A self-mocking smile twisted his lips. "Do not ask me why I care. I just do. Perhaps it is because you are so bold and determined in going after what you want. Bold and determined as I have been. I want to help you, but at the same time I want you to succeed on your own. The end result is that I have succeeded in annoying you by concerning myself with your affairs."

He raised her hands to his lips and kissed them gently, first one and then the other. "Now, if I promise not to interfere again, will you promise to come to me if you have any doubts or questions about your opponents? I know you have parents who watch over you, but I hardly think they have any more knowledge of gamesters and questionable gambling hells than you do, and you can hardly go to them without revealing your schemes for escaping the future they have planned for you."

Surprised by his earnestness, Althea looked up at him curiously. There was a sadness in his voice that told her the road to regaining his fortune had not been an easy one. There had been painful moments along the way that had etched the cynical lines in his face. He was not a man who involved himself in others' affairs; he himself had admitted that, though it was certainly common enough knowledge. Why, then, was he trying to help her? Was it truly because he wanted her to succeed? The warmth of his lips on her fingers, the reassuring strength of his hands clasping hers, the glow in his eyes as he looked down at her, all told her that he did. And for some strange reason, she wanted desperately to believe him. Even more strange was that her heart was beating so loudly she could hardly hear herself reply. "I promise that I will ask you about any questionable characters."

"Thank you."

For a moment, Althea almost thought he was going to kiss her. He paused, looked searchingly down at her, and then smiled. "And now I must get you back to the ball-room before *I* become a questionable character."

Chapter 15

As the ducal carriage rolled back to Grosvenor Square, Althea, a vague feeling of disappointment gnawing at her, stared blindly out the window. Had she wanted him to kiss her? Having grown up with a mother who was adept at creating illusions, who hid her own self-centeredness under the mask of devotion to her husband and child, who spent hours with dressmakers and maids in an effort to appear more youthful and beautiful than nature had made her, Althea had resolved to be utterly honest with herself and others [from an early age]. She had always prided herself on that honesty, and now, examining her own motives with a brutally self-critical eye, she arrived at the thoroughly uncomfortable and disconcerting conclusion that she *had* wanted the marquess to kiss her.

Ordinarily, all people were the same to Althea. Of course, some were young, some old, some clever, some not, but in general, they were just people and as such, affected her very little either way. She could dimly remember that as a very small child she had run to her parents hoping that her beautiful Mama or her handsome Papa would smile, hold out welcoming arms, and hug her tight. That had never happened. It was not that they had ignored her; no, never that. Mama was constantly adjusting her, fussing over an awkwardly tied bow in her hair, smoothing a rumpled skirt, frowning at a stain on her sleeve or a scuffed shoe. And Papa was forever admonishing her to stand up straight and carry herself as proudly as all Beauchamps did. Naturally, in an effort to win their affection, she had complied eagerly with all their strictures. She had schooled herself to become their perfect, well-behaved child, never embarrassing them with any childish outbursts of exuberance or sorrow, a tiny model of their own exquisitely well-bred exteriors, and she had never again been so unrealistic as to long for affection and attention from anyone.

It was not that she was not interested in or curious about other people. She enjoyed hearing her nurse's stories about her childhood, her governess's tales of family life, but she had never allowed herself to do anything more than listen. She had never shared her own hopes and fears, had never revealed her own dreams to anyone else.

But there was something about this man that was different. It was not just that he was intelligent and didn't hide his clever mind behind fashionable concerns. It was not just that he was a fine figure of a man. Althea was sure that there were other men in London who were intelligent, and there were certainly other men possessing powerful, athletic physiques, and men who were more conventionally handsome with open smiling countenances instead of angular features that habitually wore a faintly sardonic expression.

No, it was not intelligence or looks that attracted her to the Marquess of Harwood, but some inexplicable energy that drew her to him in a way so fundamental that it eluded all definition. There was a defiant glint in his eye, a directness in his gaze that told her he was a man who formed his own opinions, followed his own interests, went his own way, who needed no encouragement, approval, or assistance from anyone. That aura of self-reliance and quiet confidence drew Althea to him more powerfully than any witty conversation or smiling good looks could have.

She had felt that self-assurance in the strength of his hands as they had guided her around the dance floor and maneuvered her out onto the terrace. As he had held her hands in his own, his strength had seemed to flow into her. The touch of his lips on her fingers had been electric. She had sensed the pent-up passion and energy that matched her own—a passion and energy that she kept so determinedly hidden from everyone that she had hardly known herself that she possessed them until she had met the marquess. Now he seemed to bring it all to the surface, whether it was challenging her at cards, sharing his frustrations with his mother, or holding her and looking down at her with eyes that missed nothing, eyes that showed he understood who she really was. Althea could not help being drawn to him, like iron to a lodestone, until she wanted to press herself against him and feel the power and the energy that made him so different from the self-satisfied young bucks who usually surrounded her.

"My dear, you are quite ruining your gown, twisting your hands in your lap like that." The duchess shook her head in exasperation as she reached over to smooth the delicate slip of Urling's net that her daughter had unthinkingly wadded up. "Really, Althea, you should be more careful. It is almost torn here."

Slowly and deliberately Althea straightened the fingers that had been so tightly curled and let out a deep breath. This was absurd. How could she let herself be so affected by anyone? Surely it must be all in her mind, a reaction to the tension of the game with Sir Montague. The next time she saw the Marquess of Harwood, her breathing would again be restored to normal instead of this ragged and uneven gasping she fought against now; her heart would beat quietly instead of the loud drumming that now sounded in her ears; her face would remain coolly pale instead of uncomfortably flushed. The next time. She could hardly wait until the next time.

It was at Almack's that Althea next saw the marquess. Knowing his aversion for marriage-mad young ladies and their mothers she had not expected to see him. And it was not until her heart thudded uncomfortably at the sight of a tall figure in the doorway that she realized he was there.

"Would you look at that, Emily, it is the Marquess of

Harwood!" A comely young matron standing next to Althea hissed in her companion's ear.

"How very droll. Perhaps he has come to his senses and realized that ladies of quality have more to offer than those actresses and opera dancers he insists on frequenting. I, for one, shall be happy to prove it," her dark-haired friend replied, directing a sultry look in Gareth's direction. "A man of his, er, *talents* should not be wasting his time on the lower classes when there are so many women of his own kind who would welcome him into their . . ."

Her cheeks already hot at the thought of the Marquess of Harwood's lovemaking skills, Althea edged quickly away so as not to hear the rest of the conversation.

Gareth himself was wondering if he had taken leave of his senses as he paused at the entrance to the ballroom. Certainly the few delicately raised eyebrows and sly smiles of those who saw him indicated that these observers had arrived at that conclusion. Well, let them think he had lost his mind. He refused to become a creature of habit, which was precisely the explanation he offered to Sir Humphrey Fenton who, determined to be the first to spread gossip of any kind, minced over to Gareth the moment he entered the room.

"You, my lord? The Bachelor Marquess? At the marriage mart? I thought you detested anything as respectable as this temple of the *ton*."

"You should know me better than that, Sir Humphrey. I am not so simple or so banal as to avoid something just because society flocks to it. My own guiding principle is that if a thing amuses me, I pursue it. At the moment, it amuses me to be at Almack's."

Sir Humphrey tittered uncomfortably as Gareth raised a disdainful brow. "If it amuses you. Oh, very good, sir. What a devil of a fellow. He would come to Almack's if it amuses him." And he hurried off to spread the word that at the moment it amused the Bachelor Marquess to appear at Almack's.

The Bachelor Marquess, meanwhile, was not amused by the uneasiness that gnawed at him until he could reassure himself that Lady Althea Beauchamp truly was among the select throng there that evening. He was even less amused by the speed with which that anxiety vanished the moment he caught sight of her.

Then she looked up, and as her eyes met his, he was taken aback by the effect that one tiny welcoming smile had on him. Not since his salad days had a woman's smile interfered with his heartbeat or his breathing in such a way.

It was not that she looked stunningly beautiful, for Lady Althea always looked stunningly beautiful. It was that she was genuinely happy to see him and no one else. There was something about the directness, the steadiness of her gaze, that made him feel she was happy to see him, Gareth de Vere, not the Marquess of Harwood, not an eligible bachelor, but someone whose company she enjoyed. Gareth could not remember a time, except perhaps among brother officers on the Peninsula, when he had been appreciated simply for the person he was.

Slowly he made his way over to the spot where she was standing with her mother and grandmother. The Duchess of Clarendon's pale blue eyes surveyed him appraisingly. "It is a surprise to see you here this evening, my lord." The cautious note of welcome in her voice left no doubt in his mind that Althea's mother was not about to waste her time or effort on a man who sported the nickname of the Bachelor Marquess.

He flashed her the devastating smile that had even caused the notorious Harriette Wilson's unimpressionable heart to skip a beat. "I was certain that you and your daughter would be here, and since I thoroughly enjoyed my last waltz with Lady Althea, I was hoping to convince her to honor me again. I trust that she and her grandmother will vouch for me as a respectable partner."

He winked unobtrusively at the dowager who just as unobtrusively winked back. There was no doubt that the man was a rogue, but an honest one where her granddaughter was concerned. Men who wished to protect their bachelor status did not risk waltzing with an eligible young female unless they were seriously drawn to her. And from the slight flush that rose in Althea's cheeks, the dowager could see that she was seriously drawn to the marquess in return.

"Mama, may I?"

"Oh, very well. But do not forget you were promised to Cholmondeley ages ago for the next." There was no mistaking the implication in the duchess's voice that both Cholmondeley and the long-standing nature of his invitation were more to her liking than the Marquess of Harwood's offhand approach.

"I can see that I must count myself lucky to have won a waltz with the incomparable of incomparables," Gareth remarked as he led Althea to the floor.

"Oh, that is just Mama's way. She never wants anyone to succeed at anything unless they suffered a good deal to attain it."

"And the fortunate Cholmondeley? Is he a suitor of yours?" Gareth did his best to drawl laconically, but the tension rising in the back of his neck belied this casual attitude. Fortunately, for his peace of mind, he was the only one aware of the laughable contrast between his outwardly calm demeanor and his inward turmoil.

"Cholmondeley is a mere viscount, but a most biddable one, with ancient lineage and excellent manners, so naturally Mama favors him."

"So the Duchess of Clarendon is seeking a biddable son-in-law above all else. What does the Duke of Clarendon seek?"

Althea looked at him in some surprise. Why should the Marquess of Harwood even care what sort of husband her parents sought for her? "Oh, Papa, I suppose . . ." Her voice trailed off as she considered the question carefully. Ostensibly, her father's word was law in their household, but was it really? "He is far more concerned with political connections."

"But he would concede to your mother's choice."

"No, well, ah, yes, I suppose he would." Althea regarded him curiously. "Yes, now that I think of it, of course he would. But how did you know?"

Gareth smiled bitterly. "Because I know. One only has to observe them for a little while to see that."

"Yes, I suppose you are right."

There was a world of resignation in her sigh that tore at his heart.

"And is this why you devote yourself to the card room, to escape it all, to concentrate your thoughts on other things?" He could see from her expression that he had gone too far. It was not something she wished to think about. "Of course, there is also your desire to win a fortune. How are you doing at reaching that goal?"

She brightened at the thought. "Actually, I think I am doing rather well. As you know, I won ten thousand from Sir Montague and five hundred at Lady Congleton's rout, one hundred one evening from Lord Wallingford who simply would not believe a woman could beat him, as well as another five hundred from him later before I was able to prove to him that it was possible. So far, I suppose that I have won a total of about twenty thousand, which should allow me to purchase a small estate somewhere. Eventually I wish to manage a farm on my own, but for the time being I would lease the land to local farmers, except for a few acres that I would give to the poor as common land."

Gareth raised a speculative eyebrow. "Can it be that we have a radical in our midst?"

"No. Merely someone practical enough to see what the Enclosure Acts and the Speenhamland System have done to the cottagers. Papa, naturally enough, supports the acts because he feels that the land is better managed that way, and he considers it his duty to take care of the poor on his estates. He simply cannot conceive that anyone would rather have the freedom to farm and forage on their own land, risky and unprofitable as it might be, than to receive largesse from a landlord. He does not understand what it is like to have no control over one's own destiny and therefore cannot sympathize."

She spoke so fiercely that Gareth could not help smiling. If the *ton* only knew what a passionate person the Ice Princess truly was they would be shocked. "You have been reading Mr. Cobbett, I see."

"And what if I have?" The dangerous sparkle in her

eyes warned him that the lady took her politics very
seriously, but he could not help thinking, rather irrele-
vantly, how much more passion became her than icy
aloofness. Her beauty, which had always presented a
most disturbing challenge to his peace of mind, was awe
inspiring when fired by idealism.

"That is yet another peculiarity we share in common,"
he mused. "Card games and agricultural reform make
odd bedfellows, do they not?"

"You?"

"You continue to hold a rather unflattering opinion of
my character, Lady Althea. Why? I have even more reason than you do to feel that farmers and cottagers should
farm their own plots of land and be free to forage on
common lands in order to support themselves. As the
daughter of a responsible landlord, you have never seen
the misery that can ensue as the result of bad management on the part of an irresponsible owner, but I have."

Again she heard that undercurrent of pain in his voice
that seemed so at odds with the cynical gambler. It was
rapidly being born in on Althea that behind the bleak
expression in those cold gray eyes lay a sensitive soul.
She held her breath and waited for him to continue.

"When I came home after my father died, I was
shocked by the suffering I saw. Cottages that had been
neat and tidy when I left were slovenly and tumbled
down. Their inhabitants who had once been healthy and
industrious were now gaunt and listless. All of this because one man had become a slave to the gaming table
and money that had once been spent on improving the
estate went directly into other, more successful gamblers' pockets."

"But I thought he was trying to win money in order
to make your . . . his wife happy."

"Originally he was. But occasionally, when our regiment
was assigned to the Knightsbridge barracks, I saw him in
London, and it soon became clear to me that gambling had
such a hold on him that all the rational reasons for pursuing
the Goddess of Chance had gone by the wayside. He was
in the grip of a fever that knew no restraint. No words of

caution on my part had the least effect on him. In fact, the last time I saw him I warned him that he would ruin himself and we parted in anger."

"How sad for you."

They had been gliding around the room in time to the music, but now he stopped and looked deep into her eyes. "Sad for me? Frustrating, more like. He was a fool and there was nothing I could do. We had never been close, and this just made the distance between us all that much greater."

"But it kept you from ever getting close enough to him as an adult to know him or, perhaps, even to understand him. Now you never will."

The hand clasping hers squeezed it gently, warm and caressing through her glove. "What a very wise young woman you are, Althea," he whispered softly.

The warmth of his breath against her cheek sent a shiver through her. She felt as though he were embracing her in the middle of the dance floor. It was a shock to realize, as they moved back into the rhythm of the dance, that they had paused for only the briefest of moments. No one around them even seemed to have noticed anything at all, though Althea felt as breathless and shaky as if he had kissed her in front of all the patronesses and the entire exclusive company gracing Almack's that evening.

Chapter 16

As Jenny undressed her mistress and brushed out her hair that night, Althea continued to marvel how close she felt to a man she had been prepared to despise at first sight. That initial impression had begun to change with her growing appreciation for his energy and intelligence, and it had been affected even further by her pleasure at being treated as an equal and taken seriously on her own terms for almost the first time in her life. Then came their sharing of the difficulties posed by their respective parents, and now a mutual appreciation of the same political ideas.

After being introduced to so many self-absorbed, heedless young men who spared little, if any, thought for the responsibilities of their aristocratic heritages, Althea had never expected to discover a kindred spirit in the worldly Marquess of Harwood, whose reputation for gaming and women of ill repute hardly suggested that he would give a second thought to country concerns, much less the plight of the rural poor.

Althea climbed into bed that night looking forward to the next day with more pleasure than she had since leaving Lincolnshire for London. It seemed that she had a friend at last.

The next morning, however, brought a rude awakening.

Jenny appeared with her mistress's morning chocolate, wearing an anxious look. "It is Master Reggie, my lady, and he looks to be in a rare taking. Wishes to see you immediately."

"Thank you, Jenny." Althea scrambled from bed and dressed hurriedly. Her cousin rarely rose before noon. Something must be seriously amiss for him to be calling at the unheard of hour of nine o'clock.

One glance at her cousin as she entered the drawing room confirmed Althea's suspicions. Something was dreadfully wrong. The immaculate Reggie was rumpled and unshaven, his ordinarily cheery countenance pale and haggard. Clearly he had been up all night.

"Reggie, whatever is the matter?"

"Oh, Allie." He hurried over to take both her hands. "I've lost it. I've lost it all."

Lost what, Reggie?" Althea led him to a sofa and sat, pulling him down gently beside her. "Lost what?"

"All of it. Everything. My family is right; I *am* a complete nodcock."

"Now calm down and tell me what happened."

"Well"—he gulped—"I have been after the Marquess of Harwood forever to let me play against him. You needn't look at me like that, Allie. I know you warned me, but *you* beat him and, well, a fellow has his pride. Can't let it be said that his female cousin can win against the cleverest card player in town while he does not even dare to try his own luck. At any rate, it made no difference, for he refused to play against me, until last night, that is. He was in the card room at Brooks's when I looked in some time past midnight. He was among friends and in a jovial mood so I challenged him again. He declined again but his friends would not let him. They told him not to be so high in the instep, but he told them that he refused to 'pluck country pigeons.' Me, he called me a *country pigeon*! I told him that I would not suffer such an insult, that he could either meet me at the gaming table or at the dueling ground. Seeing that I was deadly serious, he finally agreed to one game of piquet. I told him that since he had chosen the game, I would choose the stakes. There was no way a gentleman could refuse, so I wagered my estate against his."

"Reggie! You did not!"

"Well, his place in Essex is worth twenty times what

Kennington is. I was compelling him to accept a wager that would force him to show all the world that he took me seriously."

Althea shook her head at the follies of male pride.

"I could see that he did not like it—you know the way his eyes narrow and it almost seems as though he can look straight through a person. But at last he agreed. He also called me a 'young fool' under his breath. I was not meant to hear it, but I did." Reggie's face darkened at the memory and he swallowed hard. "At any rate, I had rather be known as a fool than a coward."

"He asked me to set a date and offered to have the game in the privacy of his lodgings, but I was having none of that. I told him we should do it then and there. I shall not bore you with the details except to say that he beat me in very short order." Reggie paused to look at his cousin earnestly. "He is very good, isn't he, Allie?"

She nodded grimly as he dropped his face into his hands and groaned. "I do not know what I shall do. Now I do not even have the ready to buy a commission, and I *will* not go to Augustus. I got myself into this, I shall just have to get myself out."

Althea smiled and held out her hand. "I am afraid so, Reggie, but all the same, I shall try to see if there is anything I can do."

"No, thank you. It just helps to have someone to talk to, and you are a brick for not throwing it in my face that you told me not to. Oh, I wish I had listened to you!"

"I am certain you will think of something, Reggie. You can be very resourceful when you set your mind to it. Remember how you fixed the rowboat when we put a hole in it landing on the island?"

He smiled faintly at her and rose to take his leave. "Thank you, Allie. You are the only one in the family who has any use for me."

Privately Althea thought her cousin was the only one in his family worth knowing, the rest being prosy old bores pompous enough to make her own parents look positively frivolous. But it would do him no good to hear that now. "Nonsense, I am simply the only one who speaks well of you to your face. The rest are like Papa and Mama, who believe that praise spoils a person."

Reggie shook his head slowly. "No. It is not like that. You truly are good, whereas I have been nothing, but . . . Well, never mind that." He straightened up. "I got myself into this trouble; I shall just have to get myself out." His face crumpled for a moment. "But however shall I? At any rate, I shall not bore you with any more useless complaining. Thank you for listening, Allie." He turned and hurried from the room before his cousin could frame a reply.

Althea paced the drawing room furiously for some time after Reggie had left. He had told her that he did not need her help, but that was not going to prevent her from venting her fury on the perpetrator of her cousin's misery, or from taking revenge.

But all her pacing did little to help her master the anger and the corroding sense of betrayal that threatened to overwhelm her. How could the man who had seemed so sympathetic and understanding the previous evening have turned into such a monster of callousness before dawn, and to the man he knew to be her cousin!

How could he have agreed to match his own superior skill against an amiable young man who clearly possessed more hair than wit? And how could a man whose own father had gambled away his heritage deprive someone else of his?

The dreadfulness of it all knew no bounds. That the one person in all of London whom she had come to trust, yes, even to like, should behave so despicably was more shattering than Althea cared to admit. Had she been as big a fool as Reggie? Had she been duped by those shared confidences, that special light in his eyes when he smiled at her, the concern in his voice when he spoke of her plans, into thinking that she meant something to the Marquess of Harwood, that they were friends?

She slumped back down on the sofa, her face in her hands. An aching misery made her throat feel painfully tight. Tears stung her eyes, but she would not let them fall. She sniffed, swallowed, blinked hard, and stood up.

No, she was *not* going to give in to her distress like a weakling; she was a Beauchamp after all. She might as well take advantage of the one useful thing her parents had given her—pride.

Not only was she not going to give in, but she was going to triumph. She was going to win back Reggie's land, in addition to the good faith the Marquess of Harwood had stolen from her, and she was going to do it before she was another minute older.

Banging the door to the drawing room behind her in her haste to carry out her plan, Althea hurried back to her bedchamber where Jenny was tidying up her mistress's things. "Jenny, I must go out. I shall need the new walking dress that was just delivered and my azure silk pelisse."

"Yes, miss." The maid quietly did as her mistress instructed, but she was bursting with curiosity. Everyone knew that Althea's cousin never arose before noon at the earliest and spent at least two hours closeted with his valet, never appearing abroad much before three o'clock. Something must be seriously wrong. And her mistress, who had been bred to maintain an icy calm in the face of disaster, was trembling so badly that her hands shook as she allowed Jenny to help her out of one dress and into another.

"Thank you, Jenny. Now, will you discover, if you can, whether or not Mama has gone out? She spoke of consulting with Madame Celeste over material for the ball at Carlton House."

"Yes, miss. I shall not be a moment." More curious than ever, the maid went to find out what she could about the Duchess of Clarendon's whereabouts. Obviously her daughter was planning on going out somewhere, and just as obviously, she did not want her absence or her destination known.

Chapter 17

*I*n fact, Althea was forced to wait over an hour longer until the duchess's carriage rolled off toward Bond Street. Barely able to contain her impatience, she was unable to distract herself with reading or correspondence, and had to content herself with pacing her bedchamber until Jenny came to report that the duchess had left. "Thank you for doing that, Jenny. Now fetch your cloak and bonnet. We are going to pay a visit to a . . . a blackguard."

"Oh, miss, are you quite sure that . . ."

"Quite sure. There is only one thing to be done, and I shall do it." And holding her head high, Althea marched down the stairs with her maid scurrying behind her.

She kept up the pace all the way down South Audley Street until they turned the corner of Curzon Street, but her furious pace slackened as she drew closer to the Marquess of Harwood's door.

When Reggie had confided the tale of his losses to her she had been immediately ready to go do battle, but now that she had nearly reached her destination, she began to question herself. What if he were not there? She could hardly follow the Marquess of Harwood about town hoping to challenge him to a card game. What if he refused? What if she lost? *Enough, Althea,* she scolded herself. *Where is that stupid obstinate Beauchamp pride now that you need it?* Taking a final deep breath she mounted the steps and nodded to Jenny to lift the knocker.

Ibthorp's grizzled countenance remained impassive as he announced Lady Althea's arrival to his master, but his brain was working furiously. A woman calling on his master was significant enough in itself, but a well-brought-up young lady calling for the second time was a serious event. Was this the reason behind the marquess's uncharacteristic attendance at several dull but fashionable *ton* events, or his sudden decision to appear at Almack's? Ibthorp could have been knocked over with a feather the previous evening when his master had ordered him to lay out his satin knee breeches.

"Knee breeches, sir?" he had asked in amazement.

"Knee breeches," the marquess had responded firmly.

"Very well, sir." Ibthorp had followed orders as a good servant should, but his tone had clearly suggested that his ordinarily trustworthy master had taken leave of his senses.

Now Ibthorp knew why. Their caller was something quite out of the ordinary, with that regal carriage and the be-damned-to-you-all sparkle in those magnificent blue eyes.

"Lady Althea Beauchamp," he announced unnecessarily as Althea swept into the room.

"Why, Lady Althea, what a . . ."

Althea cut the marquess short. "How could you! I thought we were friends. How could you behave so despicably to anyone, but especially to someone who is like a brother to me—no, closer to me than any brother I would be likely to have."

Gareth's welcoming smile vanished and his eyes narrowed. "You have been speaking to Reginald, I gather. Young fool."

"Of course he is a fool. And you knew he was nowhere near your equal, yet you agreed to play against him anyway. And here I thought you were a man of honor. I can see how wrong I was."

"Errors in judgment being difficult to conceive of in someone as perfect as the incomparable Lady Althea Beauchamp, and even more difficult to accept." If Althea's tone had been cool, Gareth's was positively icy, his gray eyes as dark as flint in his white, set face.

"At least I *try* to behave well." Althea's heart was thudding so loudly she could hardly hear herself speak.

"A useless exercise. I learned not to attempt the impossible years ago, so I gave it up."

"Well, I have come to give you the opportunity to rectify that situation."

"How kind. Lady Bountiful here to redeem a lost soul. No, thank you. I do not need redeeming. I prefer a life without illusions. Now, if you will excuse me, I have other people to ruin." His air of sneering nonchalance was belied by the tightly clenched hands held rigidly to his side, hands so tightly clenched that every tendon, every blood vessel stood out as clearly as an anatomical drawing.

"Then ruin me." Althea sat down at a small table and pulled out a new deck of cards from her reticule. "I shall play you for all that Reggie lost."

"Very noble of you, I am sure. But what if you lose? Ladies in general have nothing but their jewels or their, ah, honor, to stake in games of chance." His glance swept her from head to toe in a way that made Althea's face grow hot and her skin tingle all over.

Some unknown and treacherous part of her made her wonder if losing would be all that unpleasant after all. Pride, however, quickly reasserted itself. "I will win," she vowed.

"But if you win he will not thank you for it." Eyes never wavering from her face, Gareth took the chair opposite from her.

"Nevertheless, I will win, and fairly, too. Do not underestimate me, my lord. I am clever enough to know if you let me win."

"You do me too much honor. I leave such outmoded chivalric ideals to fools like your cousin." But his gray eyes were softer now. The hard, bright glitter had vanished to be replaced by an expression of wary admiration.

There was no doubt that she looked magnificent with her cheeks flushed and the deep blue of her eyes made even deeper by the blue silk pelisse that she now removed, as well as the white satin bonnet. Without the pelisse she looked a good deal younger and more vulnerable, the high lace collar of her walking dress emphasizing the delicate oval of her face and the soft lines of her lips.

For a moment Gareth hesitated. Should he make her happy? All he had to do was restore the estate to her useless cousin. He glanced again at the dark, fringed eyes regarding him steadily across the table. No. She would not thank him for such weakness. She wished to beat him, to win back the estate from him fairly and squarely. Then he would give her what she truly wanted—the card game of her life.

"Very well. Let us cut for the deal." He reached out to cut the deck in half. "There. Shuffle them and we shall pick the top cards. The highest card takes the deal." He watched as she shuffled the cards expertly; her hands, slender and elegant, were as assured as she was.

Althea finished shuffling and laid down the deck. "Choose."

"King." The marquess was not a superstitious man. No successful gambler could afford to be. But he could not stop the shiver of anticipation as she announced, "Ace." As a nondealer he could surely win the first trick. And if he could win the first trick, surely he could win them all. Then the first game at least would be his.

Althea dealt the cards as unhurriedly as if she were playing a friendly teatime game of piquet with her grandmother instead of a bitter contest against a man who had been called the most formidable card player in all of London. Studying her hand carefully as the marquess discarded two cards from his hand and drew two from the stack, she very deliberately discarded three and selected three in their place.

Gareth surveyed his hand. Three kings stared back reassuringly at him. "Trio," he announced smugly. He glanced over at her, trying to read her expression, but there was none.

"Quatorze." Calmly she showed him the four aces.

He bit his lip and led the first trick. The rest of her

hand must be equally strong for her to declare her combinations. He won his first trick and the next, but it was no use, her hand was too strong and he wound up losing the game.

The next game was more evenly matched in the declaration, but this time Althea, with the elder hand, was the first to lead and thus able to take all the tricks. "Capot," she announced in the same calm voice as Gareth gnawed his lip in frustration.

His brows drew together as he frowned in an effort to concentrate more intently. She seemed to be able to picture in her mind, not only what she held in her hand but what he had in his as well as what remained in the stack. He knew that she must be looking at the cards in her own hand, remembering what had been played, then calculating what was left, but she did it so calmly and so quickly that it was uncanny, not to mention unnerving, even more so because he knew precisely how it was done yet he could not match the rapidity of her calculations.

Gareth battled her for every point, but when she announced carte blanche after the fifth deal, he knew he had lost. The best he could do was to win enough points to make a decent showing.

They played out the final hand in a silence so profound that each one could hear every breath the other one drew. The last card was finally played. Althea rose and held out a hand. "I shall take my cousin's vowel now, my lord."

Without a word, Gareth strode over to a massive mahogany desk, opened the top drawer, and pulled out a crumpled piece of paper, smoothing it in his hands as he crossed the carpet to where she was standing. Carefully he refolded it, placed it in her hands, and closed her fingers over it. "He will not take it back from you, you know, Althea. No gentleman would. No gentleman could. And no matter how foolish your cousin may be, he is a gentleman."

She could think of no reply, nor could she trust herself with one. Her anger at him and the mental energy she had summoned for the game had kept her going, but it

had evaporated the instant the last card had been played.
She had kept her misery at bay with the thought of revenge. Now that she had won that revenge, the weight
that had settled in her chest the moment she had heard
Reggie's tale of woe now threatened to suffocate her.

Forcing herself to remain calm and collected, Althea
allowed Jenny to help her on with her bonnet and pelisse; then she turned on her heel and, without a word,
left the room.

Without looking at her maid or acknowledging Ibthorp, who opened the door for her, Althea marched out
the door. She walked home as if in a trance. Still in a
trance she climbed the stairs to her bedchamber and sank
into a chair by the fire without removing her bonnet
or pelisse.

Observing her mistress's profound preoccupation,
Jenny crept silently away to leave her with her thoughts.
The little maid had never seen her quite that way before.
Lady Althea was always a model of dignified self-possession, but there was something unnatural about this
new air of resolute calm that resembled despair more
closely than it did self-possession. Her lovely face had
remained expressionless during the entire adventure, but
her blue eyes had been dark with an emotion very much
akin to pain. There was a stricken look in them that told
Jenny her mistress was suffering an agony too deep to
acknowledge to anyone.

Chapter 18

Althea went through the rest of the day and several following it in a gray fog of lassitude that she was powerless to dispel. Even the winnings that now put her so close to her goal that she could begin scanning advertisements for properties in the *Times* did not restore her spirits. The sparkle and the zest that had recently energized her life seemed to have disappeared. She felt utterly enervated and more lonely than when she had first arrived in London.

The one thing that might have brought her pleasure, restoring his estate to her cousin, was also thwarted, for despite her best efforts to inform him of the good news, she was unable to track him down. Footmen dispatched with frequent messages to his lodgings returned with no reply except that he was not there. Discreet inquiries among his friends revealed their knowledge of his whereabouts to be as nonexistent as hers.

In addition to suffering from her own listless unhappiness, Althea began to be concerned for her cousin's welfare. Surely if he had committed some drastic act after losing his inheritance, she would have heard. But there was nothing. He seemed to have completely disappeared from the face of the earth.

Finally, a week after her first frustrated attempt to contact him, Althea was brought a message that Reggie awaited her in the drawing room. Hastily tying on her cornette whose ribbons matched the lemon-colored trimming of her morning dress, she opened her escritoire, snatched the vowel handed to her by the marquess, and hurried down to tell him the good news.

Much to Althea's surprise, he greeted her quite cheerfully. "Hello, cousin. That is certainly a most fetching ensemble." He raised his quizzing glass. "Madame Celeste, I suppose. The cornette is an elegant touch. I had not thought you would trouble yourself with such frippery, but it is vastly becoming, I assure you."

Althea scrutinized her cousin carefully. Surely this air of insouciance was no more than a ploy to cover his desperate state of mind, but the color in his cheeks and the lively expression in his eyes certainly seemed to indicate a man far from despair. In fact, she could not help but be amazed at the contrast between the pale, distraught youth who had sat a week ago in her drawing room with his head in his hands and the lively young man now before her. She was so amazed by this transformation that she completely forgot the wonderful news she had to tell him, but continued to stare at him in astonishment.

"No doubt you are surprised to see me looking so well."

She nodded dumbly.

"I have been in the country. No, not at Kennington. I have been to visit Squiggy Metcalfe."

"Squiggy Metcalfe?" Totally at sea, Althea could only gaze at him stupidly.

"Yes. I was with him at Eton. His brother, Charlie, you know, is quite the man in India—father is a director of the East India Company. At any rate, he spoke to some fellows, friends of his brother and to Lord Wellesley, and it is all set. I am to sail for Calcutta the end of next week. From there I shall go to Bengal as secretary to the Marquess of Hastings, who is Governor General there and is in need of some help. In fact, I . . ."

"But, Reggie." At last Althea found her voice. "You have no need to go to India. I have won Kennington back for you."

". . . Am quite looking forward to going. They say that a man, any man, can make his fortune out there,

and society is a great deal jollier than it is here—no
starched-up old tabbies to point a finger at you, no stiff-
rumps like Augustus to prose on about the family and
one's duty to it. Yes, I think that India is just the ticket
for me. Er, what did you say, Allie?"

"I said that there is no need to go to India. I have
won back Kennington for you."

"That is very kind of you, Allie, but I really have no
need for Kennington now."

If Althea had been surprised by his previous announcement, she was completely nonplussed by this one.
"Not need Kennington? But it is your heritage."

"And one that made me feel guilty about it every day
of my life, or at least Augustus did, for not taking better
care of it. Do you not see? I am not cut out for that sort
of thing, to be a country gentleman." A sudden thought
struck him, and he turned to stare at his cousin. "You
won it? From Harwood?"

Althea nodded.

"If that don't beat all. You *are* a cool customer, Allie.
As cool a customer as I ever saw. I tell you, it is a damn
shame you cannot be a member of Brooks's."

"Thank you, Reggie. That is praise indeed. But you
cannot just leave for India in this harum-scarum
fashion."

"I am not. I have made arrangements, written letters.
I have handled everything for myself. Don't you see,
Allie, this is the first time that I have decided what I
shall do—not Papa, not Mama, not Augustus, but I have
thought it out. And I *want* to go. I think I can make
something of myself out there where I am not always
having the sainted Augustus held up to me as an example. He is a fine fellow, if you like that sort of person,
but I am not Augustus, and I never shall be. This is
something I can do. I know I can."

She was silent a moment considering what he had said.
Reggie had always chafed at his family's rigid rules, and
a good many of his foolish pranks and misadventures
had sprung from his constant efforts to prove that he
was not his older brother. He was not a useless fellow,

certainly not as useless as they had all claimed him to be, but he had just never been given the chance to be Reggie. Perhaps this was his chance. He had been enthusiastic over things before, but not as enthusiastic as this. It was more than enthusiasm. His eyes were alight for the first time with energy and purpose. Althea had never seen him look quite that way before, never seen his expression so hopeful.

She smiled and held out her hand to him. "I expect you can, Reggie, if you've a mind to."

He gripped her hand gratefully. "Thank you, Allie." A sly grin slowly spread across his face. "And at the same time I can help you escape the stuffy confines of your own family and give you the freedom to live your life as you wish to live it."

"You can? How?"

"Well, actually, *you* did it for yourself. *You* won Kennington back from the Marquess of Harwood. It is yours now. You do not have to buy an estate; you already have one. And you can use your previous winnings to make any repairs or improvements that you might wish to."

"Oh, I could not. I could not take Kennington from you, Reggie."

"You are not taking Kennington from me. Harwood took it from me. No, actually, I practically *gave* Kennington to him, nodcock that I was. You have won it back. Even if I did want it now, which I don't, I lost it, and it would still belong to Harwood if it were not for you. Kennington is all yours, Allie. I know you will do a better job of managing it than I ever did."

"Oh, Reggie!" She rose to fling her arms around his neck. "Thank you!"

"No need to thank me, Allie." He patted her awkwardly on the shoulder. "Thank that clever head of yours. Lord, I would have given a monkey to have seen Harwood's face when you won it back from him."

"He was not best pleased," she responded soberly.

"I would expect not. You are a quick-witted thing, Allie. There was never any doubt of that. I only hope that running an estate by yourself is truly what you want."

"It is, Reggie. You know it is. I have never wished for anything else."

"Every woman I know wants jewels and fine clothes as well as a devoted admirer to shower her with them." He shot a suspicious glance at her.

She shook her head emphatically, almost too emphatically, her cousin thought, watching her closely.

"Well, then, I wish you joy of it. And how do you plan to break the news to your mama and papa?"

"I do not know. How do you plan to tell your family about going to India?"

"Letter." Reggie grinned sheepishly. "To be delivered by Gregson, after I have sailed. He has no heart for the trip, so I have recommended him to a friend of mine who is in dire need of a good valet."

"I think I had better do something of the same. Once I have left and it is discovered that I have embarked on a course that makes me so obviously ineligible to be the wife of whomever they choose for me, they will have nothing to do with me. It is only while they still can hope to contract a brilliant alliance for me that they will try to control me. When they can no longer do that they will leave me alone."

"I hope for your sake, Allie, that you are in the right of it. At any rate, I must be going. There is a great deal to be done before I leave. I shall write to my agent, Duckworth, to tell him of your impending arrival. He is an excellent man, though he has had little enough help from me. He deserves a better master than I have been and now he shall have one."

"You will not leave without saying good-bye?"

He was touched by the anxiety in her voice. "No. Of course not. How could I not bid farewell to the only real family I have? I shall call on you before I go. But not a word to anyone else, mind you. I shall send you all the accounts and papers I have pertaining to Kennington. I am sure you will make more sense out of them than I have. Soon you will be able to begin your new life." And with a cheery wave he was gone.

However, beginning a new life was easier said than

done, Althea thought sadly as the drawing room door closed behind him. A man might go off and start his life over, especially armed with the introductions that Reggie was armed with. But a single, unmarried woman, especially a young one, was always looked at askance.

The money from her winnings that she would bring with her and her connection with Reggie might help, but even then it would take a good deal of convincing to win the acceptance of the respectable folk around Kennington. Having spent her life in the country, Althea knew that one could not do business, could not survive in the country, without the approval of those respectable people.

But first she had to get safely away from London and her parents. Once that was successfully accomplished, then she could worry about her reputation in the country.

Chapter 19

Althea went to bed that night in a somber mood. In the space of little over a week she had lost one person she had begun to look upon as a trusted friend, and now she was about to lose someone who had been almost a brother to her for as long as she could remember. While it was true that she had been longing to be independent and on her own since she had left the schoolroom, now that she was faced with the very real prospect of it, she found it a trifle dismaying.

The first thing to do, dutiful daughter that she was, would be to lay her plans before her parents and offer them a chance to give her their blessing. She did not expect anything from this course of action except dismay and opposition, but if by some miracle they were prepared to let her go her own way, she did not want to lose the opportunity to remain in their good graces.

They were dining in that evening. The dowager had already sent word that she was tired and would be having supper in her room. Provided with such an opportunity, Althea seized it, and when the servants had left after clearing away the main course, relaying the table, and serving the dessert, she began. "Papa, Mama, I have been giving a great deal of thought to my future and I have no wish to make a brilliant marriage. I would so much rather live a quiet life in the country. I now have enough set aside to purchase my own estate and I wish to do so, with your blessings, of course."

There was a moment of profound silence. "I have

never heard of anything so absurd. Become a rustic? It is simply not good *ton*, Althea. I am sure I have told you that times out of mind," the duchess declared.

Very deliberately the duke laid down his spoon and dabbed his lips with his napkin. "Althea, I thought we had made it clear to you that in families such as ours, marriage is not a choice, but a duty."

"I know, Papa. But I will not be carrying on the name. The line does not depend on me for an heir."

"That makes no difference. You have the blood, and you still owe it to the family to contract an alliance that will strengthen its position and add to its glory. Now that is the end to it. I will hear no more of these foolish notions. We have raised you to be worthy of your name, Althea, to ally it with the noblest families in the land. Naturally, you will do that."

"Yes, Papa." It was no use. Althea had not expected it to be, but in spite of herself, she had cherished the vain hope that if she proved steadfast in her desire not to marry they might take it seriously.

"I certainly hope that you are going to wear the new pale blue crepe dress from Madame Celeste to the opera this evening. It is vastly becoming and the embroidered lilies with the pearl trimming are sure to become the rage once you have been seen wearing it," the duchess broke in brightly as though she and her daughter had been talking of nothing but frills and furbelows during the entire meal. "And you know that Lord Spottiswode has made it a point to assure himself that you will be there so you must be in your very best looks."

"Yes, Mama." Althea could only be grateful that it was the opera and not a ball they were attending, for it would give her time to think. She was not about to give up on her dream, but she did need to develop the best possible strategy for achieving it. *Think of it as a card game,* she kept telling herself. *Consider what cards each side holds and what risks it is willing to take. It is boldness as a card player that wins games for me; it will have to be the same in real life.*

Thinking about it in those terms made it easier to plan,

and it also brought another card player to mind. *Grand-mama!* Althea had long been aware that her grand-mother was not entirely happy living as a permanent guest in her son's household. *I do not believe that she likes living under Papa and Mama's thumbs any more than I do. Then I shall offer her a chance to gain her freedom as well.*

Buoyed by this thought, Althea was even able to wel-come Lord Spottiswode to their box with a modicum of civility later that evening, and she endured his ponderous conversation with such admirable restraint that the duch-ess was able to look positively smug for the rest of the evening as she intercepted envious glances from other boxes. It was clear that gossiping tongues would soon spread the rumor the this Season's incomparable was about to make a brilliant match.

A touch of fatigue might have made the Dowager Duchess of Clarendon miss the opera, but she was awake bright and early the next morning and already immersed in the *Times* when her granddaughter knocked on her door.

She looked sharply at her granddaughter as she en-tered. "Out with it, my girl. There is some mischief afoot that I can clearly see. You only wear that expression when you are looking forward to a day slopping around the stables or when you have a very good hand indeed."

"You are correct, Grandmama. I have been dealt a very good hand indeed. And as usual, I have come to ask you to be my partner."

"Oh, what is up?"

"Reggie is going to India."

"Good. It is time that lad escaped from that family of his. Their bone-chilling respectability would dampen even the highest of spirits."

"And he has given Kennington to me."

"He has, has he!" The dowager's sharp eyes could just detect the faintly discernible blush that stained her granddaughter's cheeks. There was certainly more to this story than was being divulged, but in time, no doubt, the entire truth would come out. In the meantime, however, she banished any hint of the curiosity consuming her and forced her expression into one of polite interest.

"Yes. He knows that I want an estate of my own and he says I would be a better manager for Kennington than he has been."

"That lad has a good deal more in his brain-box than I have given him credit for."

"The thing of it is, Grandmama, Mama and Papa will not permit me to do such a thing."

"That was certainly to be expected. Henry will not rest until he has married you to a future prime minister, and your mother will not allow that to occur unless he is a leader of fashion—a combination so unlikely that you could be in the marriage mart for quite some time, I fear."

"But I loathe it, Grandmama."

The dowager's eyes softened. "I know you do, my dear." She laid a comforting hand on Althea's shoulder.

"So help me escape it all. Come with me, Grandmama. Let us go to the country and live the life *we* wish to, not the life Papa and Mama have planned for us."

"Come with you!"

"Yes. You do not like being under Papa's thumb or subject to Mama's whims any more than I do. You *know* you do not. And if you come to the country with me, it will make it a completely respectable establishment in the eyes of the neighbors. In general, I do not care about my reputation, at least not in the *ton,* but in the country, if one wants to do any sort of business at all, one at least must be respectable."

"I do not see how it is to be accomplished." The dowager shook her head, but the sparkle of interest in her eyes betrayed her desire to be convinced of the possibility of her granddaughter's scheme.

"Oh, as to that, I have thought it all out. I shall send Jem to make arrangements for a post chaise. He is devoted to me, and the promise of an eventual position as coachman at Kennington will be inducement enough. I know that Mama is planning to spend an afternoon closeted with Madame Celeste on Thursday and Papa can always be counted on to be at his club. Since we will be living simply we will not require a great deal of baggage, so it should be easy enough to slip away if we are careful. I shall leave a note telling Papa and Mama that we have gone, but not where we have gone. They will undoubtedly concoct some plausible story to account for our absence, which they will circulate among the *ton,* and by the time they discover our whereabouts, it will be too late. Besides, if you are with me, Papa can hardly force us to return even if he does find us. Oh, please say that you will, Grandmama."

The dowager would have been no proof against the pleading expression on her granddaughter's face even if she had not found living in her son's rigidly formal establishment to be a dead bore. But having witnessed Althea's misery in London, and now seeing her eyes alight with happiness at the prospect of returning to the country, she did not have the heart to refuse her.

Althea's grandmother had hoped that somehow the Marquess of Harwood, who had been figuring increasingly in the picture lately, would supply a solution that would not only be acceptable, but highly gratifying to both Althea and her parents, but apparently she had been mistaken in that hope. She had been certain that a special understanding had arisen between her granddaughter and the marquess, but Althea's eagerness to leave London, and the care and thought she had obviously put into planning her escape seemed to belie that possibility. The dowager sighed. If it was not to be, it was not to be, but it was a great pity.

"Very well, child. I shall join you in this madcap scheme of yours. I just hope it does not convince your papa that I am fit for nothing but the madhouse."

Althea rose to fling her arms around the dowager. "Thank you, Grandmama. I *knew* I could count on you to help me. You have always come to my aid, and I shall never let Papa make you go anywhere you do not wish to be. Now, I must be off to speak to Jem and Jenny and see if I can convince them to cast their lots in with me."

"Of course you can count on me, miss," was Jem's

immediate response when Althea sought him out in the stables some time later. "You saved me, and that makes me your man always. I'll be happy to do whatever you wants."

"Thank you, Jem. I am afraid I am asking you to do rather a lot. I cannot take John Coachman from his comfortable post, so I will need you not only to hire me a post chaise, but to be my groom and coachman when we get to the country."

Jem positively swelled with pride at the prospect of these new responsibilities. "Jem's your man, miss, wherever you go."

"Thank you."

Jenny, however, took a good deal more convincing. Older and more worldly than Jem, she foresaw all the many complications attendant upon such an adventure. "Oh, my lady, whatever will your parents say? The duke is powerfully set on your marrying someone important, not to mention Her Grace." The little maid looked troubled.

"I know Jenny, but they will just have to learn that they cannot control the outcome of everything in their lives. I know it is asking a good deal of you. You would be leaving an important and powerful household for a very simple establishment. And you will not be so near your family as you are at Clarendon, but Kennington is not so far distant. Naturally I shall not need the services of a lady's maid at Kennington so much as I do now, but in a household with so few servants, your position will be a great deal more important than it is now." Althea's voice trailed off as she watched Jenny struggle with the decision. There would no longer be the excitement of helping her mistress get ready for the most fashionable balls and routs in the land, but neither would she be subservient to anyone but her mistress.

Jenny wavered, but only for a moment. "I think I should like to go with you, my lady."

Althea let out a sigh of relief. "Thank you, Jenny. I shall be in need of a friendly face."

And so, the major hurdles were overcome. She had a

household, albeit a meager one. Now all that remained was to move that household to Kennington with as little commotion as possible.

It would require a great deal of work, but Althea was more hopeful about her life than she had been since her first Season had stopped being an event still far in the future and had become a reality.

Chapter 20

All the energy and invigoration that Althea's plans gave to her existence seemed to have drained from Gareth's. Since losing the contest with her for Kennington he found that he had lost all enthusiasm for gaming of any kind. Somehow, every possible opponent who challenged him to a game lacked either the wit or the spirit, or both, to make playing against him worth the marquess's while.

Oddly enough, the person who first pointed out this enervating state of affairs was the person who gave him a clue as to the reason behind it.

Maria Toscana, draped languorously across silken pillows, regarded him curiously under seductively lowered lids as he lay exhausted in her boudoir after a vigorous session of lovemaking. "My lord, it seems to me that something is troubling you. What is it?"

"Troubling me? Nothing. Do I act as though something is troubling me?"

The dancer's eyes drifted hungrily from his broad shoulders to his slim hips and powerful legs. "No. You do not *act* as though anything is troubling you, but there is a look in your eye that tells me."

One corner of his mouth quirked in a rueful grin. "You are a clever woman, Maria. Yes, something is troubling me. I lost an entire estate in a simple card game.

"You have won and lost, mostly won, fortunes on the turn of a card, my lord. You will win it back again. No one can beat you consistently. In the end you will win. You always do."

"No, Maria." He shook his head slowly. "This time I have met my match. It was not the luck of the draw that was against me this time; it was superior skill."

"Not necessarily. Are you sure she did not win against you because she had more to lose than you did?"

"She! How did you know it was a *she?*" Gareth sat bolt upright in astonishment.

"Because there is a sadness in your eyes that has never been there before. You have lost bets before, my lord. You have lost card games before as well, but this time you lost more than a card game, I think. This time it was not only two minds competing against each other. Something more than intelligence, strategy, or luck was at stake. Such a stake as that could only involve a woman."

He did not reply, but lay back among the pillows staring thoughtfully at the ceiling for some time. Nor did he say much as he dressed and bid her adieu, but the dancer knew she had been correct in her assessment of the situation. He had not only been beaten, but that protective layer of cynicism he adopted where all women were concerned had somehow been penetrated. Maria wished she knew who had accomplished such a thing, for it was a rare woman indeed that had any effect on the Marquess of Harwood.

Meanwhile, the woman in question was so busy trying to lay her plans without attracting any attention that she had not a moment's thought to spare for the Marquess of Harwood or anything else except her removal to Kennington.

Thursday, the day Althea had identified as a day when her mother's appointments with the dressmaker and linen draper, as well as several important calls, would keep her occupied for a goodly portion of the day, Althea sent Jem to the Swan with Two Necks to make arrangements for hiring two post chaises. She then set Jenny to packing the few things she would need for the trip.

"But all these beautiful gowns, my lady," Jenny could not help wailing as Althea instructed her to leave them behind in favor of her plainest morning attire and most serviceable walking dresses.

"Will do me no good in the country, Jenny. I am not going there for idle social pursuits, but to earn a living and make a life for myself. Believe me, I shall not miss them at all, nor the crushes to which I wore them." Althea turned to pick up two well-worn books lying on her dressing table. "I shall, however need these. I cannot do without Tull's *Horse Hoeing Husbandry* and Young's *Annals of Agriculture*. Believe me, Mr. Tull and Mr. Young make far better company than most of what I have experienced here in town."

Jenny sighed and turned her attention to more mundane articles of clothing—chemises, gloves, stockings, warm shawls. She did sometimes wish that her mistress would assume the role that society had assigned her, for to be lady's maid to an incomparable was no small thing. On the other hand, to be given additional responsibility for the management of a household, no matter how small, was very special indeed. Lady Althea might not gratify the wishes of a lady's maid determined to help her mistress attain the heights of fashion, but she did pay attention to a person's desire to advance herself in the world.

And which was better, after all, to be the utterly ignored maid to a society beauty or a valued servant in a comfortable country establishment? Jenny might enjoy the reflected glory of a successful London Season, but in her heart of hearts, she was a country girl, much like her mistress, who preferred a life of solid accomplishment to a few brilliant hours in the glare of fashionable notoriety.

The ensuing days passed all too quickly for the little band preparing for a new life. All of them, from Jem to the dowager to Althea, longed for the day when they would assume their new duties and take greater responsibility for their own lives. But as much as they looked forward to it, they feared the uncertainty of it all and worried lest their schemes be detected and prevented.

Reggie too was preparing for a new life, and called in Grosvenor Square the day before he sailed to bid his cousin goodbye.

"You will write to me," Althea begged.

"Of course, for I expect regular reports on Kennington from you in return." Reggie patted her shoulder affectionately. "Take care of yourself, Allie, and mind you, no wagering of the estate." He winked at her and was gone, leaving her feeling very alone. But she soon put his departure out of her mind as she concentrated on the final details of her own departure.

At last the day came. The duke went off to his club; the duchess, after unsuccessfully remonstrating with her daughter who was so weak as to give in to another headache, left for Bond Street.

An hour later a post chaise drew up at the door and the dowager, letting it be known that she had been called to visit a sick friend in Richmond for an indeterminate amount of time, climbed in, accompanied by her tight-lipped maid, Dorcas, and numerous bandboxes. The carriage rolled out of sight down Upper Brook Street toward the park where, turning the corner, it pulled up next to a second post chaise.

A few minutes later, Jenny and her mistress arrived on foot. Dorcas emerged from the dowager's carriage and climbed into one with Jenny while Jem handed Althea into her grandmother's vehicle, and they were off toward Oxford Street and the Great North Road.

Neither Althea nor her grandmother spoke much during most of the journey, each being absorbed in her own thoughts and content to watch the passing countryside after months in town. Spring was in full force. Trees were blossoming and the fields showed the soft green of tender young plants not yet covered with the dust of summer. Whenever they stopped to changed horses, Althea took advantage of the opportunity to climb down and inhale the fresh sweet scent of apple blossoms and listen to the birdsongs that were such a refreshing change after the noise and the smells of the metropolis.

The little cavalcade reached Stansted in the evening

just as the sun was sinking behind the steeple of the
medieval church and warming the redbrick tower of the
mill with its last golden rays. They clattered though the
village and headed down the Cambridge road where
Kennington lay three miles on.

As the post chaise turned into the drive, Althea leaned
out eagerly, trying to assess the state of her new home.
The soft light of evening and the earliness of the season
could be deceptive, hiding a multitude of things in need
of repair, cutting back, or cultivation. Knowing her cousin's casual approach to the more serious aspects of life,
she feared the worst in spite of his oft-voiced faith in
Duckworth's capabilities. To Reggie, an agent who did
not press him for money for repairs or insist on his active
participation in important decisions was an excellent
agent. Althea would reserve her judgment until she had
met the man and seen his work.

In the interests of secrecy, and preferring to get a completely accurate picture of the state of affairs at Kennington, Althea had communicated with no one about her
impending arrival. Apart from the letter Reggie had written to Duckworth, which merely announced a change in
ownership and promised forthcoming details, there had
been no communication regarding the new owner's plans.
She knew that such an unconventional approach might
result in a most uncomfortable first night, with no freshly
prepared meal or beds to look forward to, so it was with
good reason that Althea awaited the end of her journey
with some trepidation.

The carriages rolled up the gravel drive and stopped
under the stone portico. Daylight was fading fast, but
there was a light in the window of what must be the
kitchen wing. Althea allowed herself a tiny sigh of relief;
at least someone was on the premises.

Jem appeared at the carriage window. "Shall I knock,
miss? Let them know we are here?"

"Yes. Thank you, Jem."

The newly promoted groom, with all the exalted authority of his new station, pounded vigorously on the
door.

There was silence for some time, and then the thick oak door swung open to reveal a stooped figure who peered curiously out into the gathering gloom.

"The Dowager Duchess of Clarendon and Lady Althea Beauchamp," Jem announced grandly before scurrying back to the carriage to hand the ladies out with a flourish.

Considerably startled, the wizened man straightened out as best he could and tugged at the edges of his hastily donned jacket. "Ah, er, welcome to Kennington, my ladies. I beg your pardons for not being more, ah, er, welcoming, but we had no expectations of any company."

Althea's critical eye swept the black-and-white marble entry. Paint was beginning to peel on some of the fluted columns, but it all looked well scrubbed and dusted, as though the absence of funds for repairs did not in any way hamper those responsible for cleaning it. Peering as closely as she could into the drawing room beyond, she was able to distinguish that all the furniture was suitably cloaked in holland covers.

"I hope you will pardon our arriving unannounced, Mr. . . ."

"Crowder, my lady. It's just me and the missus and the boy Sam here as has care of the place. Mr. Duckworth, the agent, who lives in the village, did say as to how the estate had fallen under new ownership, but he did not mention any visitors. Begging your pardon, my lady, but are you related to the new owner? If we had known you were coming, we would have . . ."

"Crowder, Crowder, whoever . . ." A plump, gray-haired woman came bustling forward, keys jangling at her side.

"It is relations of the new owner, Mrs. Crowder, as Mr. Duckworth told us about, the Dowager Duchess of Clarendon and Lady Al . . ."

"My gracious, Crowder, do not keep them standing here. Your Grace, my lady, do come into the drawing room." Snatching the candle from her husband's hand, Mrs. Crowder led them into the drawing room, twitching off the holland covers as she proceeded.

Althea was relieved to note that though the upholstery beneath looked rather worn, there was not a speck of dust raised as Mrs. Crowder pulled off the covers.

"I do apologize that we are not ready for company, Your Grace, my lady, but . . . Crowder, why do you stand there gawking? Go fetch Sam to light a fire. Their ladyships must be chilled to the bone." Mrs. Crowder proceeded to light the candles in the sconces around the room as she pulled off covers at a great rate. "And once that is done, he shall fetch some water to their bedchambers. If you will just excuse me, I shall see to it that the fires are lit in your chambers as well. Not expecting company as we were, there is nothing much prepared for supper, but I have made a nice pigeon pie and could also arrange for a bit of ham and some boiled fowl if you would like."

"That is very good of you, Mrs. Crowder. And yes, if we could be shown to our rooms we would appreciate it. Jem can handle the luggage and Jenny, here, can help with the water."

Mrs. Crowder bustled off just as a gawky boy hurried in to light a fire. Althea rose to spread her hands before the warming blaze and thanked her lucky stars that the house, though shabby from lack of sufficient funds, did not appear to be suffering from neglect.

In no time at all, Mrs. Crowder had returned to show them to their rooms where the redoubtable Sam, having scurried ahead, had fires already burning. And if they had not yet warmed the rooms, they at least gave off a cheerful glow.

Preparing for bed that evening after a simple yet excellent meal, Althea reflected gratefully that Reggie, while he had not taxed his income in the slightest to make improvements upon his estate, had at least had the good sense to prize the Crowders enough to keep them at Kennington. The good couple had been somewhat surprised to discover the new owner of Kennington in the elegant young lady who had descended upon them without warning, but were so delighted to have a resident owner after all these years that they accepted the unconvential nature of that owner happily enough. Mr. Duckworth would have to wait until morning, but if he proved to be half as capable as the others, he would make a knowledgeable and useful ally indeed.

It was not until Althea fell gratefully into the enormous four-poster bed that she admitted to herself just how worried she had been over what she would discover at Kennington. Now, having seen its worn but immaculate rooms and tasted its simple but excellent fare, she felt more lighthearted and optimistic than she had in some time. She was going to enjoy making Kennington into the snug and profitable estate it deserved to be.

Chapter 21

The next morning Althea sent Jem with a note for Mr. Duckworth, who arrived at Kennington just as Mrs. Crowder was giving them a full inventory of the linen closets.

The agent proved to be a tall, thin young man who, correctly interpreting Althea's look of surprise, apologized for his lack of years. "My father was the agent for Master Reginald's father for most of his life and for Master Reginald as well. As soon as I was old enough to be put on a horse my father took me with him on all the estate business, so that by the time I went to school I already knew every inch of Kennington. When my father died several years ago, Master Reginald did not have the heart to look for another agent so he asked me. A very kindhearted young gentleman, he is, Master Reginald."

And not one to expend any unnecessary energy looking for another agent, especially one who might be older and more inclined to demand something of a reluctant owner, Althea could not help thinking somewhat cynically.

But, in spite of his youth, Mr. Duckworth appeared to have a thorough knowledge of the estate's finances and the community, as well as a familiarity with the more innovative agricultural practices of Coke and Townshend. "Most of the estate is leased to Squire Throckmorton who farms it, but if that is not agreeable to you . . ." Mr. Duckworth looked anxiously at Althea.

"I am sure that the land is admirably disposed of, Mr. Duckworth, with no need for change at the present. All that I would ask is that a small portion of land be left each year for common grazing and, as I do not intend to hunt, any wooded portions be given over to the villagers for hunting small game and finding fuel."

An approving smile warmed the agent's bony features. "That is most kind of you, my lady, and sure to be appreciated by the poorer folk, though some of the gentry may find such an idea a trifle radical. In general, Master Reginald was a kind enough landlord, but there is nothing to take the place of one who truly takes an interest in local affairs."

"I intend to make Kennington my home, Mr. Duckworth, and therefore, I plan to take a strong interest in them indeed, with your help, of course."

By the time Althea and her grandmother sat down to dinner that evening, they had a fair idea of the work cut out for them. The fields leased to the squire were in good condition, enclosed by sturdy fences and filled with what looked to be the beginning of healthy crops, but the rest of the estate—the main house and outbuildings—was in need of repair. Tiles were missing from the stable roofs, paint was peeling, and in some cases, windowsills and casements were rotting. Weeds were springing up in the drive, and the gardens were badly overgrown.

"We have tried to keep things in repair, my lady, but it is just Crowder and me, and we are getting on in years, not able to do all the work we once did. Sam is a help, but the lad is slow and not much use for anything except fetching water, sweeping, and lighting fires," Mrs. Crowder apologized with an anxious look.

"You have done well to keep the place clean, the draperies mended, and the linen in good order, Mrs. Crowder. I have no fault to find with your management," Althea reassured her. "It is too much for two people. We shall have to find you some more help. My grandmother and I are capable gardeners, so we can do a good deal there, and Jenny was a farmer's daughter before she became a lady's maid, so she will prove most useful, but I am sure you must know some likely young girls in the village and a lad or two who could work under Mr. Crowder's direction to bring things around."

"I expect that the Tubbs girls would be only too happy to lend a hand. Their father is Farmer Tubbs at the home farm, a very decent, hardworking man, but with a large family and many mouths to feed."

"The home farm." Althea's eyes brightened. "I should like to see it. When I was a girl at Clarendon, I was forever running off to visit them at the home farm. My governess finally gave up chasing me and began to teach me my sums and my geography by counting geese and sheep, telling me which animals were best grown in what part of the country, where a horse would be if it traveled for fifty miles, how long it would take a drover to get to London if he and his charges traveled a certain number of miles per day. I was even allowed to raise my own lamb, without Mama and Papa's knowledge, of course. When I grew older I would spend hours poring over the books in our agent's office, learning everything I could about all the animals there."

"Farmer Tubbs will welcome you most heartily, then, for I am sure he was always disappointed that Master Reginald did not take more of an interest in the farm. His passion is his hoggery, which is well-known throughout the county. There is no bacon so fine as Farmer Tubbs's. If you take the path that skirts the pasture and continues through the spinney and along the brook, you will find it is quite a pleasant walk."

"Thank you. If the day proves fine tomorrow, I shall do that." After the tense days of planning and a long carriage ride, Althea was eager for fresh air and exercise.

The next day dawned bright and sunny. Althea happily donned stout half boots and a leghorn bonnet and set off with Jenny in the direction indicated by Mrs. Crowder.

The walk was as picturesque as promised, and they had not gone much over half a mile before they came across the half-timbered farmhouse surrounded by its barn, dairy, and, as Mrs. Crowder had mentioned, a most impressive hoggery.

There was no need to announce their arrival, as the squawking of the chickens in the yard and the barking of a large spotted mongrel who ran out to greet them were indication enough that visitors had arrived.

Mrs. Tubbs, a large, red-faced, cheery woman, appeared at the door wiping floury hands on her apron. "We are all very happy, I am sure, my lady, to welcome you to Kennington. Mr. Duckworth rode over yesterday to say as how the new owner had arrived. I am sorry that Mr. Tubbs is not here to greet you at the moment, but he is in the stable with poor old Dobbin." She shook her head anxiously. "Dobbin is our draft horse and is feeling rather poorly at present. Mr. Tubbs is that worried about him, but I shall send Betsy to fetch him. Dick is there and can look after the horse for the time being." She turned to a towheaded girl of about six. "Now, Betsy, don't stand there gawking. Run and find your papa."

But Althea forestalled her. "No, there is no need to interrupt Mr. Tubbs. We shall just stop at the stable and introduce ourselves. But before we do, I should just like to ask . . . Mrs. Crowder spoke of your girls, Jane and Emily, I think she called them. She said they might be able to help her out. She and Mr. Crowder have done wonderfully well to keep things in order, but it is too much for the two of them, especially now that we have arrived."

The farmer's wife was happy to assure her that Jane and Emily, excellent workers both of them, would be up at Kennington first thing the next morning.

"Thank you. Now I shall not keep you any longer from your baking." Althea smiled at Betsy, who was staring at her bonnet in frank admiration, and then headed toward the stable.

She found Farmer Tubbs and a sturdy lad of about ten worriedly observing an enormous gray cart horse that leaned dispiritedly against the stall. The horse looked up as Althea and Jenny entered the stable, and the weariness and misery in its dark eyes washed over Althea so that she could think of nothing but the animal's pain.

"Ah, poor old fellow." Completely forgetting the farmer and his son, she reached out with gentle hands to rub its nose and cheek. The horse sighed wearily and rested its head on her shoulder as she stroked its neck and murmured softly in its ear.

Some minutes later, a tentative cough recalled her attention to the farmer and his son. "How long has he been like this?"

"Not long, my lady. It seemed to me the other day that he was not his usual hardworking self and then he went off his feed. The farrier came to look at him, but he could suggest nothing except feeding him bran mash with scalded water instead of corn. Dobbin is my only horse at the moment and there is so much . . ."

"It is a great worry, I know, but if you will trust me, I believe I might be able to help."

"Help? You, my lady?" Farmer Tubbs regarded the new mistress of Kennington in some surprise, but the wealth of sympathy in her eyes and the trustful way his horse leaned against her were inexplicably compelling. "It is that worried I am, my lady. I am not a rich man, and . . ."

"I know that, Mr. Tubbs. I believe that what ails this animal is a touch of pleurisy. It is in the early stages, however, and if you will allow me to send your son for my groom, Jem, to come and bring materials for a mustard plaster and some gentian, I believe we shall have Dobbin right in a very short while. I promise you, it will not harm your horse, and if he does not improve, as I feel certain he will, why then, I promise to buy you a new one."

Too bemused to do anything but nod dumbly at his son, the farmer remained transfixed while Althea grabbed a blanket and carefully covered the sick horse. "If you have bandages, it is also good to wrap the legs as well, so as to keep the animal as warm as possible."

"Yes, my lady. Of course, my lady." Rousing himself from his stupor, Farmer Tubbs hurried off to the house to procure the required bandages. The new mistress of Kennington was proving to be a most astounding young lady, but there was a ring of quiet authority in her voice. She seemed to know her way around a stable, and her gestures were the quick capable movements of someone who knew what she was doing.

When he returned from the house clutching the bandages, the farmer was treated to the even more astonishing picture of the young lady sweeping out Dobbin's stall, oblivious to the dirty straw clinging to the hem of her gray Circassian cloth walking dress. Seeing the farmer's expression she smiled half apologetically. "Please do not think I am being critical of your stables, but when an animal is ill, our coachman at Clarendon maintains that the stall must be as clean and airy as possible."

Utterly overwhelmed by the spectacle of a beautiful, fashionably clad young woman cleaning out his horse's stall, Farmer Tubbs simply nodded and handed her the bandages.

By the time Dick and Jem had returned, Dobbin was swathed in blankets and bandages from ear to hoof. Silently and efficiently Jem and Althea prepared the mustard plasters and, unwrapping some of the horse's coverings, applied them to the sides and front of his chest.

That done, Althea mixed some gentian in with the bran mash and coaxed Dobbin into swallowing a few mouthfuls while the farmer and his son watched carefully. She wiped her hands on a cloth Jem handed her, whispered a few encouraging words in the horse's ear, and stroked his nose with a comforting hand. "There. Now if you will just make sure that he is kept warm, maintain his circulation by rubbing him, and mix two drams of gentian in his mash once a day, I think you will find him looking better soon."

"You are a wonder, my lady," the farmer replied, shaking his head slowly. "And it appears to me that Dobbin looks a mite more cheerful already."

"It is not I, but Jem and the coachman at Clarendon who have taught me what to do. I just cannot bear to see an animal looking miserable, or its master worried."

"Well, I thank you for your concern. Running a farm

without a horse is next to impossible, and the only man capable of handling a case beyond the farrier's skill is over Newmarket way and powerful expensive."

"I understand, and I appreciate your trust in Jem and me. Now, I shall come by in a day or so, but in the meantime, if Dobbin gets worse, you will let me know, will you not?" Althea held out a hand.

Unused to such openness or frankness on the part of the Quality, the farmer took it hesitantly. "Yes, my lady. Yes, I will. And . . . bless you, my lady."

"And Jem here."

"And Jem."

Althea turned to give Dobbin a final pat before she, Jem, and Jenny headed home, well satisfied with their morning's work.

Chapter 22

True to her word, Althea and Jem walked over to the home farm the next day, where they found Dobbin, looking a good deal stronger, munching on his bran mash.

It is a miracle you have worked, my lady." The farmer beamed in welcome as they entered the stable. "His appetite is returning, and just look at the way he holds his head up. There is some of old Dobbin's look back in his eye."

"I am glad to hear it, Mr. Tubbs A sick animal is one of the most unhappy things on earth, for me." Althea and Jem inspected the bandages and laid their heads against the horse's chest to listen.

Jem looked at his mistress and nodded slowly.

"I agree with you, Jem. I do believe that we are out of the woods. Just continue to keep him covered and add the gentian to his feed, and I believe Dobbin will be as good as new in no short while."

"I cannot begin to thank you and the lad here, my lady."

"No need to thank me. Making Dobbin here feel better is a reward in itself. And having a prosperous and healthy home farm is all I could wish." Althea bid him good day, stopped at the kitchen door to thank Mrs. Tubbs for the help of her two daughters, and returned home to the real task of the day, which was poring over the account books Mr. Duckworth had brought her. The visit to the home farm had been a pleasant diversion from the columns of figures, but now it was time to concentrate on learning just how the estate had been run.

Althea might have dismissed her restoration of Dobbin's health as being a reward in itself, but Farmer Tubbs could not. The next day, after completing his errands in the village, he held forth in the taproom of the George and Dragon to anyone and everyone who would listen. "I tell you, it were something. There was poor old Dobbin on his last legs and the young mistress walks up and starts to work healing him as if she saved sick horses all the time. And you know Dobbin. He's a mind of his own and can be a sight mean tempered when he is off his feed. But she laid her cheek next to his and began whispering in his ear, and meek as a lamb he lays his head on her shoulder. It was as if he knew she were going to fix him up all right and tight, and she did. 'Course she says it's her groom as helped her, and to be sure he did, but to my mind it is she as did it. I saw how she made poor Dobbin look more cheerful even before the lad got there. It is as though she has some sort of magic she worked on that horse. And her a lady, too."

The other occupants of the taproom stared at him solemnly over their pints. Farmer Tubbs was usually a man of few words. It was not like him to go on to such a degree, especially over one of the Quality.

There had already been some talk in the village about the young lady, for the arrival of a new owner at Kennington, and a young lady at that, was bound to cause comment. Mr. Duckworth's revelations about the woods and pasture being open as common land for everyone only added to the talk and caused quite a stir among the poorer folk in the community. At first, no one had been inclined to believe it, but when the Mudge lad brought home several rabbits snared on Kennington land without suffering any dire consequences and the Blinkhorns' cow grazed undisturbed on the designated acres of pasture, it began to appear as though the young mistress of Kennington was a woman of her word. Certainly, she had not appointed a gamekeeper, and she had reassured Mr. Duckworth several times over of her good intentions.

In general, Kennington's new mistress kept to herself and did not mix much with the local gentry. She responded to their overtures of hospitality graciously enough, and the squire's lady, who had called on her soon after her arrival, proclaimed her to be very pretty behaved, and her grandmother not the least high in the instep, but for the most part, Mr. Duckworth's prediction that she would devote herself to the estate at the expense of socializing proved to be true.

Certainly the Crowders were able to confirm this opinion whenever they had cause to speak with the local tradesmen. "Such a hardworking young lady you never did see," Mrs. Crowder confided to Mr. Woolrich as she stopped in his shop to purchase sugar and exchange the local news.

Jane and Emily, working with Jenny to air out the linen cupboards and closets and make new curtains, reported much the same thing to their parents when they returned home laden with delicacies from Kennington's larder. "You would never know her to be such a fine lady for all the work she does," Jane announced as she reached in her basket to hand her mother some of Mrs. Crowder's gooseberry preserves, "except that she speaks so prettily and her maid says she was invited to all the finest places in London."

"And all her gowns are made of the very best materials," Emily added.

All in all, the opinions expressed by those fortunate enough to meet Kennington's new owner were favorable, and it was felt by one and all that while Master Reginald had been a most charming young gentleman, his visits had been so infrequent that the estate was in better hands now than it had been for some time.

Though involved in the more masculine business of running the estate, Lady Althea did not neglect the more traditional female charitable activities expected of its mistress. Advised by Mrs. Crowder and Mrs. Tubbs, she visited the cottages of the village's most unfortunate residents, bringing nourishing soups, comforting words, and the more material offer of fuel for their fires. It was at

one of these cottages that Tom Baldock, emboldened by
her kindness to his wife who had been laid low for some
weeks with a putrid fever, and by the desperation engen-
dered by a string of bad luck, had the temerity to ask if
she would look at his horse as well. "For it is said you
were wonderful clever about Farmer Tubbs's Dobbin.
My Charlie here has been acting most strange lately. You
never saw a gentler animal in all your life, but now he
is as full of temper as any high-blooded thoroughbred,
tossing his head and nipping anyone who gets near him.
I am sure I don't know what has come over him."

"If you will take me to him, I shall take a look, but I
am not a farrier or a veterinary surgeon, you know,"
Althea explained.

"I know, my lady. But Farmer Tubbs says you are as
clever as could stare, and he is not a man as is easily
impressed. Please look at Charlie. I am at my wits' end
over the animal."

"Very well." Althea followed the man to a rude shed
leaning against the cottage. There was loud thrashing followed by a muttered oath, and the cottager dragged out
a gangly brown horse whose laid-back ears, rolling eyes,
and bared teeth were indications enough of its ill temper.

Taking a deep breath as she locked eyes with the agitated animal, Althea approached calmly and deliberately,
murmuring soothingly, "Poor Charlie. Poor old horse.
Now let us see what is upsetting you so." Finally she
drew close enough to lay a gentle hand on the animal's
sweat-soaked neck. The horse snorted nervously, but let
her remain there stroking him and talking quietly as she
bent over to observe him more closely.

"Ahh," she muttered thoughtfully. "Yes, that is it."
Althea straightened up and then turned to the animal's
owner. "Now, Tom, if you can keep his head still, I think
I can do the trick."

The cottager gaped at her, but did as he was told,
holding tight on the leading rein so as to keep the horse's
head down and as close to immobile as possible.

Althea dug in her pocket, pulled out a clean, neatly
folded linen handkerchief, and twisted one corner of it

into a point. Then, reaching up, she pulled gently but firmly on the horse's upper eyelid while swiping gently under it with the handkerchief. She was so quick and so deft that before the horse could toss its head she was holding out the handkerchief so that Tom could see the wood chip resting on the tip. "There. Let us see if getting rid of that improves Charlie's temper any. You may let him have his head now."

Tom let go of the reins, and the horse snorted and shook his head but remained standing calmly enough. Tentatively Tom stroked his animal's neck. Charlie did not shy away, but lowered his head to nibble the edge of his master's rough coat. The cottager scratched his head in puzzled admiration. "Well, I'll be . . . You surely have a believer in Tom Baldock, my lady. I never did see such a quick change in an animal in all my life. How did you know it was something in his eye that caused him to fret so?"

Althea smiled at the man's astonishment. "You spoke of his shaking his head, which made me wonder if he had something in his ear or his eye, but the nipping and the bad temper you described made me decide that it must be the eye, which would be more upsetting to the horse. So I looked at the eyes closely and could see that one was a good deal more red and watery than the other."

"Now that you explain it that way, I see it, but it is a miracle you figured it out in the first place, and I bless you for it, lady."

"But the real miracle," he later told the crowd in the taproom, "Is that I have known that horse nigh on all its life and it would not let me get within kicking distance. She just looked at it straight in the eye and talked to it slow and comforting, and bless you if he didn't let her do her work meek as a lamb."

So it was that Althea's reputation as something of a healer of horses was established among the humbler folk of the community. It was soon discovered that she had a goodly amount of information about other animals as well, talking knowledgeably with Mrs. Tubbs about

chicken yards and the amount of space needed to ensure
that its inhabitants were healthy and active, or discussing
with Farmer Tubbs the points in favor of Tamworth pigs
over Gloucester Old Spots. But it was not her knowledge
so much as the calming effect she seemed to exert on
ailing, injured, or frightened animals that won her the
grudging admiration of the country folk. Knowledge was
one thing—it could be gotten through years of experience—but the other was a gift from the Almighty and
revered as such when they saw proof of it demonstrated
on their livestock.

Chapter 23

While Althea was slowly making her presence known in and around Kennington, her parents were doing their utmost to keep members of the fashionable world from remarking upon their daughter's absence from London.

The Duke and Duchess of Clarendon were far too well-bred to express anything as undignified as anger, distress, or even frustration at their daughter's disappearance. Privately, the duchess unbent so much as to confide to the duke the morning after Althea's disappearance that despite her best efforts their daughter had never acquired the proper appreciation for her exalted status as an incomparable among incomparables. "She would always attribute her success to her expectations—so unbecomingly cynical." The duchess had agreed to join her husband in the breakfast room that morning instead of taking her usual chocolate in her bedchamber at an hour considerably closer to noon than this.

"It is not the lack of appreciation for the reputation she has established in society that is so upsetting; for after all, one is well aware of the vagaries of fashion—a young lady who is all the rage one Season may be quite soon forgotten the next. But it is her utter disregard for what is due the family name that is so incomprehensible. One's standing in the *ton* may rise or fall, but . . ." Seeing his wife's expression of horror, the duke paused in midsentence before continuing. "Well, you know, my dear, that before you took me in hand, the Beauchamps were not considered leaders of the fashionable world by any means. But, as I was saying, one's status in the *ton* may change, but the glory of the Beauchamp name has always remained unblemished, and Beauchamps have understood and carried their duty to the family since the time of the Conqueror. We must proceed most delicately in this matter. After all, the letter she left indicated very little except that she had gone into the country with her grandmother. One does not wish to call attention to the clandestine nature of their departure by appearing to look for them. And, Mother, though perhaps a trifle too strong-minded"—he coughed delicately—"is not so strong-minded as to be thought eccentric. She will see to it that the family name is not dishonored."

"The family name!" The duchess's voice rose ominously. "Our daughter has the entire fashionable world at her feet and you worry about the family name!" With an effort, she calmed herself. "As you say, my lord, the family name has remained unblemished for centuries; it will no doubt remain that way for centuries to come; but to sustain the reputation as an incomparable, one must be constantly before the public eye. This absence will not do, I tell you. You must bring her back before Lord Spottiswode, Fotheringay, the others . . . Oh, it is too much to bear. After all the hours I lavished on her with dressmakers, milliners . . . There is nothing for it but to bring her back."

"But my dear," the duke pointed out mildly, "we have no idea where she is."

"Do be serious, my lord. Young women and their grandmothers do not just disappear off the face of the earth. Surely your mother has had some hand in this. Where would she go?" The duchess's expression left very little doubt in her husband's mind that in her opinion, the annoyingly independent-minded dowager had more than a little to do with this disaster.

"She could have gone to visit any number of friends, all of them well enough respected in the fashionable world to make us a laughingstock if I should appear on their doorsteps demanding my daughter like some overwrought parent in a novel from a circulating library. I tell you, there is nothing to be done but to remain here as we are in dignified silence." Having made his pronouncement, the duke picked up the *Times* and buried himself in its description of the previous day's debate on the Seditious Meetings Bill.

The duchess contained her irritation as best she could. Her husband confronted problems with the same ponderous gravity he brought to the rest of life. His thought processes were often slow and arduous, but once he had arrived at an opinion or a course of action, there was no changing his mind. Deliberately, she took one last swallow of tea, rose majestically, and swept out of the breakfast room to prepare for an orgy of shopping. Whatever happened, one made a much better face of it if one were exquisitely turned out. She had discovered over the years that people were far less likely to gossip about those who dressed with exacting taste in the latest fashions than those less à la mode.

Elsewhere in town, Lady Althea Beauchamp's absence was being noticed in less dignified terms. "My dear Gareth, I have not seen you with Lady Althea this age. It is a great deal too bad of you to let such a lovely young lady slip through your fingers when it is clear that she has a decided partiality for you." The Marchionness of Harwood rapped her son's knuckles playfully with a dainty ivory fan as they stood watching the waltzing couples gliding around Lady Hatherill's elegant ballroom.

"Such a naughty boy, my son." She turned to flutter charcoal-darkened lashes at Lord Battisford, who did his best to look appropriately sympathetic. "Not more than a week ago he was thick as inkle weavers with the belle of the Season, and now you would not know that he had even made her acquaintance."

"That is because Lady Althea Beauchamp is nowhere to be seen, if you have noticed, Mama," Gareth responded dryly.

"Children are such a trial, are they not, my lord?" The marchioness chose to ignore her son's unhelpful remark.

"Worrying over them is enough to turn a mother's hair quite gray."

"You cannot convince me, my lady, that you have a gray hair on your head. In fact, you are altogether far too young to be the mother of anyone, much less a man of Harwood's years."

Lord Battisford's ponderous flattery was instantly rewarded with a brilliant smile. "La, you are so *galant,* my lord. 'Tis true, however, that I was married at a *most* tender age. But tell me, who is that odd-looking woman with Sir Digby? What a quiz of a headdress, and do regard how she positively throws herself at the poor man."

Seeing that his mother was totally occupied with whetting her elderly suitor's competitive instincts by alluding to his hated rival, Gareth seized the opportunity to slip away to the card room.

But once there, he scanned the tables in vain. Neither Althea nor her grandmother was anywhere to be seen. He had half expected it, for he had not laid eyes on Lady Althea Beauchamp since she had left his lodgings in Curzon Street a good deal angrier and a good deal richer than she had entered them. It was not for lack of looking that he did not find her. Loathing himself for doing so, Gareth had shamelessly haunted all the possible gathering places of the *ton*—Almack's, the theater, the opera, ballrooms and drawing room's of society's fashionable hostesses—hoping for a glimpse of the woman who had unnervingly dominated all his thoughts, but it was no use, she was not to be found.

As he had so sarcastically pointed out to his mother, Lady Althea Beauchamp was nowhere to be seen, at least not in London at any rate. But Gareth, once he had established to his satisfaction that she was not in the metropolis, was reasonably certain as to where she could be located. It did gave him some small feeling of triumph, in the midst of the lowering feeling that he was becoming obsessed with Lady Althea, to know that he was probably more aware of her whereabouts than her parents were. He knew his lady and her talent for strategy; she would undoubtedly have done her utmost to keep the Duke and Duchess of Clarendon from discovering her until it was too late to bring her back.

The Duke and the Duchess of Clarendon were also less visible than previously at the various haunts of fashion, but they did not abstain altogether from their social engagements. Such absence would have immediately caused comment. As it was, they tried to appear just frequently enough so that the *ton* was aware of their presence, but not so much that it would be obvious that their daughter was not with them. They often arrived separately and stayed for a very short time, hoping that anyone seeing one parent in a crush of people would assume that the daughter was with the other, never staying long in one place, and hurrying out as though forced to attend another pressing engagement. Those ill bred enough to remark on Lady Althea's absence were informed in icy tones that she was kept at home by a headache but would grace the social scene when she felt more the thing. If, after that, anyone had the temerity to wonder how long Lady Althea Beauchamp's headaches lasted, they had the good sense to keep their speculations to themselves.

Gareth, on the other hand, once he had heard of Reggie's departure for India, concluded that Althea's cousin had refused to take back the estate, as Gareth had predicted, and left it in Althea's care. Having settled that firmly in his mind, the marquess discovered that London had begun to bore him in the extreme. There was no one to be found who could offer him sufficient challenge at the gaming table, and even the charms of the voluptuous Maria began to pall. The dancer's lush beauty suddenly seemed overripe, her seductiveness overdone, and the pleasures of the flesh sadly flat without any accompanying intellectual stimulation.

In short, he missed Althea. He loathed the very thought of such a thing, and hated even more that he was going to give in to it, but the marquess knew that sooner rather than later, he was going to head off to his own properties in Cambridgeshire, taking the route that went by way of Stansted and Kennington Park.

When Ibthorp finally received the orders to pack for a trip to the country, the valet was not in the least surprised. "Thought he was looking a bit down pin lately," he muttered under his breath as he carefully laid his master's cravats in the valise. "For a time there, he were looking merrier than a grig, happier than I have ever seen him. Then something happened. It is not his mother; irritating as she is, she don't affect him that way, and she has left off sending him notes. But it *is* a woman; of that I am certain." And to Ibthorp's knowledge, there was only one woman he could ever remember his master having relations with that were not purely physical.

Oddly enough, the servant was somewhat pleased by such distraction on the part of a man who heretofore had kept his emotions under the iron control of his intellect to such a degree that it had at times seemed almost unnatural. Furthermore, Ibthorp, who ordinarily left all the gambling to his master, was willing to wager a large sum in this case that the lady in question was somehow to be located along the way to Harwood. Once the marquess put his mind to a thing, he went after it, and it was clear enough to Ibthorp, at least, that the Marquess of Harwood's mind, whether consciously or not, had been set on this young woman for quite some time. So it was that Ibthorp found himself on the road to Cambridgeshire to prepare Harwood for his master's imminent arrival.

Setting out from London in his curricle the following day, Gareth felt his spirits lift the moment he cleared the city. It was a glorious spring morning, his team was eager, and he was leaving behind scenes that had become too much connected to a certain incomparable with defiant blue eyes and an amazing capacity for card games of any sort.

Once free of the traffic, he gave the horses their heads and, reveling in the speed, the smoothness of an excellent road, and the joys of a well-sprung carriage, he allowed himself to indulge in the hope that his uncharacteristic interest in Lady Althea Beauchamp had been nothing more than a diversion created unconsciously by himself to distract his attention as much as possible from his mother's irksome presence.

This optimistic fancy enjoyed all too brief an existence, however, for the moment he saw the signpost for Stanstead, the quickening of his pulses told Gareth that his preoccupation with the young woman had nothing to do with the Marchioness of Harwood and everything to with his unwanted but undeniable attraction to Althea.

He slowed as he reached the village and, hating himself for it, pulled in at the yard of the George and Dragon to ask directions to Kennington.

"It is just a few miles along the Cambridge road, that way, my lord. You cannot miss it," the ostler assured him.

"Thank you." Gareth tossed a coin to the lad whose eyes were hungrily taking in every detail of his equipage so that he could report back in the stables that a regular Corinthian, real top-of-the-trees, had stopped to ask the way to Kennington.

Just as the ostler had directed, three miles beyond the village and off to the right, Gareth saw neat fences and a gravel drive stretching between rich green pastures to end in the courtyard of a small but beautifully proportioned manor house, its cream-colored stone golden in the afternoon sunlight.

So this was Kennington. The place was perfect for her—elegant, with plenty of fertile-looking land that should support the place very well if it did not do so already. Here was an estate big enough to offer her a challenge, but not too big for a capable woman. A slow smile swept across Gareth's face. She had gotten what she wanted after all.

Cursing himself for being no better than some smitten schoolboy, Gareth strained to catch sight of her as he passed by. Suddenly, he caught a flicker of movement out of the corner of his eye and barely had time to recognize a fleeing rabbit before he became aware of the spotted mongrel chasing it.

"Damn and blast." Hauling on the reins with all his might, Gareth fought his team as he tried to swerve to avoid hitting the animal. His heart in his mouth, he struggled to bring the powerful bays to a halt. It almost seemed as though he was going to be successful when the wheel hit a rut. "Damn fool," he cursed again as he flew off the seat and tumbled into darkness.

Chapter 24

"My lady. My lady, there has been an accident, a dreadful accident. A man, a gentleman . . ." The sturdy laborer who had been repairing some of the fences Gareth had admired came panting up to the stables just as Althea was dismounting after a satisfying gallop across the fields, her fields.

"Accident? What sort of accident, Tim?"

"Carriage, my lady. The gentleman appears to be alive. I checked and he is breathing, but he is dead to the world."

Althea turned to her groom. "Jem, fetch the wagon and something from the lumber room to make a litter. I shall grab some bandages. Where is he, Tim?"

"Just beyond the turning into the drive. The horses seemed unhurt, but they did not want me tying them up."

"Very well. You stay to help Jim and I shall go on ahead." Althea ran to find the bag of salve and bandages she kept for emergencies and then hurried off down the drive while the other two went to find something to make a litter and hitch the horse to the wagon.

As Tim had reported, the horses were standing quietly enough in their traces not far from a yellow curricle that was tilted at an awkward angle on the edge of the road. A few feet beyond lay an inert form, one leg twisted unnaturally beneath it, and a curly beaver, tumbled some yards away.

Althea approached carefully, not wanting to startle an injured person who might just be regaining consciousness. As she looked down at the white-faced stranger her knees threatened to buckle under her. It was the Marquess of Harwood, no stranger at all, and yet he looked like one.

Lying hurt and unconscious, the marquess bore little resemblance to the Bachelor Marquess, the bold card player, the scourge of matchmaking mamas, and the hard-hearted gambler who deprived young men of their family estates. She reached out a gentle hand to stroke his brow, then carefully lifted one wrist to feel the pulse that was weak but steady.

The pale face, robbed of all expression except the finely drawn lines around his mouth and at the edges of his eyes, looked weary. Why had she never seen that before? Carefully, she ran her fingers through his thick dark hair, fighting the overwhelming urge to cradle his head in her lap, to hold him close and smooth the wrinkles between his straight dark brows.

"We came as quick as ever we could, my lady. And we brung us a litter of sorts." Carefully Tim and Jem laid an old door padded with blankets next to the injured man. "And we also brought a walking stick to tie his leg to as Tim said his leg was probably broke."

"Very clever, both of you. Now let us tie that stick carefully to the leg and get him on the litter." Althea struggled to distance herself from the limp figure on the grass. There was no time to reflect on the riot of emotions warring inside of her. The situation called for action and decisiveness, the cool, unruffled Lady Althea Beauchamp who could calmly survey her hand of cards while a fortune hung in the balance, not this weak-kneed stranger whose heart had leaped into her mouth the moment she discovered the identity of the injured man.

"Now you, Jem, manage the legs. Tim, take his shoulders while I hold his head and we will all lift together on the count of three. One, two, three."

They slid the marquess onto the door so smoothly that his eyelids did not even flutter. Althea sighed with relief, then frowned. The lack of response could mean that they had managed to avoid injuring him further, or it could also mean that the bump she had felt on the back of his head was severe—no way to know that until a surgeon had been summoned, and for that she would have to consult the Crowders.

Mrs. Crowder was able to assure her that Mr. Warboys, who enjoyed the highest reputation in all of Essex, did not live more than a few miles further along down the Cambridge road, and it would take Jem no time at all to fetch him, for he was always ready to come to the scene of an accident or a patient's bedside at a moment's notice.

Meanwhile, Althea could do nothing but sit by the marquess's bedside, taking in every detail of the finely shaped hands resting on the coverlet or the chest and shoulders that, freed from the exquisitely fitted coat, looked so broad and powerful she could not take her eyes from them. She had never paid much attention to men before. At Clarendon she had led a quiet life separated from the local gentry by her exalted position and closeted with her governess and a succession of instructors—dancing masters, music masters, drawing masters—all the requisite shapers of a young woman expected to take her place in the *ton* as the beautifully finished representative of one of the country's most illustrious families. With such a program of instruction to fill her days she had had little time for gaiety or socializing of any kind.

When she had arrived in town, the exquisite product of such exacting preparations, Althea had been stared at, commented upon, and gossiped about to such an extent that she had done her best to avoid even looking at men, afraid that one glance would give rise to a host of unwelcome speculation on the part of the *ton,* or equally unwelcome presumption on the part of the man.

Now, she was unable to take her eyes off this one. Recalling the first time she had seen him, casting a scornful gaze over Lady St. John's guests, Althea admitted to herself that she had always been uncomfortably aware of the attraction of Gareth de Vere's lean, intelligent face, observant gray eyes, and cynically smiling mouth. She had eventually responded to that attraction by opening up to him as she never had to anyone else. Althea had thought that her fury at his betrayal had wiped that all away, but, looking at him now as he lay injured and helpless, she knew that somewhere, in a place too deep and too private to acknowledge, no matter how much he had hurt her, she had missed him a great deal.

Anxiously Althea watched the shallow rise and fall of his chest and fought the urge to lie down beside him, to wrap her arms around him in a desperate attempt to bring him back to consciousness and health, to the sharp-eyed cynical observer, the daring gambler, not this exhausted man who was unable to respond to her solicitous caress, unable to do anything at all except lie there still as death.

"I have brought you Mr. Warboys, my lady." The housekeeper's voice broke into Althea's reverie.

"It is a great pleasure to meet the 'Angel of the Stable.'" The doctor's bright blue eyes twinkled at Althea's patent astonishment. "Come now, my lady. Surely you knew that that is what they call you. Any new resident in the district is naturally the subject of a great deal of speculation and gossip. But when the new resident is a landowner, a young lady, and something of a miracle worker where sick horses are concerned, word travels like wildfire. Actually, I did happen to hear about your skills firsthand from Farmer Tubbs. That lad of his fell from an apple tree a few days ago and dislocated his shoulder, which I was called in to remedy. And now I hear that you have a patient for me."

"Yes. Thank you for coming so quickly. The Marquess of Harwood had an accident in his curricle. I believe that his leg is broken and that he is suffering from a concussion. We have immobilized the leg, but it is obvious that it needs to be set. I do not know what to do about the concussion except keep him quiet."

"The Marquess of Harwood. Hmm." Observing the delicate flush that rose in the lady's cheeks, the surgeon refrained from further comment, but the twinkle in his eyes grew even more pronounced.

He was not the only one drawing interesting conclusions. Hovering in the background with Mrs. Crowder, the Dowager Duchess of Clarendon was indulging in a riot of speculation. Not only was her granddaughter's reaction to the marquess's presence encouraging, but unconscious though he might be, the marquess's presence in this particular neighborhood was most encouraging indeed. In the dowager's experience, sophisticated gentlemen of the marquess's stamp, especially gambling gentlemen, did not leave London in the height of the Season without a very good reason. Since his name had never been mentioned in the discussion of nearby property owners, his appearance in the vicinity could only be owing to one thing—her granddaughter's recent removal to Kennington was the reason behind the marquess's appearance in this particular spot of the country, on this particular stretch of road, at this particular time. At least there were grounds for hope.

"Your diagnosis is entirely correct, my lady." The surgeon, who had been carefully examining the inert body on the bed, straightened and nodded approvingly. "It is best to set the leg now while he is still unconscious. If you would be willing to assist me, we can begin without further ado. Fortunately it is a simple fracture, and if you were to hold the foot, so, and then pull, I can guide the bone into line."

Too surprised to speak, and too gratified by his trust in her capabilities to doubt herself, Althea nodded and moved to replace his hands with her own. Biting her lip, she waited for the surgeon's command.

"Now, pull gently but firmly. Do not worry. I believe he is too deeply unconscious to feel any pain. That is it. Slowly, slowly . . . There. We have done the trick. Good girl." He strode over to give her a steadying pat on the shoulder. "The worst thing about being a surgeon, or practicing medicine of any sort, is that sometimes one must cause pain in order to alleviate it." Expertly, he rebound the leg to the walking stick. "If this is kept immobile for several weeks, and if he keeps off it for several more, he should heal as good as new. As to the concussion, it is difficult to say. Keep him warm and comfortable and apply cold compresses to the bump on his head to reduce the swelling. I shall check back tomorrow to see how he is doing, but he appears to have a strong constitution and, as there are no other obvious injuries, I expect he will come around soon. It was a pleasure meeting you, my lady." The surgeon cast a final appraising glance at the patient, smiled at Althea, nodded encouragingly to the dowager and Mrs. Crowder, and hastened out in the same energetic manner that he had burst in.

"Well, then." Althea took her previous place in the chair next to the bed, a basin of cold water in her lap. Squeezing out a compress, she applied it to the egg-shaped lump just a little behind the marquess's right ear. "I shall ask Jenny to remove my things to the dressing room and she will bring me my meals here."

"But you must not wear yourself out nursing the marquess all by yourself," her grandmother protested. "There are many of us who can do that."

"Nursing the Marquess of Harwood is far less taxing than anything else I have been doing lately, Grandmother. Besides, you heard Mr. Warboys. He seems to think me a competent enough nurse." Althea turned her back on them, took another compress from the bowl, and laid it across the patient's brow. She then proceeded to plump out the pillow and smooth the coverlet as calmly as though no one was staring at her in astonishment.

The dowager frowned obstinately for a moment; then turning her head to hide a sly smile, she beckoned to the housekeeper and they left the room.

The afternoon drifted into evening and then into night. The patient remained as still and quiet as he had since they had lifted him onto the litter and brought him back to the house. Constantly on the lookout for the least sign of change—the flicker of an eyelid, the twitch of a finger—Althea was too preoccupied to do anything but swallow a bowl of soup. She fiercely resisted all efforts to relieve her and insisted on sitting up with the marquess throughout the night.

When Jenny brought her mistress her chocolate the next morning, Althea's face looked pale and drawn, but she was as alert as ever. "There has been no change at all, not even the slightest movement," she remarked sadly. "I fear that if this continues much longer, it is an indication there must be some deeper damage that we do not know about."

"Do not worry, my lady. He is lucky to find himself in such good hands. You have done all that can be done." Jenny had never seen her mistress looking so distressed, even over an injured animal, and in general, she worried a good deal more about animals than she did about people. The marquess was a very special man indeed to have her mistress fret over him to such a degree.

"I have certainly done all that I know to do, but is it enough?"

"I am sure it is, my lady." Jenny left her mistress gently stroking the brow of the injured man and staring down at him as though she were willing him to regain consciousness.

Chapter 25

*H*is head ached horribly and his entire body felt like one massive bruise. His mouth was dry as a dust pit, and try as he would, he could not penetrate the thick black fog that clung to him. He struggled to break free of the pain and the darkness, but nothing happened, and he lay there, trapped, helpless, and frustrated.

Then something cool and soothing drifted across his forehead and he felt his body slowly relax. He was not alone; he was not lost. Someone was there, someone who was kind and gentle. He sensed it rather than felt it, and giving a sigh of relief, he slipped back into unconsciousness.

The next time he became aware of anything, it was a soft, soothing murmur. He ached a little less though all his limbs still felt as though they were held down with lead weights. And his mouth did not seem quite so dry, his tongue less thick and cottony.

"What but thee, Sleep? Soft closer of our eyes! Low murmur of tender lullabies! Light hoverer around our happy pillows! Wreather of poppy beds and weeping willows!"

Now he could just make out words. If only he could see the speaker. He turned his head and a sliver of pain shot through him. Waves of dizziness washed over him. But then he felt a cool, soft hand on his cheek. Reassured, he pressed against it, content for the moment simply to know he was cared for.

Another hand slowly stroked his hair and he gave himself up to the solicitude of his unknown protector. He knew he should force himself into consciousness, assess his situation, and take back control of his life, but for the time being it was too pleasant to lie there, soothed by the gentle hands and the musical voice. No one in his entire life had made him feel this way—safe, sheltered, and secure—and he did not want it to end, not just yet anyway.

A drop of water touched his lips and he licked it thirstily as he tried to remember when, if ever, anything had tasted so good or been so welcome. Undoubtedly such a peaceful state was all a sweet dream from which he would soon awake, but surely he could allow himself the luxury of a few more hours of blissful delusion, just a few more hours savoring a concern so tender that he had not thought it possible. He reached up with both hands to clutch the hand that laid a cool compress on his brow, cradled his head against it, and drifted off into a dreamless healing slumber.

A soft smile curved Althea's lips and grateful tears stung her eyes. He would be all right after all. The deep sigh as he had gathered her hand to his cheek, and the heavy, regular breathing were signs of sleep rather than unconsciousness.

When the first sigh had indicated that the marquess was shaking off his comotose state, Althea had chastised herself severely for experiencing a momentary regret, a regret that vanished as quickly and unexpectedly as it had appeared. Selfishly, she had welcomed the opportunity to observe him unobserved, to run her hand through his thick springy hair, to smooth the straight dark brows, knowing instinctively that at some deep level she was bringing comfort to the unconscious sufferer. She was able to do this without worrying what anyone would think, because no one, not even the patient himself, would ever know what pleasure it gave her to be able to caress the stubbled cheek, to sense that she, and she alone, could give him what he needed so desperately. No person had ever depended on Althea before and, fleeting though it was, it made her oddly proud.

Mr. Warboys, who had complimented her on his most recent visit, had confirmed that she had a right to this pride. "You are doing an excellent job, my lady. While it is true that he has not yet gained consciousness, his color is better and his pulse is stronger, as you have no doubt noticed."

She had noticed the color and the pulse, but it pleased her to have it confirmed and to be given credit for it.

And now that Gareth had stirred, drunk the water she had dropped on his lips, and pulled her hands to his cheek, she was overwhelmed with a joy and tenderness she had not thought possible. But along with it came sorrow. He would awake and remember the anger of their parting. He would chafe at being nursed by her and demand to be taken somewhere else where he could be cared for by his valet or servants of his own. The masterful, cynical Marquess of Harwood would reassert control over his life, and the helpless patient who clutched her hand for comfort would disappear forever.

"Are you an angel?" The hoarse whisper broke into her reverie several hours later. Althea's hand had become numb in his, and her back ached from trying to keep her hand in the same position so as not to disturb his slumber.

"No, I am not an angel." So he had not recognized her, but in the dimly lit bedchamber this was not surprising. She was glad he did not know her yet. Perhaps she could enjoy a few more hours of this intimate anonymity.

"You seem like an angel to me. An angel who held out her hand to pull me out of the darkness."

"How did you happen to fall into the darkness in the first place?"

He frowned in an effort to remember. "A dog."

"A dog!"

"Yes. A liver-spotted mongrel. It was chasing a rabbit and I did not see it until I was almost upon it. I think, I hope, I was able to avoid it. Did you happen to notice, to hear how it was doing?" He clutched her hand anxiously.

"Ah. I know that dog. It belongs to Farmer Tubbs.

Yes, it is safe." Althea was both surprised and pleased to know that he was concerned enough about the animal to risk his carriage and himself to save it. But what had caused the moment of inattention in the first place? Surely the owner of such a curricle and such a magnificent team would have been concentrating enough on the road ahead of him that a stray dog would not cause him to suffer such a mishap.

"Thank goodness. I was a blasted idiot not to see it."

Althea saw the color tingeing his pale cheeks, but put it down to his anger at losing control of his carriage and team. Little did she know that he was recalling the reason for his momentary distraction. He had been looking at Kennington Park, hoping for a glimpse of its new owner, Lady Althea Beauchamp. His dark brows drew together as he focused on the face in the shadows above him. "Althea," he whispered.

"Yes." Hardly daring to breathe, Althea waited tensely for his next reaction.

A slow smile spread across the marquess's face. "Not an angel, certainly, but a most redoubtable woman, nevertheless. How long have I been here?"

"Nearly a week."

His eyes narrowed in an effort to concentrate as he scanned her face intently. It was pale and there were dark circles under her eyes, but in spite of that, she looked happier and more relaxed than he could ever remember seeing her. "And you have nursed me the entire time." It was a statement rather than a question.

"Yes."

"A most redoubtable woman, indeed. And a kind one as well." Odd to think that the capable hand that shuffled and dealt cards so skillfully could be so gentle and so comforting, that a mind clever enough to beat him and a spirit daring enough to risk everything on the turn of a card could also heal. Undoubtedly she had consulted with a surgeon or a physician, but it was her healing presence that had eased his pain, that he had felt pulling him out of the fog of unconsciousness, watching over him and keeping him safe and warm. "Remarkable," he whispered again as he closed his eyes, worn out with the effort of speech.

Relief washed over Althea. It seemed that he was going to allow her to care for him a little while longer. Still holding his hand, she laid her own head back in the chair and, for the first time since the accident, allowed herself to fall into a true sleep.

When she awoke, it was daylight, or the beginning of it at least. Guiltily she looked over at her patient, but he was sleeping quietly, a smile on his face. A ray of sunlight slanted across the bed throwing into relief the high cheekbones and the hollows in the unshaven cheeks. It was such a sensitive, intelligent face. How could she have thought it arrogant or mocking?

His gray eyes opened as he regarded her seriously. "You are still here."

"But of course I am still here."

"Thank you." He did not seem inclined to talk, but lay there surveying the room and his injured leg, assessing the situation.

"We sent a groom to your lodgings in London, but no one was there. All that could be discovered was that you had left for the country and that your valet had preceded you."

"Poor Ibthorp. He must be wondering where the devil I am. He went to Harwood to prepare things for my arrival. It is not too far distant from here, near Newmarket."

"We can send Jem to fetch him for you. I am sure you will feel much more the thing when you are cared for by a proper valet." So he had been heading for his estate. What madness had allowed her to indulge in the crazy hope that he had been on that road because he knew it ran by Kennington, because he knew she would be there? It must be the lack of sleep, she told herself. Why else would she entertain such foolish thoughts? She had certainly never indulged in such absurd fantasies before.

"Thank you, but I have no complaints about the care I have received thus far." He seemed happy to lie there quietly, accepting the quirk of fate that had brought him into her care.

And indeed he was content. A queer sort of lethargy had overtaken him, and the man who ordinarily would have been struggling to be up and about, attending to his affairs, taking care of everything, found it more pleasant than he ever could have imagined possible to let someone else look after him.

Once he had returned to full consciousness, Gareth spent a good deal of time over the next few days sleeping, but as he healed, he begged her to read to him.

"What shall I read?"

"Whatever you were reading when I first awoke."

"Keats's *Sleep and Poetry*?"

"Yes, I enjoyed that. So soothing."

Althea looked at him curiously. The Marquess of Harwood did not seem the sort for poetry. Indeed, sometimes, when she looked up and found his eyes fixed upon her, she wondered whether he was even listening at all, so lost in thought as he appeared to be.

But as his strength slowly returned, so did his energy. He moved more restlessly in bed and struggled to see out of the window as she plumped his pillows for him. Althea began to bring up the *Times* to read aloud to him, and invariably they would fall into discussions of one topic or another.

A few days after the marquess regained consciousness, Ibthorp arrived to relieve Althea of a good deal of his master's care, bringing with him a groom to look after his horses. "They are merry as grigs, sir, and eating their heads off," the groom reassured his injured master moments after he had looked over the team. "No need for me, sir. They are in excellent hands here."

Althea could not help shooting a triumphant look at her patient when they heard this.

From the moment he had regained consciousness, the marquess had fretted about the welfare of his thoroughbreds, and no amount of reassurance on her part could convince him that she and Jem were capable of looking after them adequately.

In fact, despite his groom's reassurance, Gareth continued to concern himself with their welfare until Althea, thoroughly exasperated by his lack of faith, wrung permission from Mr. Warboys for his patient to visit the stables on the same litter that had carried him from the site of the accident.

Chapter 26

The very next morning, after the surgeon had given his permission, the marquess was carried out to the stable to see for himself the state of his team. Gripping the shoulder of his valet as Jem and Tim supported the door he reclined on, he turned toward Althea as they approached the stable. "I want you to know that I do appreciate your care of my team, but naturally I have been concerned, for they are so high-spirited that it is difficult even for me to approach them close enough to discover if anything is amiss. Truly, it would take someone with whom they are very familiar to do so, and even then it is a risky business indeed."

Gareth sensed that his lack of faith had touched a nerve, but even he, notable whip that he was, had discovered some time ago, to his own chagrin, that the man at Tattersall's had understated the case when he had warned the marquess that the bays were high-spirited. *You'll never find sweeter goers than these two, my lord, but they are touchy, sir, very touchy.* The man had been very insistent upon this point and he had been entirely correct. The bays possessed incredibly sensitive mouths and flew like the wind, but they were temperamental in the extreme.

A low whicker greeted them as they entered the stables, and Gareth, his eyes adjusting slowly to the gloom, was surprised to see two handsome heads appear eagerly over the stalls. Ordinarily they snorted and stamped their hooves at the approach of anyone, especially a crowd such as this.

"Hello, my lads." A soft voice at his side responded to their greeting.

Gareth watched in astonishment as Althea acknowledged the bobbing heads and another low whicker before bestowing a lump a sugar and a friendly pat on each of them. Then, to his utter amazement, she opened the door to the first stall, entered, stroked Achilles' velvety nose, and took hold of his bridle to lead him out.

He followed as meek as a lamb and stood patiently flicking his tail as his dumbfounded master surveyed him for signs of the accident.

There was the faintest hint of a cut on its outside hind leg, but other than that, the animal appeared to be in superb health and the best of spirits. In fact, Gareth could not remember when he had seen the horse looking so calm and relaxed.

"Looking right fit, ain't he, my lord?" Gareth's groom flashed his master a sly smile.

Damn the man! He was laughing at him. Actually, they were all laughing at him. They knew that his cattle were as contented and as well cared for as they had ever been in their lives, but they were all waiting for him to acknowledge it. And with that acknowledgment would come an important admission about himself and a certain remarkable young woman that he was not quite prepared to face at this particular moment.

Gareth de Vere, Marquess of Harwood, might be able to admit that, as an injured man, he needed to rely on another's care; he might even concede that he had been forced to accept that care from a woman. But he was not about to admit that anyone, especially a young woman, was able to handle his team.

"Happen you don't know what they call my lady in the village, my lord," Althea's own groom ventured.

"Hush, Jem." His mistress silenced him with a frown. "That is neither here nor there."

"No, Jem. I do not know what they call her in the village, but I feel certain that you are going to enlighten me," the marquess responded grimly.

"Yes, my lord, I am." Too intent on defending his

mistress to be intimidated by his lordship's icy undertone, Jem stared back at him defiantly. "They call her the Angel of the Stable, and it ain't just because she knows how to heal ailing animals. It's because she knows how to talk to them. I don't mean talk to them like 'How are you today?' and 'What do you think of the weather we're having?' But it's like she understands what they are thinking. They know that and they trust her. Take these lads, here, for instance—as rare a pair of tearers as I ever did see—they are gentle as lambs with her because they trust her."

Jem's rare grin illuminated his face for an instant. "You see it, sir. I know you do. And I do not blame you for being a mite put out. After all, you must be a bruising driver yourself and a connoisseur of fine horseflesh, if your team is anything to go by. And I'll be bound that you are a man who has not met his match. But our lady here is something altogether special. It is a magic she has, and there is no mistaking it. Ask anyone around these parts and they will agree with me."

Jem stopped, gulped, and reddened in embarrassment as if suddenly recognizing his temerity in flaunting his mistress's talents in front of a man who was clearly an experienced whip himself.

"I thank you for your enlightenment, Jem." The harsh note in Gareth's voice cause Althea to scan his face anxiously for any signs of pain, but he seemed to be resting comfortably enough, his injured leg thoroughly supported by the door they had laid across two sturdy chairs.

She could not know, however, the conflicting emotions warring in his breast. First and foremost was relief that his own stupid moment of inattention had not brought harm to a magnificent pair of animals. But this relief was closely followed by chagrin that someone else had been left to care for them and that that someone else had done a superb job of it, better than he could have.

Gareth watched silently as Althea returned Achilles to his stall and brought out Ajax who, slightly less temperamental than his partner, was actually affectionate with her, rubbing his head against her arm and nuzzling her ear.

There was no doubt about it: Noted whip and rider that he was, Gareth had never in the year that he had owned the team established the bond with these animals that Althea had in little over a week's time. Added to that deflating fact was the speedy recovery both animals had made, not only from the wounds, superficial though they were, but also the trauma of the accident. He was forced to admit that Jem was right. It was nothing short of a miracle.

But a cynic of the Marquess of Harwood's stature did not believe in miracles, and when they returned to his room, he questioned his caretaker closely. "And just how did you happen to come by this appellation that your groom alluded to, the 'Angel of the Stable'?"

"Oh, that. It is nothing. You know how credulous country folk can be."

"I do," he responded doggedly. "And I also know that it takes a very long time for country folk to accept a stranger in the neighborhood, especially someone who has arrived straight from the metropolis. And it takes even longer for that stranger to establish a credibility, especially where country matters are concerned."

"As I said, it is nothing. I have merely helped out a few people who are too poor to afford the services of a veterinarian."

"Is there not a farrier in the village?"

"Yes, of course there is."

"I see." Clearly she had done more than the "nothing" she claimed to have done. And clearly she was unwilling to admit to any of it. The more she dismissed this private and unusual side of her character, the more he wanted to know about it, which was a rare departure for someone like Gareth, who lived aloof and independent from his fellow man, who protected his own privacy at all costs, and who ordinarily respected others who wished to do so. He found himself feeling utterly frustrated by her obvious wish to avoid any and all confidences.

Refusing to look into those penetrating eyes that were fixed so intently on her, Althea turned to leave the room, but before she could, he caught her hand and pulled her down onto the chair next to the sofa where they had lain him after his visit to the stables. "Please do not turn away. I wish to understand this. Why do you not want to admit to having used your hidden talents and special powers to help these animals and their owners?"

Gareth continued to stare at her, willing her to look at him, but she remained silent, still avoiding his gaze. Did she not trust him enough to share this important part of her life with him? Usually he avoided the intimacy of shared hopes and dreams, for it required the listener to reveal something on his own part to the speaker and he avoided such revelations at all costs. But in this instance he wished to share. "I only ask because I admire anyone who can communicate well enough with an animal to earn its trust."

Althea stopped trying to free her wrist from his grasp and he pressed his advantage. "When I was a lad, my horses and my dogs were the only friends I had. They lavished more attention and affection on me than my parents ever did, and they were certainly far more trustworthy. They meant everything to me. When I later joined the cavalry I met some excellent fellows, comrades who would do anything, risk anything for one another, but it was still my horse I relied upon in battle, my horse whom I trusted with my life. And it was the suffering of the horses in these battles that made me grow to detest the military life. Agonies of wounded men were nothing to me compared to those of the noble beasts who carried them. And I could do nothing to help them."

Tears stung his eyelids as he recalled these painful memories and he paused, swallowing hard. "After all, it is man who makes war and these poor animals who bear the burden of man's idiocy. I was just beginning to think I could bear it no longer when my father died a ruined man and I was forced to return home. But I kept thinking about these poor beasts long after I left the battlefields of the Peninsula. Then one day I overheard a friend talking about attending an auction of wounded troop horses where he happened to stand next to the renowned surgeon Sir Astley Cooper, who astounded the entire crowd by buying twelve of them. My friend later heard that Cooper had taken the horses home to his estate, removed all the bullets and grapeshot from the animals, and given them all the solicitous care these old warriors deserved. The minute I heard that I resolved to do the very same thing. I wrote to Sir Astley to learn more about it, and now I have a dozen or so on my own estate who have been rehabilitated by the great man himself. It is one of my greatest joys to see them occasionally form together in a line and charge across the pasture."

"You? I would not have thought—" Suddenly aware of what she had been about to say, Althea broke off in some confusion.

"You would not have thought what?"

"Well, I . . ." Uncomfortably, she twisted and untwisted the ribbon of her jonquil morning dress between her fingers. "You do not seem to be, er, a, well . . . You do not seem to be a sentimental sort of person."

"Because I prefer to keep my thoughts and feelings to myself instead of forcing them on anyone who will listen? How can you be surprised at that? After all, *I* am not the one who is called the Ice Princess; you are. And yet you are here doing just what I would wish to do, helping suffering horses."

"That is different. You are cynical and scornful of society. My demeanor, which won me the name of Ice Princess, was not adopted out of a scorn for society."

"Then why were you the Ice Princess?" Gently he pulled her over to the sofa next to him so he could look deep into her eyes.

"Because I . . ." Althea bit her lip as painful memories of greedy eyes and covetous smiles came rushing back to her "Because I did not like being the object of attention and desire on the part of people who knew little or nothing about me beyond my family and my fortune. People who knew little and cared less, but intruded into my life, forcing me . . ." She shuddered and fell silent. "I did not want those people to know anything about me. I did not want to satisfy their need to know, just for the sake of knowing, any of the details of my life."

"Did it not occur to you that some of them might have been genuinely interested in you?"

"Believe me, they were not," she replied acidly, a bitter smile twisting her lips.

"But you told me you disliked being treated as an object. If you allow no one to know you, then that is how they are forced to treat you."

"Better that than the other."

"But the more I came to know you, the more I discovered that you were not a vain and haughty beauty who enjoys reducing men to abject, slavish admirers, but an intelligent, courageous, and thoughtful woman who possesses talents far beyond those of the ordinary person." Gareth tilted her chin to look deep into her eyes. "A woman who is worthy of admiration, not for her family or her fortune, but for her character. Is that not what you want, to be understood and appreciated for who you really are?"

His face was so close to hers that she could feel his breath against her lips and she could barely hear the words he said over the pounding of her own heart. She had always avoided looking into men's eyes before, for fear of what she would see there, but now she could not look away. In the gray depths of this man's eyes she could see reflected back at her the person she wanted to be—a person, not a thing, someone admired for her work, not for her possessions.

Althea felt herself being drawn deeper and deeper into a whirlpool of intimacy and closeness. She did not resist, but leaned closer as his arm pulled her to him and their lips touched.

She felt as though all the breath had suddenly left her body, and with it had gone her will. She was helpless to do anything but revel in the warmth of his lips on hers. In the oddest way, it was the culmination of what had begun that long-ago evening in Lady St. John's ballroom. In spite of her annoyance at him, she had been drawn to him because he was different, because he did not join the throng clamoring around her. After that, every time she saw him, everything she had discovered about him had drawn her inexorably closer to him until she was in his arms. Had she always secretly longed to be there? Althea could not say, but for the moment she only wanted to experience the powerful connection between them, the indescribable current that flowed back and forth between their minds, their hearts, and their bodies.

At the same time, she was deathly afraid of the irresistible pull he exerted on her. She had run away from London and risked incurring the wrath of her parents precisely because she had not wanted anyone to have any power over her and now she was relinquishing herself to a force that dominated her more completely than her parents ever had. True, the power her parents exerted had come from without while the power the Marquess of Harwood held over her came from within herself, but that made it all the more compelling and all the more threatening. Either way, she was in danger of losing herself.

Summoning all her strength and all her willpower, Althea pulled away. Unable to utter a word, she raised a shaking hand to her lips. What was she to do now? What she wanted, shockingly enough, was more. She longed to twine her hands in his hair, to pull his body close to hers, to feel the power of it against hers, to share everything with him, her body as well as her mind.

Gareth caught his breath as he looked at her. She had never been more beautiful. Her parted lips were slightly swollen and red; her cheeks were flushed, and her eyes sparkled. She wanted him as much as he wanted her. He had only meant the kiss to be a confirmation of his belief in her, but it had become so much more—a proof of how much he wanted her, how he had longed to be near her, to touch her, to hold her, since the very moment he had lain eyes on her. In all his previous liaisons with women he had never experienced such a thing, this irresistible attraction. In the ballrooms with people around, or in his lodgings with her maid watching, he had had control of himself, but now he was helpless in the face of his desire.

But he detected something else beside a sparkle in her eyes. There was a wariness, an unease. He had seen it before in the eyes of wild animals. It was the fear of being caught, of being trapped.

Summoning up all his willpower, Gareth gently laid both hands on her shoulders and set her away from him. "Forgive me, Althea. I did not mean to alarm you. I just wanted you to know that I admire you. And I thank you for sharing your healing powers with me, since I know you care about animals a great deal more than you care about humans."

A reluctant smile quivered at the corners of her mouth. The wary expression disappeared. "You are correct about that. Luckily for you, my lord, your team looked to be in better shape than you did, so I concentrated on you. But now I must go because I promised Jem I would take a closer look at their wounds the moment you were assured of their well-being. The cuts on their legs are healing nicely, but they still need to be looked after."

He gave a crack of laughter. "Go along then, Althea. This patient is most grateful for your care, and he cannot thank you enough for healing him."

But as she rose and hurried out the door, he could not help whispering, "You may have healed my body, Althea, but what have you done to my soul?"

Chapter 27

$\mathcal{M}$r. Warboys called at Kennington the next day and pronounced the marquess fit enough to move about the house with the aid of a crutch. "But mind you, not putting any weight on that leg, my lord. I have seen more sporting gentlemen and former cavalry fellows than I care to remember, thinking that they can do more than they should when they have broken something. So I am giving you fair warning that if you put that foot to the ground you will walk with a limp and ache in damp weather for the rest of your life."

Gareth grinned at the surgeon's ferocious expression. "have no fear sir. I may be a 'former cavalry fellow,' but I do have sense. By the way, how did you know that I was a 'former cavalry fellow'?"

"A man does not develop the muscles that you have without spending hours in the saddle, and I do not mean jaunting around the park or riding to the hunt. Besides, you have that look about the eyes that says you have seen a good deal more of life than most of us."

"You are a clever man, Mr. Warboys. I believe that I shall take your advice."

"See that you do"—the surgeon shook an admonitory finger at his patient—"or you will be the worse for it, believe me." The fierce expression relaxed into a smile. "Actually, you *do* look as though you have more sense than most of those crazy lads in the cavalry, which is to say, not much. However, you have someone looking after you who has an excellent grasp of such things. I suggest you listen to her. You owe a debt of gratitude to Lady Althea, here, for your excellent and rapid recovery."

"Believe me, I owe her a great deal more than that."

The tone of his voice and the wealth of meaning in his eyes brought the color rushing to Althea's cheeks.

So that is the way it is, the surgeon thought as he left the room. *I knew there was more to this than met the eye. I hope he is worthy of her.*

Mr. Warboys would have been astounded to know that the marquess asked himself that very question a number of times in the ensuing days, for once he was able to be up and about, Gareth begged Althea's permission to accompany on her daily routine.

At first she was reluctant to share her life with him to that degree, but she was no proof against his pleading. "Please," he begged. "If I have to remain here in this room any longer, I shall die of boredom, and all your good work would be for naught. You would not wish to rescue a man and nurse him back to health only to have him fall into a decline through utter boredom. I know you must have a great deal to do for you have spent all your time attending me, away from your own duties."

The quirked eyebrow and crooked grin coaxed a reluctant smile from Althea. "Very well, sirrah, but no interfering, mind you. I realize that you know a great deal more about running an estate than I do, but the only way I am going to learn is by doing it on my own." Her tone was light, but the intensity of her expression warned him that she was very serious. This was her dream and she wished to succeed or fail on her own terms, with no assistance from anyone else.

Gareth respected her for that. No other woman he had met was ready to take such responsibility for her life, no other woman except, perhaps, Maria. But certainly he had never met a woman of his own class who did not automatically assume that it was some man's duty to look after her and provide for her happiness as well as her welfare.

Yes, he respected her fierce independence, but as the days wore on, he found it increasingly difficult to honor her command not to interfere, for the more he saw how hard Althea worked, the more he wanted to help her achieve everything she was striving for.

With his injured leg carefully protected by piles of pillows, the marquess was able to sit with Althea in her gig as she drove around the estate. He listened intently as she pointed out the fences she had had mended here, the drainage ditches that had been dug there, showed him the fields she was renting to this farmer and to that, the pastures she had turned over for common land and the small woods where she allowed the villagers to hunt and gather fuel for their fires. He heard the excitement in her voice and saw the glow of pride in her eyes as she shared her plans with him, and more than anything in the world he wanted to make it all happen as she planned, to protect her from all the inevitable small disasters and disappointments that occurred in the running of any enterprise the size of Kennington. At the same time, he respected her intelligence enough to be confident that she would be realistic enough to have prepared for these disasters and strong enough to deal with them when they came along.

Gareth had never found himself in such a quandary. He longed to help her, yet at the same time he was desperate for her to succeed on her own. He wanted to give her advice gleaned from his own experience, yet he wanted her to discover the joy and satisfaction that came from figuring things out for herself. He wanted to pour money into Kennington so she could have it restored immediately to the state she envisioned it in the future, but he wanted her to savor the pleasure of watching it grow and flourish over time through her own planning and hard work.

Tossing restlessly in bed at night after a day spent overseeing fields, fences, and tenant farmers, or having passed the day watching Althea bent over ledgers as she balanced accounts or pored over agricultural treatises, the marquess realized at last that it was not so much that he wanted to *do* it all *for* her, as he wished to be allowed to *share* it all *with* her. Lady Althea Beauchamp was planning everything as carefully and intelligently as the Marquess of Harwood ever could, expending as much attention on all the small details as he would, calculating, balancing, weighing all the factors as strategically and with as much foresight as he had ever brought to bear on any problem, and she was facing those problems and their inherent risks with the same boldness and the same calm courage that he would have mustered.

But even being allowed to share this with her was a very tricky business indeed, as he discovered one morning after breakfast. Althea's grandmother had disappeared into the library with the *Times* and Althea and the marquess were left in the breakfast room to enjoy the sunlight flooding in through the windows and the view across the green fields to the village in the distance.

"I am letting the fields I have not rented out lie fallow this year while I decide what I shall do with them," Althea replied to Gareth's unspoken question as he surveyed the landscape. "But I have almost decided that some of them will be turned over to the sheep, using Townshend's four-fold rotation system."

"Sheep!"

"Yes, sheep. What is wrong with that?"

The bristly tone should have warned him, but too intent on his thought process to pay complete attention, Gareth ignored it. "Well, it takes more capital at the outset to purchase the stock and hire a shepherd. Of course, one needs a thorough knowledge of livestock, and then there is the worry of their health, finding good shearers when the time comes, and . . ."

"And you do not think I am capable of such things?"

"No, no. I did not say that. But it would be far wiser at first to try a simple crop such as grain until you have acquired both the capital and the expertise to do the other."

Althea rose. "Naturally I appreciate your advice, my lord, but I have already determined to do things this way."

"Lady Althea, I beg . . ." Gareth grabbed his crutch and struggled awkwardly to his feet, but before he could rise, she had sailed from the room. "Blast!" he muttered, dropping back into his chair. "The girl is as obstinate and independent as . . . as . . ." *As I am,* he acknowledged to himself ruefully. Not only had she refused to listen to him, but it was quite clear from her clipped tones, squared shoulders, and raised chin, that she thoroughly resented his interference in something she was determined to do herself.

But the most upsetting aspect of the entire episode was the destruction of the understanding that had begun to spring up between them. Gareth did not see her again until dinner, which was a change in their routine because heretofore, she had sought out his company, checking on his leg, inquiring after the bump on his head, and staying to discuss whatever topic was occupying her mind at the moment. And at dinner, though she was pleasant enough to him, her conversation lacked its usual animation and her eyes were cold, devoid of the special warmth he had come to expect when she looked at him.

This coolness disturbed him more than he cared to admit. He had come to count on a firm hand helping him up and down, gentle fingers smoothing his hair as she checked the now almost invisible bump on his head. He missed the comforting closeness that, until Althea had begun nursing him, had been utterly lacking from his life. Gareth longed to get it back, but he did not know how. Any other woman would have been won over by a smile or an apology, but not Althea. He had not angered her as much as intruded into her life. She was not mad at him; she had simply retreated into herself to protect her privacy and independence.

The next day, however, luck was with him and the marquess was given an opportunity to retrieve his position. After breakfast, yet another meal where the conversation was confined to the superficial, he made his way to a bench on the terrace. Althea had gone off to write letters and Gareth, feeling uncomfortably at loose ends without her companionship, sought out a warm spot in the sun where he could smell the scent of spring flowers wafting on the occasional breeze, listen to the birdsongs rising from the meadow, and figure out what he was going to do next.

Mr. Warboys had pronounced him well enough to travel by the end of the week, providing that he promised to take the journey in easy stages and protect the leg well. Until now, Gareth had been loath to leave. He was enjoying Althea's company too much, more than he had ever enjoyed anyone else's before. Here, in her own element, the reserve with which she protected her privacy had vanished and she made an excellent and interesting companion. She was more open, honest, and forthright than any gentleman he had ever known, much less lady, and this made him relax in turn and open up to her as he had never opened up to another person. But now that openness was gone, and its loss saddened him, made him ready to leave.

Hurried footsteps and the rustle of paper broke into his reverie and Gareth looked up to see Althea striding along the terrace, angrily crumpling up what looked to be a letter. Seeing him, she came to a dead halt. A frown of annoyance clouded her expression and she turned to go.

"Lady Althea." Quick as a cat, Gareth caught her wrist and pulled her down on the bench beside him. She struggled in his grasp, but he was far too strong for her to free herself without an undignified struggle. "Please do not go. I wish to apologize for what must have seemed an intrusion into something that was none of my concern."

"There is no need to apologize, my lord. It is not an offense to offer advice."

"But it is not the way to show someone that you admire what they have accomplished and that you trust their intelligence and judgment enough to know they will accomplish more. It is just that listening to all your plans, I became so interested in the problems that I forgot they were not mine to solve. Certainly I would have resented anyone telling me what to do." He smiled ruefully. "And I would not have been so gracious as you were at calling it to my attention."

The smile, the light of understanding in his eyes, and the sincerity in his voice filled her with a warm feeling of happiness. So he *did* realize what he had done to annoy her. No one else, except possibly her grandmother, would have understood how important it was to her to know she could do it all on her own, that she did not need to depend on the care of anyone else to survive and flourish. Which brought to mind the letter that had sent her racing to the terrace in search of fresh air and sunlight to calm the anger that threatened to overwhelm her. She frowned and crumpled the paper tighter in her hands.

"If I were to guess, I would say that I was not the only one threatening to interfere with your plans."

"What? Oh, this." Althea looked at the wad of paper. "It is not unexpected. In fact, I am surprised that I had to wait this long. My father has discovered my whereabouts and I am pleased to report that he has disinherited me."

"Disinherited you, but why? Just because you left town to take over the management of an estate that was in crying need of repair?"

"Yes. But mostly he has cut me off because I disobeyed him. He is not accustomed to having his authority challenged, much less flouted. Actually, I am relieved that he cut me off. I was far more afraid that he might come to fetch me back." She tossed her head and laughed bitterly, but the sparkle of tears at the corners of her eyes told Gareth that she was hurt by it all the same.

"Of course he is not really disinheriting me, because Clarendon and all the rest of the Beauchamp lands were never mine in the first place. But he has declared me to be no child of his any longer. Naturally, my mother agrees with him and they have settled what was to be my dowry on a distant cousin. It is not that I am worried about it because I never wanted any of it anyway, not the brilliant marriage or the public life of someone who is wife to the wealthy, influential husband they would eventually choose for me, but I wish . . . I wish . . ." Her voice was suspended by tears.

"What do you wish?" Gently, he gathered her hands in his.

"I wish they had cared enough about me to try to understand and not to punish me for doing what I did. I tried to be the Beauchamp my father wanted. I learned everything about our estates. I studied the politics that were his life. I know how to ride and hunt as well as any son he could have had, but it was not enough even to win his attention for a moment. All he wanted was for me to bring him a son-in-law worthy of the family. I told him that I could run Clarendon for him, and for that fool Vivian who will inherit it when Papa dies. I told him he could count on me to see that Clarendon would remain a seat worthy of the Beauchamps, which it will not under Vivian's indifferent care. But he would not even listen to me." The tears were running unchecked now down cheeks that were pale with frustration and despair.

Gareth felt his own eyes stinging. He thought he had never seen anyone look so tragic. His heart aching for her and her hurt and loneliness, he pulled Althea gently into his arms.

She buried her face in his neck and wept as she had never wept before. All the longing for love and approval that she had never allowed herself to acknowledge came pouring out, as she clung to him, desperate for the strength and comfort he offered. She had never wanted the wealth, or the power, or the envy of the fashionable world. All she had ever wanted was for someone to see how hard she was trying to live up to what was expected of her. And she had lived up to almost all of it except for one thing—a brilliant marriage to a husband who would be chosen for her by two people who had not the least understanding of the person their daughter truly was. She had been the perfect accomplished young lady, the perfect mistress fulfilling all her duties on the estate where she grew up. She had struggled to cultivate her mind, to learn every housewifely accomplishment as well as its masculine counterpart in estate management, but to no avail. None of her efforts had been noticed, much less appreciated.

Helpless sobs racked her slender body as Gareth gently stroked her shining dark hair. He had never known a woman to cry so deeply, and he ached with the desire to comfort her. But he felt powerless in the face of such despair. What could he say that would make any of it less painful? He, too, knew the fury and the hurt of trying to satisfy a parent who would never be satisfied, for whom even the greatest of efforts would never be enough. But he had given up hoping for approval long ago, had given up caring about the good opinion of someone he had come to scorn. Althea had not given up, until now.

"Hush. My poor girl. You must stop crying or you will make yourself ill. Hush, Althea." He held her close, whispering into her silken hair, stroking her shaking shoulders until at last the sobs had subsided and she lay in his arms exhausted by her misery.

Gently he cupped her chin in one hand, forcing her to look up at him. "Of course you deserve better than that, Althea. You deserve the love and respect, the admiration of everyone who knows you and cares for you. But your parents do not know you. They never will. They have deprived themselves of that joy. But it does not mean that you are not valued for who you are by other people. For those who can truly appreciate you, you are the Angel of the Stable, a mistress who is bringing hope and prosperity to the countryside around her estate. I may be crippled for the moment, but I am not deaf, nor am I blind. I see the difference you have made in people's lives here. I hear the respect in their voices when they speak of you. No, you will never have the appreciation or understanding of your parents, but all on your own, without the benefit of your family connections, you have won the respect and appreciation of everyone around here, and that is no small thing."

A tremulous smile quivered on her lips. "I expect you are right. And I shall just have to be satisfied with that. The other was a dream, of course, a dream that would never have been realized even if I had done exactly what they asked. But I have done this for myself." She twisted in his arms to gaze with pride over the green fields stretching off into the distance.

"And Kennington"—he leaned forward to whisper in her ear—"is perfect for you. I am sorry that I took it from anyone, but I am glad you won it back again."

She did not answer, but leaned back against him and reached up to clasp one of the hands that was holding hers.

The last bit of constraint between them vanished and they sat quietly for some time, silent with their own thoughts but sharing the pain they both had suffered and the deeper understanding that had come along with it. At last she turned to him, her eyes soft with gratitude. "Thank you for understanding." She laid a finger on his lips as he opened his mouth to reply. "And thank you for being honest with me, for not pretending that in time my parents would come to understand me or care for my happiness. That is what a true friend would do." Then, still holding one of his hands in hers, she lifted it to her lips and kissed it. "Thank you, my true friend." Suddenly shy, she replaced his hand in his lap and hurried away.

Chapter 28

Too surprised to react, and hampered by his injured leg, Gareth remained glued to the bench staring at the hand in his lap, a tender smile curving his lips. It was rare that anyone thanked him, especially for something as intangible as sympathy and understanding. Knowing how much it must have cost her, he was doubly touched, first for her appreciation of his honesty and secondly for acknowledging it.

And who could have ever imagined that the Ice Princess would kiss a man's hand out of gratitude? But as quickly as he acknowledged her gratitude, Gareth admitted to himself that he wanted more than gratitude. With each passing day he wanted her, all of her, more than he could remember wanting even the most seductive of his mistresses.

The unwilling but magnetic attraction he had experienced the moment he saw her had only grown more powerful since he had become acquainted with her. He had hoped that after their kiss, the craving to touch her smooth, white skin, and feel her lips under his own would have been satisfied. How naive he had been. What had been simple desire before that kiss had become an ever-present hunger after it, and he found himself recalling their interlude in the most vivid and compelling detail several times a day. Instead of helping him put Althea out of his mind, that kiss had made him think of very little else.

It was time to get away, time to leave before he lost

his soul completely. At the same time, he really did not want to leave, did not want the idyll to end, for he had never been so happy in his life, so content just to enjoy life's simple pleasures.

The surgeon made up the marquess's mind for him when he visited the next day. "Well, my lord, I have to admit that I did not think you would follow my advice, but you have, and I would say that if you follow my instructions for your journey just as faithfully, you should be able to make it home in fine fettle. Keep your weight off the leg for another few weeks after that and you should be as good as new. No headaches or dizzy spells, eh?"

Gareth shook his head. The only dizziness he had experienced had nothing at all to do with his accident and everything to do with living in close proximity to a beautiful, desirable, and maddeningly independent woman.

"Good. Then I shall take my leave of you and wish you the best of luck." The surgeon shook the marquess's hand and then, nodding to Althea, hurried out the door.

She smiled at the surgeon and then turned back to Gareth. "I expect, then, that you are most eager to be on your way home now that Mr. Warboys has given his approval."

Was it only wishful thinking, or did he hear a wistful note in her voice? "Yes. I have been gone far too long, especially since I have a two-year-old who will be racing this year at Newmarket. Ditchley, my trainer, is a most excellent man, but it is time I was there to oversee things. What with the other horses in my stable that he is training as well, he has more than he can handle with the race fast approaching."

"And are you as successful at winning fortunes on the turf as you are in the card room?"

Gareth smiled and shook his head. "My horses are quite a different thing altogether. It is not so much the betting as the breeding, the raising, and the training, especially the training, that interests me. At the moment, what I have spent on building up my stables, purchasing bloodstock, and raising Apollo to fulfill his racing potential is many times over what I could possibly win."

The light in his eyes and the eagerness in his voice revealed to Althea yet another side of the Marquess of Harwood. Almost boyish in his enthusiasm as he admitted to this heretofore hidden passion, he seemed a very different man from the jaded gambler. It was obvious that horses and racing were his true interest in life, and Althea could not help feeling just the tiniest bit hurt that he had not revealed this side of himself to her before.

Of course, the moment she had lain eyes on his team, she knew that the marquess was a connoisseur of fine horseflesh. His concern for his team's welfare had only served to confirm the importance these animals held for him. But it was clear that they were a central part of his existence, and now, just as he was on the verge of departure, she was hearing about it for the first time.

Later, as she asked Mrs. Crowder to prepare a hamper for the marquess's upcoming journey, Althea reflected on how little she had actually learned about the marquess's life despite their many conversations. All the days they had spent together during his convalescence had been devoted to discussions of her hopes and dreams for Kennington. It had been such a luxury for her to have someone knowledgeable to talk to that she had rattled on like a regular jaw-me-dead. To be sure, she had always confided in her grandmother, but the marquess had more practical and recent experience to share with her than the dowager and, Althea admitted guiltily to herself, it was much more enlivening to share such things with an attractive man whose crooked grin and smiling eyes conveyed a wealth of appreciation and admiration such as she had never before experienced.

Althea had shared her life with him, but until this moment he had not shared much of his with her. This discovery, coupled with the thought of his imminent departure, made her feel oddly bereft.

Sitting on the terrace that evening, enjoying the golden haze cast by the setting sun, Gareth could not help noticing this somber mood and remarking on it, hoping against hope that his leaving was at least part of the cause for it. "You are unwontedly serious tonight, Lady

Althea. I should have thought that the prospect of ridding yourself of a troublesome guest and regaining control over not only your time, but your chambers, would be cause for celebration."

Too honest to admit to anything but the truth, Althea smiled a little sadly. "You are right. I will have more time to devote to my own projects, but I shall miss our conversations." *And I shall miss you,* her heart added.

Even though he knew how different she was from other women, Gareth had been expecting the standard coquettish denial, and he was unprepared for the effect of her simple reply. A lump rose in his throat as he looked down into her deep blue eyes, eyes that did not dissemble as so many others did but mirrored her every thought. Gently he took her hand in his. "And I shall miss you."

He longed to pull her to him, to kiss the slightly parted lips, to feel her heart beat against his, to share physically the intangible bond that drew them together wherever they were—ballrooms, card rooms, sickrooms, stables. But he knew if he began, he would not be able to stop with just a kiss.

Fighting for control, he stroked her slender fingers with his other hand. Did she want him as much as he wanted her? Sometimes he thought so. Sometimes as he had lain on his sickbed, eyes half closed, watching the expression on her face as she looked at him, he had thought he read more than simple concern for his welfare in her eyes. He had thought that he had seen the glow of desire flicker in them for a brief moment at least.

But perhaps he had only imagined it, an imagination fueled by his own longing. For he had definitely heard, more than once, the revulsion in her voice and seen the anger in her eyes when she had railed against the greedy, loathsome advances of her unwelcome suitors. Was he just another man to her, someone who threatened her independence and her peace of mind? His rational side told him that he was different from the others, that she trusted him, that she enjoyed his conversation and his company. At the same time, the intensity of his own desire made him unsure of anything, of everything. To someone who had established iron control over his own existence from the moment in his childhood when he had discovered the frailties and unreliability of his own parents, this dreadful state of uncertainty was as unwelcome as it was unusual. Perhaps, after all, he was glad to be leaving Kennington, glad to be returning to a life where he would once again be his own master.

"Come." He released her hand to strip off his coat and lay it across her shoulders. "The mist is beginning to rise, and I am sure you are beginning to feel the chill."

There was nothing for Althea to do but acquiesce. Untangling her skirt from one of the crutches that had slipped off the bench, she rose, pulling his coat more tightly around her as she reveled in the warmth and masculine scent that lingered in it. She sensed that he had been going to say something more, but then had thought better of it. What had he been going to say, or going to do? She almost hoped he would kiss her again, but then again, she was afraid of what her response would be.

In the past, it had been easy to avoid men's kisses. All she had had to do was see that look in their eyes and her stomach would knot in disgust, her body grow cold, and her face freeze into the disdainful expression that had won her the name the Ice Princess. But every time she saw that look in the marquess's eyes, she experienced an entirely different reaction; her face felt as though it were aflame, her bones melted, and her entire being ached with a hunger she did not dare think about, did not dare acknowledge, for fear of what would happen if she did.

It was a lucky thing for her peace of mind that he was going tomorrow, for without his constant presence to remind her of her feelings for him, surely she would stop continually wondering what it would be like to press not only her lips but her naked body to his.

Chapter 29

But as the marquess's recently repaired yellow curricle made its way slowly down the long gravel drive away from Kennington, both Gareth and Althea were beginning to suffer from second thoughts.

Althea was the first to sense the emptiness after Gareth had left. When he had first arrived as a patient in her home, when all her healing skills were truly needed, she had fretted over the other duties she had been unable to attend to as she remained sitting watch at his bedside. Later, when he had been able to be up and about, and she actually had the opportunity to return to those duties, she realized that whatever had originally seemed so pressing while she was preoccupied with nursing him had either dwindled into unimportance or been handled by Mrs. Crowder, Jenny, and her grandmother. Of course, once the marquess had been well enough to view the estate and ask questions about it, she had managed to let entire hours of time slip by without noticing or regretting it. Later on she would take herself to task for not accomplishing all that she planned to do each day, but would find herself indulging in the luxury of another such conversation the very next day.

Finally, she had given up feeling guilty altogether, promising herself that she would work twice as hard once the marquess was gone. But now he was gone and, somehow, she no longer had the energy for tackling any of the projects she had set aside in order to enjoy the marquess's company. Now, freed from his distracting presence, Althea found herself simply going through the motions of these tasks in a most desultory fashion. She would stare at columns of figures without seeing them for hours on end or listen to reports from Jem, Mrs. Crowder, or Mr. Duckworth without hearing a word they uttered. And all the while, at the back of her mind, she would be recalling what Gareth had said about this, or the look in his eyes as he had commented on that, remembering over and over again the strength of his arms around her, the warmth of his lips on hers, and the light in his eyes that made her feel understood, appreciated, and important.

She told herself that it was just a normal reaction to unusual circumstances. She had never had to care for anyone as she had cared for the marquess. No one had ever needed her or depended on her as he had. Naturally, she had felt close to him, and now it was taking time to readjust after the pressure of the added responsibility. She told herself that what felt like emptiness was simply exhaustion from nursing the marquess coupled with the worry over his recovery. Once she had gotten some rest, she would feel much more the thing, and her natural energy and enthusiasm were bound to return.

But deep in her heart, Althea knew that fatigue was not at the root of her strange lethargy. True, she had been working harder than ever before, even before the marquess's arrival, and caring for him had only added to her work, but she had also felt more alive and active than ever before, more ready to take on anything, and she knew that it was his presence that had inspired her.

All her life, Althea had longed to be on her own, in control of her own destiny, with no one telling her what to do. But just when she was beginning to enjoy that hard-won freedom, the marquess had reappeared in her life to prove her utterly and completely wrong. Now she knew that a life shared was a life richer and more fulfilling than any life she spent alone, no matter how much she worked, no matter how much she studied or tried to improve her mind.

There was nothing to do but force herself to think of

Kennington and the people who had come to depend o
her, to remember that running her own establishmen
had been her dream long before the Marquess of Har
wood had appeared on the scene. It would be her drear
again. All she had to do was to concentrate on that an
forget about Gareth de Vere and the way his gray eye
glinted when he was amused or how his mouth crooke
into a sardonic smile that included her in his ironic viev
of the world. All she had to do was to forget the wa
he made her feel whenever he was near her—breathless
alive, filled with a tantalizing longing. All she had to d
was forget that he had offered understanding, suppor
and a genuine enthusiasm for what she wanted to d
with her life.

Surely he would write, just to let her know that h
had arrived safely and that his recovery had not bee
affected by his journey?

Althea had no idea how strong this hope was, but th
dowager, observing her granddaughter looking eagerl
down the drive several times a day in the hopes of seein
a messenger, knew precisely how much she longed fo
some word from the marquess. The dowager did too
Even in London, she had sensed a bond between th
marquess and her granddaughter. She had been disap
pointed that Althea's skill at cards had won her so
quickly the longed-for prize of her own estate and re
moved her from the marquess's fascinating influence
During their card games, Althea's grandmother had no
been too immersed in the play to miss the gleam of admi
ration in her granddaughter's eyes every time their oppo
nent captured a trick. Nor had she missed the way a
clever sally on his part coerced Althea into uncharacteris
tic laughter. There had never been any doubt in the dow
ager's mind that two people who had been isolated from
the rest of the world by their own cleverness were now
reveling in the discovery of another person equally as
clever who could offer both appreciation and challenge

When Althea had exclaimed over the coincidence tha
had caused the Marquess of Harwood to suffer an acci
dent at their very gates, the dowager had smiled slyly and

kept her own counsel. She knew that men like Gareth de Vere did not frequent country roads in a sporting curricle on a whim. If the Marquess of Harwood was driving by Kennington Park, it was because he knew very well where he was and very well who now lived at Kennington Park. In fact, the dowager was willing to hazard a guess that he had been investigating the estate now owned by Lady Althea Beauchamp, if not planning to visit it, when the mishap had occurred.

The period of the marquess's convalescence had only strengthened the bond between him and her granddaughter. More times than she could count, the dowager had interrupted silent exchanges of understanding passing between the two of them. She had witnessed the tenderness with which Althea watched over the injured man, and the way his eyes sought her out whenever she was in the room. And more than once the dowager had been surprised to see a look in those eyes that could almost have been called reverence. The Dowager Duchess of Clarendon was willing to bet the very fine Beauchamp diamonds not yet ceded to her daughter-in-law that the Bachelor Marquess had never looked at another woman so worshipfully, so longingly, in his entire life as he looked at Althea.

But nothing had come of this extremely promising situation and now he was gone, leaving the dowager to await word of him as eagerly as her granddaughter did. Watching Althea forcing herself to concentrate on her daily tasks, the dowager felt for her granddaughter's suffering. She longed to reassure Althea that the marquess would be back. Years of experience and observation told her that he would return, but it was clear that Althea was doing her best to avoid all mention of the marquess, that the unexpected pain of missing him made her all the more eager to forget him, all the more eager to wipe all memory of him from her life as quickly and thoroughly as possible. So the dowager kept silent and bided her time.

Was the marquess suffering equally from the loss of her granddaughter's companionship? Althea's grandmother wondered. She hoped he was, but in general gentlemen had far more resources at their disposal and considerably more distractions to take their minds of upsetting reflections than females did.

Both the dowager and her granddaughter would have been gratified to learn that while Gareth was less quick than Althea to come to the realization that he had left a very important part of his life back at Kennington, he too was suffering from the same disturbing second thoughts and sober reflections as she was.

When he eventually reached Harwood, Gareth was faced with a mountain of correspondence and questions from his agent that had been held in abeyance until his return. At first this pile of work and his tendency to tire easily after his accident, kept him too occupied to pay attention to anything except the tasks before him. However, the second week of his return, as the marquess was digging out the last letter from the pile to be read and answered, he was suddenly struck by the purposelessness of it all.

Why am I doing this? he wondered. And for whom?

Gareth mulled these questions over that evening as he sat alone at dinner staring into the fire, absentmindedly spearing peas on his plate. Unlike most, if not all his acquaintances, he had always been a thoughtful individual who sought out the reasons for things, the explanation behind them. But he had never, until now, questioned the reasons for his own existence.

Now it all seemed so very empty. Yes, he had rebuilt Harwood and repaired all the damage caused by his father's neglect and his mother's expensive and insatiable appetite for fashion and luxury. Yes, he wished to build the best stables for his horses and provide the best breeding and the best training for these animals that he loved and admired. But still the question remained. Why? What did it matter? Who cared what he accomplished?

For years Gareth had sought only to live up to the standards he had set for himself, but now, suddenly, that was not enough. He took a drink of wine and then another and another. He knew very well what he thought of himself and what he was trying to accomplish. What did she think?

That unnerving question remained with him all the next day as he watched Apollo and his trainer going through their paces, as he inspected the new mare he hoped to breed with Apollo, as he drove his curricle around Harwood surveying fences and pastures, cottages and outbuildings in much the same way he had surveyed Kennington not long ago with Althea. Would she approve of the improvements he had made to his tenants' cottages? Would she admire the fat, fluffy sheep grazing contentedly in the rich green pastures? Would she notice the thought and care he had put into the design of his stables?

In fact, Gareth spent more time picturing her at his side, her eyes alight with interest and enthusiasm, than he did concentrating on his duties, and when he finally returned home that evening, he welcomed the chance to retire to the library to write the letter he had been composing in his mind all day.

Initially, he had meant only to send word that he had arrived safely and to thank her again for her care and her hospitality. But as he had tried the message out first in his mind, seeking just the right words to convey how much it had meant to him, without making her feel that he was being was too effusive, the short note of thanks had somehow grown into a lengthy epistle telling her all about Harwood and asking her for details about her projects at Kennington.

By the time Gareth finally sat down to write, his head was bursting with several pages worth of communication to be put on paper. But at least the transcribing of all these thoughts eased the hollow feeling of loneliness that had been nagging him since he had driven away from Kennington. And as the ink flowed onto the paper, he could picture her reading the letter, smiling at his assertions that Ajax and Achilles were quite bad tempered now that they no longer had the Angel of the Stable attending to their every need. He cherished the thought that her hand would be holding the paper where his now rested. How simple and sentimental the thought was, but how true.

Writing to her almost felt like speaking to her. And as he filled one page and moved on to the next, Gareth realized how much he missed just talking to Althea.

No, he thought later as he lay in bed staring at the ceiling and remembering the comforting way she had plumped his pillow and smoothed his coverlet, it was not her conversation he missed. He missed her. Achingly and longingly, he missed her.

And what was he to do with himself until he saw her again? When would he see her again? What could he do to ensure that he did see her again, for she would never reappear in London, and he could not be forever having curricle accidents at her front door.

Chapter 30

Oddly enough, it was a remark of Ibthorp's two days later that suggested the solution to this last question. The marquess had set aside that day for the annual consultation with Mr. Wilkins, the veterinary surgeon who not only examined all his horses, but also advised him on the optimal conditions for their care and feeding. It was Ibthorp who suggested that the surgeon not only examine the racehorses, but also the marquess's recovering team. Gareth had made the acquaintance of Mr. Wilkins in the Peninsula where the young man, fresh out of training, had been assigned as the veterinary surgeon to Gareth's regiment. There was something about the man's calm demeanor even in the most horrific of situations that had soothed and reassured everyone around him, men and animals alike, and it had not taken Gareth long to realize that Mr. Wilkins was not only a skilled surgeon, but also a natural healer whose presence kept many a tense moment from turning into a disaster.

Mr. Wilkins, in turn, had been drawn to the young cavalry officer who, no matter how weary or in how much pain himself, had always taken the time to see to it personally that his animals were well fed, watered, rubbed down, and made as comfortable as possible in all weathers and all conditions. All cavalry officers were concerned for their mounts' welfare as a matter of course—a soldier was only as good as the horse he rode—but this particular officer had been unusually devoted, making sure of his horses' emotional as well as physical well-being. Wilkins, who firmly believed that the mental state of man or animal was key to its physical state, had become friends with the young officer and taught him all that he could about equine physiology and diseases.

After Gareth had left his regiment, he had kept in touch with the veterinary surgeon, and when he had begun to think about breeding racehorses, he had tried to convince Wilkins to leave the regiment and work for him. The young surgeon had appreciated the offer and the trust and confidence that lay behind it, but he had regretfully declined for the simple reason that he felt his skills were more needed in a regiment whose quarters and whose needs were subject to the varied fortunes of the cavalry and the whims of politics than they were needed in a stable where the welfare of its inhabitants was the owner's prime concern. He had, however agreed to pay a yearly visit of inspection.

Gareth always looked forward to this visit, but now it took on even more importance when, prompted by Ibthorp's suggestion and the surgeon's obvious surprise at seeing the marquess with a cane, he realized he had a favor to ask. "Yes, Wilkins, as you can see, I had a bit of a mishap in my curricle," he said in response to the surgeon's query about his cane. "I believe that I suffered the worst of it, but Ajax and Achilles did receive a few minor cuts and scrapes. I would appreciate it if you could take a look at them as well."

The surgeon examined the injured legs on both animals, who fretted nervously under his observation. "Yes, I can see they were a bit cut up, but they seem to be recovering nicely." He patted Achilles' shining neck. "Nor do they seem the worse for wear, as high-spirited as ever and not the least upset by the affair."

"That is because they had superior care," Ibthorp volunteered. As Gareth's former batman, Ibthorp was almost as familiar with Mr. Wilkins as his master and, having been the one to greet the surgeon upon his arrival at Harwood, was now accompanying the two men on their visit to the marquess's team. "By a right proper young lady who appears to be almost as gifted as yourself, sir."

"Oh?" The surgeon raised a curious eyebrow, but he was less taken aback by the servant's assertion than he was by the master's reaction. He watched in some surprise as a flush stained the marquess's high cheekbones and a self-conscious look stole into his eyes.

"He is referring to Lady Althea Beauchamp who, as you can see from my own recovery, is skilled at nursing both humans and animals. I was completely unconscious for several days after the accident, and my leg was badly broken, yet you see me now before you almost completely unaffected by the unfortunate incident."

Mr. Wilkins was inclined to disagree with his former military companion. As far as the marquess's physical health was concerned, it was clear that he was recovering magnificently, but there was an almost regretful sadness, a loneliness in those gray eyes that had never been there before. This Lady Althea might have completely restored him physically, but emotionally she had obviously left a significant impression.

"She is a great deal like yourself, sir, begging your pardon, sir, but she has that same sort of magic." Ibthorp refused to let the topic drop. He had been observing his master's curious lethargy for some time and had arrived at the conclusion that there was only one remedy for it— Lady Althea Beauchamp. Being the loyal servant he was, he had developed a plan to improve his master's state of mind and was now putting that plan in effect, covertly of course, but with all the energy he could muster.

"A rare young woman, indeed, this Lady Althea, if Ibthorp is to be believed," the surgeon remarked later that evening as the men drank a convivial glass of brandy in front of the fire in the library.

"Oh, Ibthorp is correct enough, all right. With his own eyes he saw Ajax and Achilles greeting her more eagerly than they ever did me, and submitting to her tending their injuries as meekly as lambs. What he did not see was her beating me soundly at both whist and piquet, soundly enough to win a snug little estate from me."

"Beat you, Gareth, at cards?" The surgeon smiled and shook his head in disbelief. "She must be a very clever young lady, indeed."

"There is not the least doubt about that. A more formidable opponent it has never been my pleasure to encounter. She has a mind that absorbs and remembers every detail, and a spirit bold enough to take advantage of her opponent's slightest weakness."

"Along with a heart gentle enough to bring comfort and healing to both high-spirited animals and men. A remarkable woman indeed."

"Yes. A remarkable woman who has struggled to become the remarkable person that she is, virtually on her own, with no help from anyone."

"Come, now, Gareth. Even I, uninterested as I am in these things, am aware that Lady Althea Beauchamp is the only child of the Duke of Clarendon and, if rumor has it correctly, is the darling of the *ton*, not to mention the Season's most eligible heiress."

"You are entirely correct in saying that she has been born with all the advantages of family and fortune that a generous Providence could bestow, but she did not receive those gifts for which she longed the most, appreciation and understanding."

"Both of which you have taken it upon yourself to supply."

Gareth grinned. "You were always too clever by half, Wilkins, but yes, I do wish to shower her with whatever her heart desires. And though she does not know it yet, she wishes to become a veterinarian, perhaps not a surgeon such as you, but at least more skilled than she is now in the art of healing. Of course, no woman could attend the Royal Veterinary College, but she could be an apprentice to someone like you and she might learn just as much that way."

"She could," Wilkins agreed evenly enough, but his eyes were bright with speculation, "and then what?"

"And then, since she lives a good deal closer to Harwood than you do, she could look in on my horses on a more regular basis. Of course, I would still continue to consult with you, but I intend to grow the racing stock at Harwood to such an extent that it will eventually require more attention than your annual visits can give, thorough though they may be."

"Ah." Enlightenment dawned in the surgeon's face. Personally, he thought that what his old friend was angling for here was a wife, not a veterinarian, but that was something he would have to discover on his own. "Naturally the lady must be busy with her own estate, but if, during the winter months when both she and I will be less busy, she can spare the time to visit me and to study, I think something might be arranged—if she is interested."

"Thank you, Wilkins. I knew I could rely on you. I guarantee that you will not be disappointed in her."

"Disappointed in a woman approved of by the Bachelor Marquess? I highly doubt it."

Gareth went to bed that night in a better frame of mind than he had been since leaving Kennington. It was Ibthorp's mention of Lady Althea that had set him thinking about it, but the idea of improving his stables and helping Althea develop her natural gift at the same time had been all his own. He could not wait to add this news to his letter.

No. He could not wait for the news to reach her in a letter. Letters were too slow. He wanted to see her face when he told her of his idea. He would deliver his own letter, tell her of his wonderful plan, tomorrow.

Entering the marquess's chamber with his coffee the next morning Ibthorp was astonished to discover his master up, freshly shaved and dressed, and in better spirits than he had seen him in some time.

"You were correct, Ibthorp, when you spoke so admiringly of Lady Althea's care for the team. She does have a talent, and it would be a dreadful shame to have that talent wasted. I have spoken to Mr. Wilkins about it and he has agreed to teach her all that he can."

"Excellent, sir. That should please the lady very much, sir, I would think."

"I think so too. The moment Mr. Wilkins leaves this

morning, I intend to drive over to Kennington to lay the plan before the lady myself."

And bring back a bit of the spirit that has gone out of you since you bade her good-bye, Ibthorp added silently as he turned away to hide a triumphant smile.

Chapter 31

So it was that later that day, Althea, looking out from the window at the top of the stairs in the hopes that she might see a messenger bearing news of the marquess's safe return, saw the marquess himself bowling down the drive in his curricle.

"Gracious," she squeaked, pulling off the apron she had donned that morning to help Jenny air some of the spare bedchambers. She raced back to her own chamber where she tried to tidy up before the looking glass, tucking in stray locks of hair and wiping a smudge off her nose. Never one to linger long before the glass, she suddenly found herself most discontented with her looks on this particular day. Her nose really was far too long and there were dark circles under her eyes. She looked pale and drawn. Why had she not noticed before how tired she looked?

"My lady. My lady. His lordship is here!" In her excitement, Jenny burst into her mistress's chamber without even stopping to knock. Like the dowager, the maid had also cherished high hopes for the marquess and her mistress, hopes that had been dashed when he had driven off toward his own estate, what felt like ages ago. But now he was back, and from the sparkle in her mistress's eyes and the slight flush rising in her cheeks, the maid could see that Lady Althea was already aware of his arrival.

"Thank you, Jenny. Show his lordship to the library and see that he is offered some refreshment. Inform him that I shall be with him directly." Drawing on years of rigorous training, Althea tried her best to smile serenely and appear utterly unconcerned, but her heart was thudding so hard it was difficult for her to breathe and her knees felt extremely uncertain.

Why was he here? What could he have possibly come for? And how could she have longed for his return as much as she was now discovering that she had?

If Althea thought her pulses became disordered and her knees grew weak at the sight of the marquess's curricle, it was nothing to what they became when she entered the library and found him smiling down at her with that special light in his eyes and that quizzical lift of one dark brow.

"My-my lord." She hated herself for stammering, especially when she saw that his smile broadened as she stumbled over the words. She would have felt a great deal better if she had known that seeing her again Gareth was overwhelmed, as always, by his powerful attraction to her, an attraction that made his mouth go so dry he could not even speak, much less stammer a response to her greeting.

"I am delighted to see that you are continuing your excellent recovery." Althea nodded to the cane that he was managing to use in place of the crutches.

"What? Oh, yes, that. I had intended to write you about it and to say that I had reached Harwood safely, but there was so much to do, so many pressing things to attend to that I never . . ."

"There was no need to write. I quite understand, I assure you." But why was he here now? Could it be that he had missed her company as much as she had missed his?

"Althea." She looked so lovely standing there, those amazing dark-fringed eyes shining bluer than he even remembered, that he almost forgot why he had come. God, she was beautiful! God, he had missed her! "I beg your pardon. I mean *Lady* Althea. I came because I have just had a most singular idea. My friend Wilkins, the veterinary surgeon attached to my old regiment, has agreed to take you on as a student. And once you become sufficiently skilled you can replace him in looking after my horses." In his eagerness to share his wonderful plan, he blurted it out without any sort of explanation or preparation.

"I can what?" Althea felt as though he had thrown a bucket of cold water over her. She hoped he had come simply to visit her, simply to see how she was doing, or, at the very least, because he had been thinking about her as much as she had been thinking about him—every day and every hour that they had been apart. She hoped he had come because he had discovered that he was as lonely without her as she was without him. But no, he had come because he did not trust her to manage her own life. He did not trust her to manage the estate well enough to be successful—the estate she had been clever enough to win from him—so he had come to arrange her life for her.

"That is most thoughtful of you, my lord, but I believe I have shown myself capable enough of looking after my own welfare that I do not need anyone else's assistance." Her voice was brittle and her eyes as cold as the ice that had given her her nickname.

"No, Althea. You do not understand. It is because you have such a gift, because my own horses prefer your care to mine, because there is a magic in you that I have never seen in anyone, except possibly Wilkins, that I had this idea. I do not wish to arrange your life, but it seems a terrible waste if you become so involved in running your own estate that this talent of yours is not given the chance to develop to its full potential."

"Just as terrible a waste as the *ton*'s most eligible heiress retiring to the country to live out her days in rustic spinsterhood. I thought that you, unlike my parents, cared for my happiness, but now I see that you are no different from them, except that you are possibly more clever. Good day to you, my lord." Althea swept from the room and slowly, deliberately, climbed the stairs, praying all the way that she would not dissolve into tears before she reached the privacy of her own bedchamber.

"Althea, no." But it was too late. Not only had he not convinced her of the brilliance of his plan, he had now destroyed all hope of seeing her again. Biting his lip in anger and despair, Gareth walked back to his curricle and headed for home, to emptiness and loneliness, to a life that had suddenly lost all interest for him.

He had barely cleared the stone gateposts at the end of the drive and sprung his team when he reined them in again. She was right. He *was* trying to arrange her life, but not for the same reasons her parents were. They had been doing it out of vanity and pride. He was doing it out of desperation, because he wanted her to be with him. Because he loved her.

Trying to control his rising excitement, Gareth carefully turned around his team. Who was he trying to fool? He did not want Althea as his veterinarian; he wanted her as his wife! And if he had not been so intent on laying his plan before her, he would have told her that he had come up with the plan because he missed her, because he was seeking a reason for her to be at Harwood. Surely she had missed him as much as he had missed her. After all, she had been happy to see him when he first arrived, had she not? She had been happy until he had blurted out his plans for her future.

Gareth racked his brains trying to recall the look in her eyes when she first entered the library, the expression on her face. Damn! If only he had not been as nervous as a schoolboy at the prospect of seeing her again, too nervous to read the signs that the Bachelor Marquess had always been able to read in every other woman's eyes. But he had been. And now he did not know if the signs had been there or if he had just been hoping desperately that they were.

This time it was the dowager and not her granddaughter who saw the curricle coming back down the drive. Having heard Jenny announce the marquess's arrival the first time, the dowager had taken up a strategic position in her own bedchamber where she could hear voices in the library and look out over the drive. She had witnessed the curricle slowly departing, heard the door to her granddaughter's chamber shut more firmly than usual, and her heart had sunk. But now, the curricle was returning. Surely such indecision could not be indicative of anything but love.

Smiling slyly, she hurried down to make sure that she was the one who answered the door. "Good day, my lord," she greeted the astonished marquess. "You are surprised to see me at the door. Surely you know how little we stand on ceremony here. Do let me call my granddaughter. She will be delighted to know that you are here, so dull and cross as she has been without you here to amuse her."

There! That should show the man which way the wind blows. And almost hugging herself with glee, the dowager hurried off in search of her granddaughter.

"But, Grandmama, I am not feeling quite the thing. You entertain the marquess," Althea protested when informed of the astounding news that, not content with accepting her rejection of him and his plan, the Marquess of Harwood had had the nerve to return.

"What, tell the marquess that the woman who had the temerity to win an estate from him at cards is too missish to admit that she is glad to see him? That she has suffered the megrims since the moment he departed?"

"Grandmother! You would not say such a thing! Besides, it is not true."

"Is it not? Not only could I say it, I will say it if you do not go down to him yourself. It is as plain as the nose on his face that the Marquess of Harwood as been as blue-deviled as you have been since he left. Now hurry along and tell him that you have missed him before I tell him myself."

Thus it was that, hastily checking herself in the looking glass for the second time that day, Althea half reluctantly, half hopefully, descended again to the library where Gareth was pacing back and forth as fast as his injured leg would allow.

"Althea." He limped forward, his expression very different from the one he had worn before. Now it was tense and pale, and, Althea could not quite believe it, but he looked uncertain.

"My lord."

"I beg your pardon. I went about things all wrong before. But it was because . . . because . . ."

"It was not a question of *how* you went about them, it was . . ."

"It was because I missed you so desperately."

Althea felt her defenses beginning to crumble. She tried to rally the last remnants of her anger to protect herself—against she knew not what—against the desperate urge to throw her arms around him and welcome him back.

"I said it all wrong. I tried to tell it to you all at once so I could convince you to say yes, so that you would come to visit me at Harwood, so I could count on seeing you again. But I got it all wrong, and I misled you. I misled myself."

"I had hoped that . . ."

"I love you."

"You what?"

"I love you, Althea. I always have. Since the moment I saw you at Lady St. John's rout. I thought that I loathed you. I wanted to loathe you as I loathe incomparables like my mother, like your mother, selfish women who know the power of their own charms and use it without conscience. I thought you were one of those women. But I could not hate you. You were so damned beautiful, so aloof, so pure, and so unimpressed by your own beauty that I could not help myself. I was drawn to you and I could not stay away in spite of myself. I have never been able to stay away from you, not then, not when you left London, not now. I cannot live without you. I do not want to live without you. I want you to be my wife."

Wordlessly, Althea sank down onto the sofa. All she had wished for was to hear him acknowledge that he had missed her. She had not expected *this,* did not know how to react to this.

Carefully, Gareth lowered himself next to her on the

sofa and cupped her chin in his hands. Gently he brushed his lips against hers until they parted beneath his. Slowly he slid his hands down her neck, caressing the warm column of her throat before burying his fingers in her hair and pulling her to him until he felt the quiver of her response. All his pent-up desire broke as he devoured the warm, soft flesh he had longed for for what had seemed like forever. He had wanted her so desperately, for so long, that his hands trembled as he pulled her into his arms and lay back against the pillows of the sofa.

He looked down at her, her eyes half closed, her cheeks flushed with desire, and he ached with the beauty, the promise, the longing of the moment.

Slowly Althea's senses stopped reeling. At the first touch of his lips, the quivering that had taken control of her the moment she saw him seemed to explode into a chaos of sensations—touch, taste, scent, heat, and longing. All she wanted was to feel her flesh against his, to satisfy the ache of loneliness that had tormented her since he had gone. But now, looking up at him, at his eyes blazing with an intensity she had never seen, she was afraid, afraid of losing herself to this overwhelming desire to become part of him, never to let go ever again. What would this do to her newfound independence? If she allowed herself to give in to this longing, would she ever have control over her own life again?

But she wanted him. She wanted his love. She wanted the life he offered to share with her. And she wanted her own independence It was all too much. She must be strong. She must not give in now. Her eyes filled with tears.

"What is it, my love? What is wrong? Have I hurt you?" Instantly and intently aware of her change in mood, he searched her face for some clue to the uncertainty he read in her eyes.

"Gareth, please. I cannot."

"Cannot what, my love? Just tell me. I will do anything."

"I am afraid."

A slow, tender smile spread across his lips. "So am I. We are a rare couple, you and I—the Ice Princess and the Bachelor Marquess. We value nothing so much as our own independence; is that not true?" He raised one quizzical brow.

He did understand. A wave of relief and gratitude washed over her.

"I promise you that I shall try to protect your independence as vigorously as I have protected my own all these years. But what I have discovered recently, to my utmost chagrin, is that without you independence is merely loneliness and not worth protecting. But I swear to you I will not try to influence you in your management of Kennington if you promise not to take over the management of Harwood, which I very much fear you will once its inhabitants come to love you as Kennington's inhabitants love you. After all, my horses already mind you better than they mind me."

Althea gave a watery chuckle. "You make it all sound so remarkably simple, but I know such things are not simple."

The teasing smile vanished as he gathered her hands in his. "Althea, in my heart I know that this is the love I longed for all my life but never found. In spite of what my heart says, my head tells me that it is too good to be true. Which should I believe, my heart or my head? It is an enormous risk for you. It is an enormous risk for me. But we are both gamblers, Althea, ready to take enormous risks to win enormous prizes in the end. Please, Althea, say you will share your life with me."

She thought for a moment, but her heart already knew the answer. "Yes, Gareth, I will."

He kissed her for a long, breathless moment. When at last he drew away he looked down at her, his eyes alight with tender laughter. "Unfortunately, my love, in your bid for independence and control over your own life, you have fulfilled your parents' fondest wishes and contracted an eligible alliance after all. Of course, the de Veres may not be as wealthy or as powerful as the Beauchamps, but my family is certainly as ancient and illustrious as yours. However, I do beg of you not to let a such a small thing as parental approval stop you from becoming my true love and my beloved wife."

Althea chuckled. "I promise you, Gareth, I will not . . ." But she was allowed to say no more as his lips again closed over hers.

Chapter 32

*I*t was not until the deepening dusk brought Jenny in to light the candles that they broke apart.

"Begging your pardon, my lady, but I thought you might wish some light. And shall I send Sam in to lay a fire?"

"Do come in, Jenny." Althea, still clasped in Gareth's arms, smiled at her maid. "Jenny, I am to be married."

"Yes, my lady. I know."

"You know?"

"Her Grace told me."

"Grandmama told you that?"

"Yes, my love." Gareth chuckled at his betrothed's expression of utter astonishment. "Though I am loath to break it to you, it appears that your grandmother saw the truth of it all long before you did—that you and I are meant for each other. Had you not agreed to become my beloved wife, you would have had her protests to contend with as well as mine."

"Oh." Althea digested this piece of information for a moment. "In fact, then, this choice of mine is no choice at all, but a conspiracy of . . ."

"Hush, my love." The marquess put a finger to her lips. "Your grandmother saw, and very rightly, that we could not live without each other. Nor do I wish to do so for a moment longer than I have to. The truth of it is that I am so eager to begin our life together that I shall continue on to London from here to speak to your father so we can be married here at Kennington as soon as possible."

"Papa, and Mama?" Althea grimaced in a most unladylike fashion. "They will never . . ."

"Trust me, sweetheart, I shall make them come around. After all, I have been dealing with my mother for years, and she is far less reasonable than your parents are."

"Your mother, at least, should be pleased."

"Oh, she will be pleased, well enough." Gareth chuckled bitterly. "Until she realizes that our marrying will make her the Dowager Marchioness of Harwood. Being a dowager is not quite in my mother's style, especially when the daughter-in-law is an incomparable of incomparables, a diamond who won far greater acclaim in the *ton* than she ever did."

"Oh, dear." Althea maintained a straight face, but her eyes were dancing with suppressed amusement.

"Exactly." He grinned in return. "The vanity of an aging beauty is a tricky thing, very tricky indeed."

"Perhaps Lord Battisford?"

"I quite agree with you, love. As I see it, Lord Battisford's days as a widower are numbered. Now, that is enough of such unpleasant prospects. Let us begin happily by telling your grandmother of our plans."

The dowager had no need for an announcement. One look at their happy faces and fond glances at dinner that evening told her all she needed to know. She was reminded of her own dear Harry and of happier days when she too had had someone with whom to share her life. "I can wish nothing more for you two than that you may have the same joy in each other that Harry and I did." She beamed happily at both of them as she helped herself to a hefty portion of roast veal. The past months at Kennington had made her feel ten years younger, and now, seeing her granddaughter's face alight with love and happiness, she felt younger than that, as young, if not younger than her own daughter-in-law. The dowager chuckled at the thought. "Lord, I would give a monkey to see your mother's face, Althea, when she hears the news."

The dowager was correct; the Duchess of Clarendon's

face was something to behold several days later when her husband called her into the library to inform her that he had just given the Marquess of Harwood permission to marry their daughter.

"You what!" Astonishment gave way to annoyance as the duchess struggled to maintain her customary air of well-bred composure. It was aggravating in the extreme to discover that she had not even been part of such a momentous discussion. After all, she had been the mastermind behind her daughter's Season—arranging numerous trips to the milliners, spending hours closeted with dressmakers, seeking introductions to the most illustrious members of the *ton* and avoiding those of inferior reputation. And now the intensive and elaborate campaign was ended, just like that, without anyone even consulting with her. "But the man is never seen in the *ton*, if he can help it, nor is he intimate with the sort . . ."

"He frequented the *ton* enough to meet Althea," her husband pointed out reasonably enough.

But this infallible logic only served to infuriate the duchess even more. "And I positively will *not* endure the encroaching manners of that . . . that *mushroom!*"

"What mushroom?"

"The Marchioness of Harwood!"

The duke raised his eyebrows in mild surprise. "Do try to calm yourself, my dear. She is a de Vere after all and while the de Veres, naturally, are not so illustrious as the Beauchamps, they are almost as ancient a family and nearly as respected. At any rate, it is a great deal better than no marriage at all, and infinitely superior to having a daughter whose whereabouts are a mystery. They are to be married at Kennington, which, it appears, Reggie settled on Althea before haring off to India in that ridiculous fashion."

"Kennington! Married at Kennington! Have you completely lost your senses, my lord? *You* may have given your permission for our daughter to marry some . . . some . . . Well, at any rate, *you* may have given your permission, but *I* will not allow a daughter of mine to be married anywhere except St. George's, and certainly not in some hole-in-the-corner fashion in some village church." The duchess sniffed loudly and turned on her heel only to be stopped by her husband's next words.

"Harwood informed me in no uncertain terms that it is their wish to be married at Kennington. Believe me, the man was quite definite about it." The duke fiddled uneasily with the silver letter opener on his desk as he recalled Gareth's exact words. *All her life Althea has asked for very little and worked very hard to live up to what was expected of her. It is time that those who demanded so much of her give her something in return.* There had been no mistaking the tone in the marquess's voice. The duke, despite his exalted station, his years, and his illustrious lineage, had recognized the voice of command, and acquiesced.

"I will not be seen . . ."

"And we shall make a journey to Kennington in order to see the thing properly done," her husband continued, utterly ignoring his wife's outraged expression.

Elsewhere in town, the news was received with precisely the mixed emotions that Gareth had predicted. "Congratulations, my dear. Of course I *knew* she was the one for you the moment she made her appearance. Nothing but an incomparable of incomparables would do for my only son. After all"—the Marchioness of Harwood turned to smiled coquettishly at Lord Battisford, who had come to escort her to the exhibition at the Royal Academy—"he is the son of one who was accounted something of an incomparable in her time. And certainly, the family and the fortune are all that one could wish for. I do trust, Gareth, that you have spoken to the duke about the settlements. In addition, her manners are excellent and her person most elegant. Not so elegant, perhaps, as some . . ." The marchioness paused for a moment as the full implication of her own words sank in. "I do think, Batty, that perhaps we should settle our own affairs before the wedding. After all, one would not want any other joyous events to detract from the celebrations of the young people."

"What? Oh, er, yes. Quite so. Whatever you say, my

dear." Lord Battisford wore the helpless smile of a man giving in to the inevitable. "I shall procure a special license immediately."

Doing his best to stifle his amusement, Gareth offered the pair his congratulations and hurried off to Rundell and Bridge's to order a simple band of gold. He smiled to himself as he sauntered along Great Marlborough Street. Who would have thought that the prospect of slipping a ring on a woman's finger would bring him, the Bachelor Marquess, so much joy?

The festivities celebrating the marriage of the Marquess of Harwood to Lady Althea Beauchamp, though simple, were abundant. Tenants and villagers from both Kennington and Harwood partook of the quantities of food laid out on trestle tables on the lawns behind Kennington, for Gareth had made sure that there were plenty of wagons to transport all the loyal folk who had served his family through its darkest period of financial reverse.

While the holiday atmosphere owed much to the fineness of the day and the never-ending supply of ale, roast beef, pigeon pies, and other delicacies too numerous to count, the people of Kennington and Harwood alike shared a genuine feeling of joy as they took part in the happiness of the two who had worked hard to ensure the comfort and prosperity of their respective estates. And more than one romantic young maid remarked as she observed the bride and the bridegroom sharing a secret smile every now and then that they looked just like the prince and princess in a fairy tale.

Not everyone, however, participated in this general spirit of festivity. Though she would never have admitted to agreeing with a single notion put forth by the new Lady Battisford, the Duchess of Clarendon and Gareth's mother were alike in considering the entire thing to be a dreadfully rustic and most paltry affair indeed that could not be said to boast a single guest worth knowing, besides themselves, of course.

The rest of the crowd, unburdened by such delicate sensibilities, enjoyed themselves thoroughly, far into the evening, and it was a very groggy but happy throng that climbed aboard wagons returning to Harwood in the wake of the carriage that carried the happy couple.

Left standing on the steps of Kennington as the carriage rolled down the drive, the duke was astounded to perceive his mother being handed into a second carriage of her own. He strode over to the carriage window. "What is this, Mama? We have made arrangements for you to return to town with us in the morning."

"Thank you, Henry, but I have been invited to join Althea and Gareth at Harwood."

"Join Althea and Gareth? I have never heard of such an absurd notion. The proper place for the Dowager Duchess of Clarendon is at Clarendon or at Clarendon House when we are in town."

"But, Henry, I do not enjoy myself at Clarendon or Clarendon House. I shall enjoy myself at Harwood. I find the company of Gareth and Althea both stimulating and amusing. However, you, Henry, I am sad to say, are an old stick, and your wife is a dead bore." The dowager smiled triumphantly as she shut the window and the carriage rolled off down the drive leaving the duke to stare helplessly after it.

In the carriage ahead of her the bride and groom were sharing similar sentiments. Looking down at Althea nestled in the crook of his arm, her head resting on his shoulder, Gareth thought he had never seen her looking so relaxed. "Happy, my love?"

She tilted her head to smile up at him. "Yes, Gareth."

"Good. From now on I intend to make your life so thoroughly enjoyable and interesting that you will not even think of spending a moment of it without me ever again."

Penguin Putnam Inc.
Online

Your Internet gateway to a virtual environment with
hundreds of entertaining and enlightening books
from Penguin Putnam Inc.

*While you're there, get the latest buzz on
the best authors and books around—*

Tom Clancy, Patricia Cornwell, W.E.B. Griffin,
Nora Roberts, William Gibson, Robin Cook,
Brian Jacques, Catherine Coulter, Stephen King,
Ken Follett, Terry McMillan, and many more!

**Penguin Putnam Online is located at
http://www.penguinputnam.com**

PENGUIN PUTNAM NEWS

Every month you'll get an inside look at our upcoming books and new features on our site. This is an
ongoing effort to provide you with the most
up-to-date information about
our books and authors.

Subscribe to Penguin Putnam News at
http://www.penguinputnam.com/newsletters